Seer of Windmere

Michelle Janene

Seer of Windmere

Michelle Janene

STRONG TOWER
PRESS

Sacramento, CA

Strong Tower Press
Sacramento, CA
strongtowerpress.com

Publishers Note: This is a work of fiction.
Names, characters, places, and incidents are either
products of the author's imagination or used factiously.
All characters are fictional, and any
Similarity to any person living or dead is entirely coincidental.

Cover Art by: D's Creations and Designs
Images: Celtic Heart and Infinity: Simeon, VD/Depositphotos.com
Moons: Tristan3D/Depositphotos.com
Mountains: JanMac/Depositphotos.com
Girl: Mihail Guta / ShutterStock.com
ISBN: 978-1-942320-16-6

Author's Note

Dear Reader, I wanted to make you aware, that while you are about to read an overtly Christian fantasy, I have taken a small liberty. Much in the tradition of our Jewish Brothers and Sisters, I have replaced the common names for God, our Lord, with His attributes. In the Jewish Scriptures we find, The God who Hears, God with Us, My Healer, My Banner, and so many more. This is how my characters express their relationship with the Triune God, as the characteristics He displays. I have quoted from the Geneva Bible, to add to the old world flavor, but I have also replaced the name God, and Lord, with the attributes of His character to keep in agreement with the rest of the story.

I have not done this to offend or make light of my Lord and Savior, but rather to extend what I know of Him, as relatable and accessible to all—no matter the realm from which you hail.

May the Lord God, by all His many names, be praised. May He alone receive the glory. And may you, dear reader, be blessed.

--Michelle

Chapter 1

Destiny has an annoying habit of being inconvenient. Two full moons' crossings away from his throne, and still Kaldreck had found no maiden whom he believed to be the one the Divine had chosen for him. And there remained little of Windmere left to search.

"The Lord High King grows weary of this quest, it would appear." A deep chuckle rumbled through Malic.

"Does not your backside ache from spending the cycle of both moons in the saddle? A whole season has passed since we left our homes in Hearthrop."

"Oh aye, but I do not search for my calgent. Mine awaits me in my home near your great palace."

"I am sorry to keep you from her so long, my friend. There is but one great city left to search."

"Come now, Kaldreck, no woman would grant your spousal request with such a weary scowl. Though I fear the possibility of finding her in Dusk Bay is not so great as to offer you many potential maidens."

The guards before them slowed and Farn came back to draw alongside his king's mount. "Lord High King, forgive the delay, but the village of Illgrove has heard of your approach, and they beg you turn aside to rest and refresh with them."

Kaldreck's burdened shoulders sagged, "And I am sure their finest maidens stand ready to attend me as well?"

Malic roared with a mighty laugh. "Is it not why every village —no matter the number of their huts—calls you to turn aside?"

Kaldreck groaned and rubbed the base of his aching neck. His gaze moved to the road before them, and his mouth opened to refuse.

"It would hurt their pride to refuse them at least a look, Lord Kaldreck." Farn's voice remained a hushed rumble from deep in his huge chest. "We have missed no other and it would be a great slight to Illgrove to refuse. There are maidens of suns past you may still return to, but what if your One and Only dwells here? You know no other will satisfy the longing in your heart, or heat the blood in your limbs."

"Lord High King, why do we delay? Dusk Bay is yet many degrees of the sun ahead?" Renwald, his seer, called. Even though his dark hair was cut shorter than any of the other men, the straight black locks spilled over his forehead obscuring his eyes, something Kaldreck did not like in a man.

"Illgrove has invited us for refreshments." Kaldreck nodded his head toward Farn indicating they would accept. The warrior returned to the lead position and turned the company to follow the messengers to the east, away from Dusk Bay.

"Why go to such a small village, my lord?" Renwald chided. "Dusk Bay would hold more promise."

Kaldreck turned to consider the man who never, in all their

journeys, had tried to turn him from any settlement. "For the simple reason we have stopped at all others. She may dwell here."

Renwald snorted, "In Illgrove? Naught good could come from such a far-flung, insignificant patch of mud."

"We go all the same." Kaldreck's tone was firm, and the seer slipped to the rear of their party.

The village of Illgrove was much larger than Kaldreck would have thought possible for its location so far from all the others. Close to thirty huts crowded around the large central square, and more lay off in the distance. "What commerce feeds this community, Malic?"

"Fishing, I would think."

Kaldreck followed his captain's pointing finger south of the village to a large lake. "Fish and wool, it would seem." Kaldreck's gaze fell on mounds of wool waiting in dozens of wagons.

"Of course, the fine wool of Illgrove is well known, my lord. I should have remembered."

Kaldreck laughed, "That knowledge would fall to my steward, Halfort, not the captain of my guard."

The warriors riding ahead of him parted, and Kaldreck saw the throng of maidens gathered at the far end of the square. He glanced over them, seeing the same expressions he always did. Women seemed to come in but three emotions when they were in his presence. There were those hopeful mothers and two-mothers standing on opposite sides and wringing their anxious hands. The next group consisted of the eager maidens who stepped in front of the others, titling their heads in shy smiles and fluttering their lashes at him with infatuated sighs. And finally was the collection of shy maidens fearfully standing as far from him as possible. They secretly hoped he would not choose them, but he looked on all.

He sat atop his wide destrier and glanced at every face. Blonde, dark haired and red heads—short, tall—lean and plump—those who had come into their full womanhood and those with but small buds beneath their gowns. They were all the same. Faces unending. Until his eyes lighted on one maiden firmly planted in the middle of the others. Like their island home, which sat in an unending expanse of the violet sea, she stood different than the others.

Her unremarkable brown hair lay bound behind her and not loose like the others. She neither cowered at the back, nor did she clamor for the front. She did not seem to have any readable emotion upon her face. She merely looked on him as though he were any common trader come to visit, not the Lord High King of all Windmere. She held his gaze without interest—and this intrigued him. He leaned toward his captain and told him to bring her when he had concluded his introductions with the elders.

Kaldreck dismounted and was given a deep observance by all gathered. Farn took the tall-backed chair provided by one of the town's elders and positioned it out of the harsh blue-white glare of the midday sun under an awning to the left of the square. Two more of his guards collected one of the many benches and placed it before the chair.

"Welcome and give honor to the Lord High King of Windmere. May his reign see naught but peace. May his home overflow with sons. And may he rule for a thousand years in friendship with his people and service of the Divine."

Kaldreck had heard the traditional greeting more times in the last moon cycles than he ever wished. Farn passed the cup of friendship to his page who sipped to assure its harmlessness, as Kaldreck gave his blessing. "May the sun and the Divine's favor never set on Illgrove. May its people be found in good health, and prosperous. May kindness between neighbors never end."

Kaldreck took of the cup and drank deeply. A sour wine assaulted his tongue. It took all his will to swallow it down and not spit it from his mouth over the good people of Illgrove. He exchanged pleasantries with the elders and spoke with many of the people while working his way to the chair awaiting him.

Once he sat, a surge of enthusiastic maidens stepped forward as though one organism. Guards intervened to hold them back.

Malic's voice rang out like a roll of thunder. "If the Lord High King seeks your company, you will be escorted to sit before him." Many jumped. That big booming voice was one of the features Kaldreck liked best about his friend.

The hopeful maidens groaned and moved to the benches positioned on all sides of the large square. This plaza provided enough space for the entire community to sit for common gatherings and festivals.

Once the masses dispersed to hover nearby, Malic stepped forward with the maiden who'd caught Kaldreck's attention earlier. She bowed low and sat on the bench before him. The drab tan kirtle that hung loosely over her body made her figure indistinguishable. He noted her dainty hands and small bare feet. Her neck was slender, and her small oval face carried no extra plumpness. Mirth tickled him, for it mattered not what she looked like. If the Divine had chosen her for his spouse, she would stir him regardless of her physical features.

Her smoky eyes struck Kaldreck the most—swirling gray, like a fire when water is tossed upon it. They stared at him without a single emotion he could read. Her slender lips, more pink than red, were held straight with neither reaction or sentiment. She did not lower her gaze or employ her womanly wiles with him but sat straight-backed and quiet.

"May I ask your name?"

"Ellianna, my lord."

No fear quieted her voice and no vibrato raised it. She stated the fact as if she talked about the mundane with an acquaintance.

Her entire demeanor—everything he saw and heard—intrigued him and he settled into the chair with anticipation, as at the beginning of his great quest. She was like no other. But was she the one?

Though he grew weary searching, his heart raced thinking he might be seated before the woman who would touch him where all others had failed. Ellianna in her drab, shapeless, tattered dress would not be considered a striking beauty, but how would she appear in an elegant gown? Her hair arranged pleasingly? Would she become the desire of men?

A jealous pang pricked his heart. If she were his One and Only, he would hate every other man who looked on her with longing.

But was she the one?

He couldn't wait to find out.

Chapter 2

"Ellianna, do you know why I have come to Illgrove?"

"You are Lord High King of all of Windmere. As law requires, since this is the third year since the crown was awarded you, that you must find your calgent—your One and Only who is for you alone. The one who will bear you many strong sons."

"And what would you do if you were found to be such?"

Still she gave no emotion for him to read. "I am loyal to the Lord High King. I would fulfill my duty."

"Duty?"

She nodded without speaking.

"If I choose to take you with me, would you try to flee?"

"No."

"Would you lie to me, Ellianna?" He smiled, hoping for some reaction.

She remained quiet for some time. "An occasion might arise when I would find it necessary to lie, my lord."

Kaldreck nearly choked on the frank honesty.

Malic attempted to appear uninterested in their conversation as he stood with his back to them. Though he looked out on the others, he titled his head to catch her answer.

"What occasion might you foresee, Ellianna, which would require you to lie to your calgent and king?"

"If the words of truth would bring more harm to my lord than the saying of them would merit."

Malic raised his chin, looking out at the others again, but Kaldreck noted his nod of approval. She was honest and answered any question he put forth with the same thoughtfulness and directness.

"Would you find leaving your home distasteful or painful?"

She shrugged, and the loose garment fluttered around her. "I work hard here and find pleasure in my toil. I might become bored if I were to sit about in priceless gowns only to preen like an arrogant wintercock with people forced to wait on my every need."

He laughed and brushed his curly locks from his face at her notion of how she thought the High Queen spent her suns. "I am sure we could find something of worth to occupy your time." He considered her. "You do not approve of servants?"

"A true man or woman should be glad for the work of his or her own hands and not be forced to labor against their will. Villiant has many who help with his lands and flocks, but all do so for a fair wage and the dignity of freemen to choose for whom they would work."

Again Malic's head nodded.

"If you were selected my calgent, what would you expect of me?"

For the first time, her gaze wavered from his. She looked down at her hands resting in her lap, then raised her head toward the fields. When her eyes again looked upon him, they swirled with emotion she could not hide though it never touched the calm of her voice. "Only to be treated with kindness and not to be lorded over as if I had not a thought in my own head."

Kaldreck sat a little straighter and Malic again turned to consider her. "Would you not expect me to love you?"

"The need of the Lord High King is for strong sons and a stabilizing force in his palace while he is out protecting the lands of his people. Love is not required for such, just a willing mate of some character. Love and passion can be found in the arms of another."

Kaldreck's fist slammed down on the arm of his chair. "Such entanglements are forbidden,"

"Yet such taboo does not seem to stop all manner of men from partaking in them."

"True, but I vow I will not."

Her gaze dropped from his again, "It would still not assure your love." She tossed her head, and her long braid came to teeter on her shoulder for a time. "It would matter not. I only said I would not expect it of any who claimed me calgent."

He leaned forward pressing for some clear emotion. "Have you not wanted to seek out your One and Only?"

Her gaze fluttered away for a moment, then she addressed him with a firm directness. "I am well aware my face carries no great beauty, which is the source of the fire that runs hot in men's blood. I am of greater age than many here, from that lack." She waved her hand out as she glanced back at the other maidens who glared with visible hatred at her. "I am unwanted, but I am content to work with Villiant's bot until such a time as a man finds me of some value to him."

Saddness gripped his heart.

"My Lord High King, the midsun meal is being laid," Malic said with a tip of his head.

He had not noticed the sifting degrees of their blue-white sun. Ellianna now sat within its rays as they fell from directly overhead, though the heat did not seem to bother her.

Now was the chance to test the veracity of what his heart was telling him. He stood and reached for her hand. He had done this with scores upon scores of women since beginning his quest. Thus far, every hand had felt cold in his. With new hope, he reached for Ellianna. She rose without his help and curtsied low to the ground, her sloppy garment becoming a pool of fabric around her. She then relinquished her hand to his still outstretched one.

Her grip was strong. As her fingers closed around his palm, a fire erupted in his blood, racing up his arm to his pounding heart, which broke into song. 'Elli-Anna' it sang with the two parts of its beat. Did she feel it too? Naught registered in her face. She pulled her hand from his, dipping low once more.

"I have greatly enjoyed your company, Ellianna. May we speak again after the meal?"

Her brows drew together, and she looked out at all the waiting maidens. "There are others who seek your favor, my Lord High King. Would you not prefer a more charming or beautiful one to share your sunsinking?"

"I would choose only you."

She inclined her head with the same blank face. "As you wish, my lord."

Shunned and ostracized by the other maidens, Ellianna moved to a bench far removed from everyone and ate alone. Kaldreck's heart ached because of her isolation and for the song she had stirred in him. His men surrounded him as he moved to a table and the trays of waiting food.

Renwald, to his left across the table, spoke first. "The mounts are prepared to leave as soon as you are sated, my lord. We can still make Dusk Bay by nightfall."

Kaldreck's gaze moved to Ellianna again before he turned to Farn. "Make arrangements to remain in Illgrove for the night. I am not yet ready to depart this charming village."

Renwald sneered over his shoulder at Ellianna. "She cannot be the one, my lord. She is plain and simple. Not the proper sort to carry the title High Queen."

"Seer, you have directed me to all manner of frivolous women. If you had true vision, should you not have led me directly to my one? I will stay, and I will spend the afternoon with her." To Malic he said, "You may send the rest home. I will speak with no other but her this sun."

The seer grumbled, and his captain nodded as he stuffed a bit of succulent bot in his mouth. Apparently the citizens used them for more than wool. The meal was good with much bot and many fruits from the trees growing in the forest they had crossed earlier.

His gaze upon Ellianna, Kaldreck rose to return to his chair. She sat waiting for him on a far off bench but stood as he sat once more.

His attention was drawn by a shriek of one of the maidens—a gangly youth with shoulder length unruly hair. Having learned she would be given no audience with the Lord High King, she erupted in a wild outburst. Ellianna entered the aisle between the many benches to make her way back to sit with him. The distraught maiden suddenly broke from a guard's grasp and she lunged at her.

Kaldreck stood out of concern for her. Her next actions nearly sent him back in his chair, however.

Ellianna blocked the charge with ease, sending the other girl sprawling into the benches with a crash. The enraged maiden sprang to her feet and flew at Ellianna again. Before she could be struck, Ellianna scooped up a jahala stick used to knock the juicy fruit from lower branches and beat her away with it. She struck the girl hard on the shoulder sending her off balance. Still she came. Ellianna then thrust the bulbous end into the girl's middle doubling her over in pain. With a quick strike high between the shoulders, the combatant slumped to the ground at Ellianna's feet.

All stood transfixed in silence until Kaldreck thumped the gold breast piece of his armor. His warriors followed suit on their silver armor and howled the call of the volif as praise.

Ellianna dropped the stick, and Malic led her to stand before Kaldreck. He smiled to see her cheeks awash in pink. She sank to the ground before him. "Forgive me, my Lord High King. I acted most rash and unbecoming of a Windmerian woman."

Kaldreck pulled her to her feet feeling the burning in his blood afresh. "I applaud you, Ellianna. You remind me of the warrior queens of old. Where did you learn such skill?"

She looked at him for a time, her eyes blinking wildly, stirring the smoke within. "I have spent many turns around our sun tending Villiant's bot, my lord. Out of need to protect them from the volif and the great hairy monsuit, I have learned to fight."

He tilted his head in amusement. "I wonder at the extent of your skill." He considered her for a moment and without turning his gaze said, "Malic, your sword."

"My lord?" he protested.

"Malic, I am the Lord High King. I tell you, give the maiden your sword." His words were firm but full of mirth. "You will not harm me, will you, Ellianna?"

She swallowed hard. "Not out of malice or will, but I make no such promise for my sheer clumsiness."

Malic drew his blade and turned the hilt toward her. She took it, but the weight dropped the tip against the hard-packed earth with a thud. She stepped back, dragging it with her. Using both hands, she tried to lift it. The gleaming weapon swayed but the length of a foot off the ground, then dropped again. She looked up at him. "Perhaps a smaller instrument would suit better, my lord."

It was not a chastisement but a statement of fact. Kaldreck laughed. "I forget what a mighty weapon my captain wields." He looked about his men and saw his page sitting near. "Goffray, your arms."

The young man stood quickly and untied the strip of leather from his waist.

Kaldreck took it by the tip of the sheath, laid the guard across his forearm, and offered the hilt to her.

She grasped it and drew it from its home. She again stepped back and tested the weight and feel of it in her hand just as any warrior would do.

"Are you ready, Ellianna?"

She gave a quick nod and followed him into the center of the square where room had been made for them.

As soon as he turned, he set his blade to flight planning to come within a safe distance of her chest. She blocked his strike, pushed it aside, and lunged with a thrust of her own.

"You are fearless," he breathed in wonder.

"Have you ever seen the size of a monsuit, my lord?"

He came at her again, "Would meet you eye to eye when astride a destrier, I wager. And that is while standing on all six paws. They are much taller when they rear. Green hair as thick and tough as the forest behind Hearthrop and a roar that would weaken the blood of any warrior."

She dodged his blade and spun to his side.

He whirled to catch her before she gained her balance, but she stood ready for him and came at him with four repeated strong blows upon the end of his sword. The vibrations from her attack sent his arm to shuddering.

He moved for a better angle still, and she whirled from him again, though this time her agile legs became tangled in the fabric swirling around her. She began to fall toward him, and her face filled with terror, the first clear emotion he saw from her this sun. She yanked her blade close to her body and contorted until she turned from him and fell upon it.

Kaldreck's sword fell with a muffled clatter and he dropped to his knees beside her.

Chapter 3

Kaldreck's blood ran hot as he turned Ellianna over while his heart froze in fear. The Merciful was never cruel. To be introduced to the only one destined for you only to have her die within degrees of meeting her—this would be beyond dreadful.

Laying across his lap, Ellianna's eyes were wide—the smoke within still. She shuddered and gasped, in her terrified state, "My Lord High King?"

He smiled. "I am unharmed, Ellianna."

A long breath slid from her, her eyes closed, and she relaxed back into Kaldreck's hold. "The Merciful be praised," she whispered.

Kaldreck smiled at the use of one of the many names for their single God. "You have been hurt, Ellianna," he said and waived Balmson, his healer, forward.

"It matters not, as long as I did no harm to you."

"It matters to me."

Her eyes fluttered open and she pulled from his grasp. As she sat, pink again kissed her delicate cheeks. Blood seeped from the cut in her chin and dripped down the front of her garment. Still, she would not allow Kaldreck to assist her further.

Balmson knelt and examined the wound. "'Tis small but will require sewing."

She shook her head splashing more blood about. "There is no need for such trouble. A bit of yaro root pressed on it will staunch the bleeding and draw the cut together as it dries."

"But what of the scar, mistress? Without sewing it will be large and jagged."

She smirked, wiping blood on her sleeve, "Saving me one small scar would do naught to add to my beauty. Do not fear over me, healer. The mark will matter little."

Balmson treated her as she requested and Kaldreck helped her stand, holding her hand longer than was appropriate to savor the song in his heart. "You handle yourself well with a sword and now herbs. Tell me what you know of the state of our lands?" Kaldreck led her to the bench. She paused to look at him before she sat.

A wry humor twisted her mouth. "I know well of the healing properties of the yaro root, for as I told the Lord High King, I am quite clumsy." She continued to stand.

"Will you not sit and talk with me further?"

"If you can find enjoyment in the company of such a fool, I will do as you wish."

She slipped onto the bench and eyed the darkening blood on her garment as it dried in the sun. Her eyes clenched closed and her hands clasped so tight in her lap they lost all color.

"I see no fool in you, Ellianna."

She looked up at him, a slender brown brow arched above the questioning stare.

"I have found an honest woman with strength of character I

see in few others. I am honored to have met you this sun. May the Divine bless you with all good things."

She turned her head from him, but he saw the color rise to her cheek, bright and vivid even in the shadows where they now sat on the opposite side of the square.

After a moment she seemed to collect herself. She straightened and looked upon him once more. "You asked of the lands, my lord. Windmere is at peace and has been for some time due to the strength of the Lord High King and his mighty warriors. It will not always be so, for the heart holds much wickedness and is too easily corrupted. One must always watch with earnest least the enemy take the kingdom while her leaders are unaware. Peace is the best time to lay spies and seek the downfall of an enemy. Relations and bonds should continue to be forged for they may be Windmere's warning of coming trouble or her help in time of calamity."

Kaldreck could not fight the smile consuming his face. "You are wise beyond many of my scholars, and add to that, a keen intelligence, and the strength of a warrior. You would serve a king well." Kaldreck's gaze caught on Renwald who glared at Ellianna's back from the far edge of the seating area. "I do not think my seer approves of you."

"Perhaps he fears being replaced."

"Are you a seer, Ellianna?"

She sighed with a toss of her head. "One of my ancestors was a seer of some renown, but I do not possess the gift. For my family, the power only comes to those who are joined in deep love with their calgent. The intertwined love of two hearts is said to awaken it."

"And you do not think you will find such a love?"

"It seems unlikely, my lord."

She looked at the degree of the sinking sun as it moved between the huts lining the area behind him. "Do you need to leave, Ellianna?" A pain gripped his heart at the thought of not being with her.

"Villiant expects me to have dinner prepared when he returns from the fields."

"You have spoken often of this Villiant. Who is he?"

"My father."

"And your mother?"

"The One called her twelve sleeping seasons ago, my lord."

"May the Comforter ease the pain of your loss." He rose to his feet and she followed. "I will allow you to take your leave, but I must ask you to return on the morrow."

She looked at him, the crease returning between her brows.

"I leave in the morning and I would see you," he requested in a whisper.

She dipped low saying, "As you wish, my Lord High King."

"I have just one last thing to ask of you?"

She inclined her head and remained silent.

"Are you still a maiden?"

Her eyes narrowed on him and something akin to lightening flashed in their smoldering depths. "I have been claimed by no other professing calgent, and I am not a woman of loose morals, my lord."

He bowed fighting to suppress the smile at having evoked an

emotion from her, though it be wrath. "I meant no disrespect on your honor. It is simply a question, which must be asked."

"Perhaps it could be a question to start a conversation and not one at the end of many degrees of the sun spent together."

The smile would not be contained any longer. "A point well taken, Ellianna. I bid you safe journey home."

She gave a quick jerk of an observance and spun away, the skirt of her gown twirling angrily.

He watched her walk from the center square to the east until she disappeared over a rise.

"Is she the one?" Malic asked.

Kaldreck shrugged and moved inside the home provided for him.

"You are a fool of all fools, Elli," she chided herself when the village square lay well out of sight. "You just had to go into the village this sun of all suns. Had you not been so eager to deliver the wool, which was not destined to leave for two sun risings yet, you would have learned too late of the noble visitor. You babbled like a fool… to the Lord High King. And nearly skewered him besides. His spouse!" She snorted. If it was not so completely out of the realm of all possibility, merriment might be found in the thought. She fumed at herself all the way home.

"Girl, where have you been all sun? The bot need to be penned, and I expect dinner, now," Villiant yelled from the doorway of their house.

Ellianna picked up her pace as she neared the home she shared with her father. Puffs of thin smoke trailed up from the roof hole over the central fire pit—at least one task was already done. She also took notice that the thatch needed replacing before the sleep season when the entire world lay dark and lifeless waiting for the Divine to bring it back in the wakeful time.

"Girl, hurry up!" Villiant bellowed, his round face red as flames.

She flew through the leather-covered doorway, but still he managed to slap her. The action sent her off balance, and she stumbled toward the fire. Only a hurried twist saved her a serious burn.

"Lazy, clumsy, fool. That's what you are, girl. Good for naught at all."

She staggered on her feet a moment and moved to the fowl lying on the sideboard waiting for her to pluck and prepare. Villiant sat at the small table he once allowed momma to share with him, but now had no room for her. His fingers drummed over its worn surface, as he glared.

"I asked where you've been," he snarled. His own hair fled his hot-tempered head. A small band now only grew over his ears, dark and greasy. Villiant abhorred bathing. His short beard stood on edge as he fumed at her—naught like the Lord High King's that seemed to brush his wide firm jaw and crinkling in a pleasing manner over his lip as he spoke.

Villiant's massive fist slammed down on the table overturning the unlit candle and sending it rolling to the floor.

Ellianna neither jumped nor cowered. This was the way of things in her home. If her father was not yelling at her or striking her, he must have caught some dreadful chill that kept him abed. Even those times were short lived, for he did not trust her to oversee his possessions for long.

"I went into the village to deliver the wool to be taken to market."

"Where is the payment?"

She brushed feathers from her hands, reached for the small pouch hanging around her neck, and pulled it from under her tattered dalmatic. She yanked it free of her braid and tossed the coin-filled bag onto the table in front of him.

Villiant snatched it, dumped its contents on the table and counted it, twice. "All here," he grumbled and put the coins in a pouch which always hung at his waist. She would collect her bag later as he left it on the table.

"Depositing wool could not have taken all the degrees of the sun, even for you." He paused and growled at her. "I heard tell, the Lord High King was in the village square all sun." He laughed a hateful sneer. His tone mocking and hurtful, "Did you stand among the maidens and sigh at the lord."

"I tried to leave as all the hopefuls gathered on the east end of the square. Several of the mothers pushed us into a tight group and I could not get free of them until he appeared."

Villiant snorted his doubt. "Then you just had to sit there and gaze at his lovely face?"

"When the maidens moved forward for their moment with the Lord High King, I turned to return home."

"Still you have not said why it took you all sun." He looked at the mark on her chin. "Clumsy dolt. What did you do to yourself now? Is that what delayed you. You wasted the sun sitting along side the road weeping over an insignificant hurt?"

"I cut it on a sword." She poured water from a bucket over the small fowl, and her stomach tightened for she knew there would be little to eat this night. Villiant ate his fill first, and he would be sure to consume this whole bird.

Villiant rose to his full height—over a head taller than her and twice as wide as her slim frame. His bulbous finger wagged out at her. "What manner of humiliation have you brought on my house now? What horrid offense did you comment before the Lord High King that he found it necessary to point his sword at you?"

She continued to cut open and clean the bird, numb to his tirade. "I did naught to my king." She reached up and pulled down a pouch of herbs to rub into the cleaned skin. "Airamena came after me. I knocked her senseless with a jahala stick. It must have intrigued the Lord High King for he offered me the blade of his page, and we sparred in the center of the square."

Villiant dropped back to his three-legged stool with such force he nearly toppled. "You crossed blades with the Lord High King?" he stammered.

She secured the fowl to a spit and placed it over the flames. She wiped her hands on the front of her clothes. They were already stained with blood and would need a deep cleaning tonight before she returned to see the king off in the morning. "As you tell me at all times, I am clumsy and fell on my own blade."

He roared with laughter. "What did the Lord High King do after he saw you for the fool you are?"

"He had his healer tend me, and we resumed our conversation."

The laughter cut abruptly. "Conversation?" A snarl turned his lip.

"As I tried to leave after delivering the wool, the Lord High King took a seat in the shade on the edge of the gathering place. I made my way through the throngs of anxious maidens, but one of his warriors approached me saying the king wished me to come and speak to him."

His fist hit the table once more. "And you skipped off happily?"

"The man was a mountain. Twice your size, with a head the size of the boulder in the middle of your field you curse at all sun. He wore a long black beard so thick it was divided into five sections, four of them braided and wrapped in leather. His arms were as large as jahala trunks. It was not as if I could have done anything to elude him."

She started to turn the spit as the fat dripped into the flames with sizzles and licks of flame. "I did try to dissuade the man, for I was sure the king had meant for him to bring another. He was certain, and he led me before the Lord High King, and I sat on a bench all sun talking with him."

"What did he want?" he growled.

"He searches for his calgent."

His roar of laughter drowned out the sputter of the meat and her stomach's grumbling. "You think he came to pick you as his queen?" He laughed until he struggled to breathe. "A clumsy old fool like you—the next high queen. When hamsouls fly."

"Of course he will not choose me. I know not why he wished to talk all sun. Perchance he wanted only an afternoon's respite from the clamoring of silly maidens and saw I would not swoon over him. It matters not for he leaves on the sunwake. There shall never be another thought about it."

"Other than I shall have to compensate Boyiam for the pain and distress you caused his daughter when you injured her and stole her chance at the king." It was some time before he continued. He wiped the merry tears from his eyes as they narrowed on her. "You are forever costing me girl. Would have been better had you never been born."

She stood and pulled the spit from the fire placing the whole steaming thing on the wooden tray before him. "Well I know it." She moved the pitcher of sour wine to the table and then stepped toward the door.

"Where are you going now? Off to get another glimpse of your king?"

"To pen the bot for the night, then to the creek for water to clean when you are done, and to wash my garment." *And if the Provider is gracious, to find a root or two to eat along the way.*

As the flap over the door slapped back into place, he called after her with a mouth full of food. "See to it you go no farther. I'll not have my reputation in the village tarnished any more by you this sun."

Chapter 4

The orange meadow grass brushed cool under Ellianna's feet as it swayed in the breeze, tickling her ankles. The bot on the hill lowed at her. With a heavy sigh, she turned from the path to the stream and climbed the trail to their pen. The hairy rust-colored creatures stood around the gate eager to enter and eat of their favorite grain. "Yes, yes I will see your bellies full too, before I give thought to my own aching middle," she groaned.

She put her hip into the shoulder blade of one male and shoved. He stood too close for the gate to swing open. He turned his head and rubbed against her legs raising the hem of her skirt and bumping her sore chin with the arc of one of his great curved horns.

She sunk her finger into the wool near a long floppy ear, noticing the half circle and a small pointed mark carved in it branding them as Villiant's creatures. "I fear you are the only one who will ever care if you see me each sun, old man." He lowed at her again. She pushed him harder being mindful to stay clear of the sharp hooves all around. "If you will not move, you cannot eat." The stubborn brute would not budge. She sighed, looked about the field, hefted her skirt, and climbed over the poles of the enclosure.

She went to the feed trough and scooped up a handful of the grain that Villiant grew higher on the hill. Walking back to the gate, she tossed it out a short distance. The bot chased after it moving far enough to open the enclosure, and when they had finished rooting for every small kernel, they galloped into the pen.

She secured the gate and went to the creek. Having no other clothes than those she wore, she stepped into the chilly mountain-fed water and sunk down into a deep hollow. She struggled out of the heavy coarse garment and, picking up a rock and a root, scrubbed at the stains. Her garment lay near full of holes before the blood was as faint as she dared scour it. She pulled the thing back over her head and grabbed for the bucket she'd left on the bank. Filling it, she dragged herself, with some difficulty, out of the water.

The breeze now blew harder. Her teeth chattered, and she trembled so much she sloshed water from the bucket. Her stomach soured, for little wood remained when Villiant's dinner was complete. He would not allow her to add more no matter if she froze. She believed he secretly hoped she would freeze to death so he no longer had to contend with her. It was also the reason she believed he never mounted a proper door on their home. He slept in the one small room off the central space with a well-stoked fire in a proper fireplace. His heavy wood door remained closed tight. She slept opposite the table where he dined staying as far from the flapping leather covering as possible. She had no pallet or pillows. She did possess one small blanket she had knit herself with wool her mother had given her shortly before she passed. Villiant hid it from her when he was most angry.

Thankfully, this night, the blanket remained. She stood over the coals of the central fire and warming and drying herself as best she could before removing the well-cleaned carcass from the table where he'd left it. She threw it in the refuse pile and washed the table and tray leaving it on the sideboard to dry.

As she curled under her small covering, still damp and shivering, she allowed herself a moment to think on the man who had occupied her entire sun. He stood taller than Villiant by about a hand, shining armor covered his broad chest in sparkling gold. He wore his hair loose at his shoulders, and it reflected the golden glow of his breast piece along with intertwined locks of warm brown. His hair formed a myriad of swirling ringlets all around his head and coiled when he moved.

A slim smile tugged at her lips as she considered how handsome those ringlets would look on any woman. His high square cheekbones and a firm angular jaw tempered them. Neat brows cut straight lines over keen eyes the color of the shallow part of the bay.

The hand he offered her was rough and hard likely from his time training or in battle. But though much larger than her hand, it was gentle. She felt again the sensation dance on her skin at his touch. The memory stirred something else more like a dream.

Before her the Lord High King stood alone. He smiled.

She could not speak for the hold of his gaze.

"Ellianna," he whispered her name, and the tingle his touch evoked raced over her entire flesh. Then he stepped forward, and his lips brushed her temple with a searing heat.

She jerked upright scraping her back against the rough mud wall. She shook the fancy from her thoughts and chided her pounding heart. "You are a fool of all fools, a worthless child who was good for naught in all your nineteen turns around the sun. It truly would have been better if you had never been born. Better that than to hope for a thing that is impossible. Love is not within your future. Accept that and you will suffer less pain, fool," she muttered as she lay down again.

Kaldreck lay upon the pillows of his borrowed bed in a hut gifted him for the night by a prosperous merchant. He laid thinking of Ellianna, a wide grin stretching his lips. Her stormy eyes, which held his without fear. The bud of a nose that crinkled when Balmson put the salve on her narrow chin. The strength and agility of her movements as she sparred with him, sword in hand. The blush of her cheek and the sad contour of her lips. How would it be to taste of those lips?

How many maidens had he seen, and how many had he sought to speak to? None had stirred his blood like Ellianna. None had made his heart sing. She stood before him again, eyes churned with… joy. "I am yours, and you are mine."

Fire erupted deep within his heart, and he bolted off the pillows with a gasp for the pain of it.

"My lord?" Goffray asked groggily from where he slept near the door.

Kaldreck waved the page back to sleep in the flickering light of a low candle as he sat on the side of the bed and struggled to catch his breath. Never had any of the maidens ever visited his dreams.

Ellianna slept fitfully after she allowed herself to think on the king. He would be gone soon and her life—such as it was—would continue as before. She prepared a thick gruel of grain and bot milk, warmed over the fire. She used more than she was supposed to and lapped up several fingers full before Villiant emerged from his room. She could not meet the king with her stomach so ruckus. She had done more than enough to embarrass herself already.

As he stepped from the door into the predawn light, Villiant grumbled from the doorway of his chamber.

"Your gruel is prepared, and ale is in the pitcher," she said.

"And where do you think you're going?" he snarled, rubbing his eyes.

"To say goodbye to the Lord High King."

Villiant seized her arm and jerked her back inside. "You fancy to waste another sun on your foolish folly?" He raised his hand and struck her across the sore cheek he marked at sunsleep.

She did not cry out nor shed a tear. He had done worse. "I do as I was bid by the Lord High King himself. He bade me come at sunwake and see him off." She squared her shoulders and tipped her chin at him. "It is your choice, Villiant. Do I go, appease the king, and fulfill his request, or will you invoke his wrath and suffer for it?"

He released her.

"I should be back in time to lead the bot to pasture." She turned and strode away.

Chapter 5

The blue hue of the waking sun kissed the home at the east side of the square as Ellianna crested the last hill. Noting the distance and the degree of the sun, she picked up her hem and ran the last half league. Hidden behind the last hut, she paused and quieted her breathing before she moved again toward the village center.

The king faced the path she walked and rose as soon as she came into view. A smile filled his face. Kaldreck moved toward her, and they met in the center of the square where they had sparred.

Ellianna fell in a deep curtsy, "The Divine bless you, my Lord High King. I hope your sleep was pleasant and your waking joyful."

Kaldreck took her by the arm and pulled her to her feet. He did not return her greeting. His firm lips turned in a deep scowl.

Kaldreck raised a hand to brush her cheek with a tender thumb. "Who has dared strike you, Ellianna?"

So used to the pains she experienced under her father, Ellianna had forgotten about the strikes she suffered since she'd last see Kaldreck. Ellianna's fingers reached up and explored the place he had brushed. She shrugged, "Villiant." When he did not seem to understand she spoke again. "My father, my Lord High King."

Kaldreck's jaw became rigid. His eyes narrowed and darkened as if the water they resembled was tossed by a storm. A rumble tore through his chest. No longer did the gallant king, who laughed and talked kindly, stand before her. Now Ellianna faced a warrior. A man trained to kill, and he moved to draw his sword.

"Malic!" he roared, though the man stood but a few steps away.

"Aye, my king?"

"Make ready to leave. I would put this village behind me at once. But I have a matter you must see to first."

"Aye, my lord."

Malic turned and walked back toward the other guards, another man taking his place behind the king.

"Prepare to leave," Malic bellowed.

The king's soldiers redeployed with well-trained movements.

The Lord High King then turned and stood beside Ellianna.

"People of Illgrove, be the first to hear and bear glad tidings. My heart has chosen my calgent. The Lady Ellianna is to be the next High Queen."

Some maidens sighed their gratitude of not being chosen. Others whimpered. Mothers wailed. Even those attempted to call out their blessings.

Ellianna's heart had stopped beating in her chest, and no air remained in her lungs.

"Good people of the village of Illgrove, now your status will grow for not only do you produce a fine wool, but you are the growing-home to our High Queen," Kaldreck called out with joy.

Ellianna's legs trembled like they were made of straps of fresh leather about to give way under her.

Kaldreck turned to Ellianna now, a smile once more softening his face. "Do you consent to come with me to Hearthrop and be my love, Lady Ellianna?"

Still no air graced her lungs, but she managed a nod.

"I promise to love you always."

Now Ellianna really did need to sit before she collapsed. She staggered back a step, and the king's strong hand took hold of her above the elbow and steadied her. Not a thought remained in her head. Ellianna stared uncomprehending as Malic returned leading a mount the size of a small hut.

"I am here to do your bidding, my lord." Malic's deep voice rumbled her insides.

Again, the warrior stood beside her—angry and powerful. Kaldreck's words were soft at first. "You said your father raises bot, is that not right, Lady Ellianna?"

She did not realize he had spoken to her until her name whispered across his lips. Ellianna could but nod.

"Find someone to lead you to where the lady dwells with her scoundrel father, and seize all his bot. It will be payment to our lady for the pain and injury she incurred at his hand."

"Aye, my lord." Malic found a farmer's son who knew the way and seated him on the mount behind him. Malic called two guards, and they all rode off toward her home.

The king took her hand and led her to a bench. "Balmson."

Stuttered heartbeats clamored in her aching chest, and she gulped in air. She waved the healer away as he reached for her. "My

Lord High King, there is no need," she stammered. "It is much less than I have suffered at his hand before."

A frightful growl, akin to a monsuit's, rattled the king's chest. He knelt before her. "I should have him killed."

Seeing the mighty king on his knee caused her to jump to her feet. Dizziness flooded her addled mind, and she swayed.

"My lady?"

The strength of Kaldreck's hands filled Ellianna as he held hers, making her insides flutter. She nodded slowly. "Are you sure it is me you seek, my lord?" Her voice was a soft whisper for she feared to say the words too loud.

A tender smile filled his face and danced in his eyes. "It is only you who has made my heart sing, Ellianna. It is you and none other."

She took a slow step, following where he led toward the mounts that awaited them outside the central square. She had only traveled a short distance when his earlier word brought her up short. "My Lord High King, you intend to drag along one hundred and thirty bot?"

"I did not know the wealth of your family," he mused.

She glanced down at her worn garment. "Villiant is a tight-fisted man who sees me as a great burden on his affluence."

Once more the flash of anger washed over his face. "You shall never want again, my lady."

Before Ellianna could respond, several men from the town stepped forward bowing low.

Kaldreck turned from his lady, still seething at the bright welt on her fine cheek, to the men before him.

"My Lord High King, perhaps we might be of assistance. The bot are slow walkers and cannot be forced to move quickly. They will greatly slow your return home, but there may be another way."

"Continue."

"Many of us in Illgrove have long admired Villiant's superior stock. We could purchase them from you, for a fair price, and you could carry the coin home rather than contend with the beasts."

Kaldreck called his field marshal, "Do you know the worth of bot, Farn?"

"I have spent many suns in the market with Halfort, my lord. I believe I could judge the worth of an animal."

"Good. Go wait for Malic to return with the lady's herd then sell them to any interested for a fair coin."

Farn stood on a bench and called out to those gathered. "The Lady Ellianna wishes to sell her herd to any who find them of worth. I will collect my tools and meet the buyers at the last bench." He pointed to clarify.

With his ink and quill and scraps of prepared hide, Farn began to barter with the those who came forward—which were many.

"Do you require anything before we leave, my lady?"

Ellianna slipped to the bench behind her and shook her head.

"There is no treasure you wish to bring with you? Something your mother left you perhaps."

She raised empty hands. "I have not but what you see, my lord."

Lowing drew their attention as Malic dropped from his mount handing the reins to Goffray before coming to stand before them. His chest was puffed out and his hairy chin held high. He placed his great fist before Ellianna.

"I drew blood to avenge the injustice visited upon you, my lady." A red smear lay across his wide knuckles. "I also took this from him." He handed her Villiant's money pouch.

She looked up at him, eyes wide, but as was proper, Malic did not meet her gaze. "Thank you, my lord. None has ever done the like for me before."

Her breath was airy and full of awe. Kaldreck feared her heart would go out to another, and he drew her attention. "It shall be forever more. This I swear to you."

She nodded and stared without focus.

Farn concluded the business and brought a fat pouch of coins to him. Kaldreck judged the weight in his hand. "A goodly sum."

"The animals were of the highest quality and the buyers eager. The lady has near two hundred saltars."

Ellianna gasped as Kaldreck placed it in her hand with the other. "My lord…"

"'Tis a small token of what the man owes you, my lady. Take it and be at peace." He closed her fingers around it, savoring the fire the touch afforded him.

"All is prepared, my lord," Farn called from near the mounts.

Kaldreck stood, and Ellianna rose beside him. Her motion seemed to be instinct and not willful, for she still stared unseeing into the distance. "Bring the queen's mount," Kaldreck called.

Those gathered sighed their appreciation as a fine white destrier was led toward him. He pulled a length of white silk from the leather bag behind his saddle, and the men draped it over the mount's neck.

"Shall we go home, my lady?"

She stepped forward glanced down at her loose garment and seemed to come to herself. The smoke once more whirled in their gray orbs. "May I ask for but one moment, my Lord High King?"

He nodded, and she turned to leave him. She whirled back and with some hesitation held out her wealth toward him. "Could I trouble you to find a safe place to put this?"

He smiled and reached out his hand. She poured one bag into the other, removed one coin, wrapped the string tight about the top, and sat it in his palm. She curtsied and hurried toward a nearby shop. Kaldreck motioned to a man to join her within, and a guard followed them inside what appeared to be a tailor's shop. Kaldreck smiled believing she wished to purchase a new gown.

When Ellianna returned she looked no different. She still wore the same tattered garment and he wondered what she sought in the shop. She reached for the saddle, which was nearly beyond what she could grasp. Malic knelt and offered his cupped hands to help her. She considered him for a moment then lifted her skirt and placed a bare foot in his hands. In doing so revealed the men's breeches she now wore under her skirt. Once in the saddle, the skirt of her garment slid to above her knees, but she remained modestly covered.

The rest of the men mounted, and they turned toward home at last. Kaldreck's heart knew no greater peace.

Chapter 6

Ellianna worked to find a comfortable spot on the wide mount and looked at the warriors arrayed around her. They were assembled in a neat procession. Farn, a dark-haired warrior with an easy smile, led the way with another warrior beside him. Two more men followed next, then Ellianna rode between the High King on her left and Malic on her right. The thane was the largest of Kaldreck's guards, but his penchant for merriment and roaring laughter proved him a gentle soul.

Goffray and the healer, Balmson, followed behind her. The healer looked odd among the glinting metal clad warriors with their heavy cloaks of deep blue-purple streaming in the wind. The thin Balmson, in contrast, wore a short-sleeved tunic that came to his thigh and tight leggings. All he wore only brown and dull except the bright orange sash tied around his waist, which marked him as a healer of the highest order. He resembled the blades of grass in the surrounding fields. He had a wide forehead and a narrow jaw, and when Ellianna turned to look at him he inclined his head.

Goffray, riding next to him, behind Kaldreck, sat stooped under the burden of his large expanse of chain mail. He was a slim youth not yet fully grown—though he was probably only a few turns younger than her, appeared more youthful. Under his mail he wore a gambeson and carried the king's standard, both were in the king's colors of blue and purple. The colors blended and swirled into one another like the sky at sunsleep.

Behind Goffray and Balmson rode a row of three soldiers: the mark of the king on their silver breast pieces gleamed in the sun. As on the standard, each warrior wore the insignia of a mighty monsuit paw lifting a great star into the heavens. Behind these came a wagon with two warriors riding on its forward seat. Three more mounted warriors closed the ranks of their party.

Among these last few was a man she had seen in passing. He seemed to blend in and lurk around the edges of her vision. Even now as she glanced back on their number, he maneuvered his mount to ride almost hidden by the wagon. He wore an all black satin short tunic and trousers, and his black hair was cut short. Ellianna shivered when she caught a glimpse of him at a turn in the road.

"My lord," she turned to Kaldreck. "Who is the man in black with you?"

A wry smile twisted his lips. "Renwald, the royal seer I mentioned to you." He turned his head to look directly at her and lowered his voice. "I have seen no benefit in having him near. However, all the kings of the past have retained at least one seer as part of his council."

She remembered Kaldreck speaking of the seer's dislike for her, but she hadn't turned to see which man he'd been talking about. Ellianna looked ahead as the procession moved off the narrow lane from Illgrove onto the wide, well-worn road beyond.

"Have you traveled far from your home, my lady?" Kaldreck asked.

"I have never been this far west of the village. I have walked much of the open grazing land to the east, but I have not visited any other villages, and I have never seen a city."

His back became straight and his chest, covered in golden armor, puffed up. "Then it will be my great honor to show you our lands, my lady."

The few citizens of Illgrove who'd journeyed with them, now called, "The Divine bless Lord High King Kaldreck. The Divine bless the future Lady High Queen Ellianna." They repeated the chant several times before turning back to the village.

Farn called for an increased pace and the mount beneath her began to trot sending her bouncing in every direction as she struggled to keep her toes in the stirrups. One hand tightened on the reins and the other grasped a handful of silky mane. She tried to clamp her knees about the beast to keep from falling, but he was too wide to get a good grip.

"Farn, hold!" Malic bellowed beside her, causing her to startle and nearly fall.

Kaldreck eased his mount closer and his steadying arm held her.

Malic stepped down and moved toward her. "Forgive me, my lady," his voice rumbled, and his face held a deep scowl. "I have failed to adjust your stirrups properly. I would never have forgiven myself had you been injured."

The mount beneath her now stood still and she worked her

way to a straight sitting position once more. "There is no need to fret, my lord. I am sure my own inexperience is to blame."

As Malic moved to the other side of her mount, Kaldreck considered her. "Have you never ridden before, my lady?"

"I have sat atop such creatures in my youth but never any this large."

Malic laughed. "The Lord High King has the best breeding destriers in all the land. They are mighty in battle and fear little." He took her bare foot and placed it in the cold rough metal of the stirrup, then growled low. "This will not do. One moment, my lady." He walked back to the wagon and returned a short time later with an expanse of leather drawing a large knife from his belt.

Malic took her foot and sat it on the cloth to judge the size he would need and cut an ample piece. He tested it on her foot and cut another of similar size. Then setting them over the neck of her mount he cut several long lengths from the remaining leather. Tucking the last bit in the bag behind her saddle he took one cut piece and two thongs and covered her foot before placing it in the stirrup once more. "Is that comfortable, my lady?"

"Yes, thank you, my lord."

He moved to the other foot and bound it likewise. Placing it securely in the stirrup he asked her to stand on them. He shook his head and adjusted them further.

"Lady Ellianna, do I dare ask why you do not wear coverings on your feet?" Kaldreck's eyes flashed with anger again and it tainted his words.

"It seems as though the wise king has already guessed. Villiant saw no point in wasting his coin on something I would quickly outgrow."

"Surely your feet have not grown in many turns." His gaze looked out to stare into the orange, yellow, and green trees around them.

"No, but by then my feet were accustomed to walking the earth, so again, he saw not the need to provide them."

"I can still send back men to put an end to him," he growled.

He turned, and she noted the fire blazing in his eyes. "No, my lord. You have done far worse to him by depriving him of his one true love. You have stripped him of all his wealth. There is little money in the poor grain he grows for the bot, and he has naught else. He will grieve that loss far deeper and longer than the loss of his life."

The fire cooled, and he looked on her once more with tenderness. "You are wise, my lady."

She shrugged.

Malic asked her to stand in the stirrups again this time nodding at the results of his work. He mounted and waved Farn to continue. As the pace resumed Malic gave instruction. "First, my lady you must feel the rhythm of your mount. As it moves between strides, there are two bounces." He took a moment to show them to her as their destriers trotted along the road. "Now it is fine to bounce atop the animal the entire way, but the jostling tends to cause the rider's rump to ache quickly. What is better is to stand in the stirrups for one of the bounces and sit for the other. Once again he showed her what he meant and soon she tried it.

Ellianna struggled for a time.

"Feel the rhythm, my lady. Up, down—up, down." He smiled

and praised her when she succeeded for several strides. "Now as a new rider, I will say, your legs will be tired by sunsleep, but we will not keep up this pace all the way to Hearthrop. Farn, I think, hopes to reach a certain ford of the Vaulrey River before sunsleep because there is a good clearing on the far side." He watched her technique again. "You are a fast study, my lady. By the time you reach home, you will be much more comfortable for any future travels."

"Thank you, my lord."

He grunted, and they fell into a quiet ride for a time.

Ellianna's head swiveled following Kaldreck's finger as he pointed out rivers, mountain peaks, and other landmarks. She squinted her eyes to glimpse a few features through the sea of trees, which extended in every direction as far as she could see.

Ellianna's legs burned. The endless bouncing indeed made her rump ache. She tried riding with the tempo of the mount below her, but what she wouldn't give to get off the beast and walk.

Chapter 7

The sun descended on its arch. The men talked and laughed as they passed water skins back and forth. With each league, Ellianna grew more uncomfortable bouncing along the road. When she thought she would burst if she did not speak, she turned to the king. "My lord, how far will we ride this sun?"

"Until near sunsleep, I would imagine. The men are anxious to be home."

"Will we not stop?"

"There will be no villages to stop in."

Ellianna squirmed in her saddle. "My lord?"

"Farn, halt!" Malic called. "Men check the woods are safe, take care of your needs in shifts. Let us have some nourishment as we rest a moment. My lady, if you would come with me, I will find a safe place for you to attend to private matters."

"Thank you," she sighed.

Kaldreck placed his hands around her waist and lowered her to the ground. She seized hold of his shoulders, as her legs felt like mother's pudding and would not hold her weight.

"Give it a moment for the blood to flow through them properly," he told her. His words brushed her temple, and the memory of his dream kiss heated the spot.

As promised, feeling soon returned, and she moved toward the trees where Malic led her, another guard followed. The thane stomped into the tree line with a roar swinging his huge sword. Birds took flight with angry cries and unseen creatures fled deeper into the underbrush. He walked back toward her where she stood as still as she could on the edge of the tall grass. "You should be safe, my lady, but do not venture in too deep. We must be able to get to you quickly." He planted his feet with his back to the trees. Shoulder to shoulder with the other man, their hands rested on the hilts of their weapons.

"Thank you, my lord," she mumbled again as she wobbled out of sight.

Well relieved, she emerged from the woods to join Malic and the other soldier. "Thank you, my lord."

"The men vanish to the trees as they have need and rejoin us," he commented as he offered his arm to her. She recalled seeing some riding in front disappear for a time and now understood. "It is not safe for you to be alone, so speak as you have need."

She set her hand awkwardly atop his near the elbow, "I will."

He took her hand and placed it on the back of his.

He smiled as they started walking, but she found he never met her gaze. He would face her, but he would look over her, or to the side. As they joined the others lounging upon the ground, she noted they looked at her in the same manner. Staring passed her, never meeting her eye to eye.

She slowed as they neared the men. They sat relaxed, chewing on dried meat, and sharing hunks of cheese and bread given them by the people of Illgrove.

Malic pulled her forward until Kaldreck motioned for her to join him on a log among the men. He offered her some cheese, but she refused it. He tried some bread next. Again she would not take it from him. "My lady, I know you are hungry. I have heard the complaints of your belly."

Heat rushed to her cheeks. "But you are not finished, my lord."

Kaldreck took her wrist and turned over her palm pushing first the bread and then the cheese into her small hand. "From this sun forward, I want you to think no more of that foul wretch, Villiant. You will never go in want again." His words were harsh, and she turned her head from his wrath—only to see every warrior offer their meal to her.

Kaldreck watched the kindness of his men and praised the Provider for their good hearts. Then it happened—the corner of her mouth turned up. She smiled at them and dipped her head shyly. The glimpse of gladness on her lips washed away the hatred he held in his heart for Villant. He was a beast of a man, but he had sired his One and Only. For that he would do no more to the man.

"Thank you, my lords, but this is more than sufficient for my needs," she told them quietly.

Several of his men shifted, glancing at one another, and returned to their meal. Kaldreck leaned in to speak into her ear. "It is only proper to call true lords of the land by such a title. With the exception of Malic, who has his own holdings, all here are but humble warriors."

She looked up at him her smile gone, and her brow furrowed.

"Then how is it proper to address them, my lord?"

"By name."

"And if I do not know their name?"

Kaldreck nodded and turned to his men. "Warriors of Windmere, present yourselves to your future queen."

The men leapt to their feet and formed a line before her. Each in turn stepped forward, bowed, and gave his name. When all fifteen men—save Renwald—completed the task, they sat or moved to see to the animals in preparation for resuming the journey.

"How ever shall I remember them all?" she whispered as she nibbled on the hard, dark bread.

"I will help you."

She finished the last of her small meal and wiped her fingers on her skirt.

Kaldreck stood and offered her a hand. She took a few steps toward their mounts and sighed.

Kaldreck laughed, "There are but a few degrees of the sun before we make camp for the night. The next sun will be easier for your time in the saddle now."

She nodded without comment, and Malic boosted her up once more. She bit at her lower lip trying to find a comfortable spot and once more bounced along atop her great beast.

Chapter 8

The sun painted the sky in turquoise and violet, with a hint of deep green as they sloshed across the Vaulrey River. Water filled the leather wrapped around Ellianna's feet, and she wiggled her toes in the uncomfortable soggy warmth. A clearing came into view on the far side. A ring of rocks with its charred center lay near the middle. The grass lay flattened in patches. The men dismounted and dispersed to the tasks needing to be done.

Again, she found herself struggling to stand even with the king's strong grasp firm about her waist. It took longer this time for the feeling to return and she set about rolling her ankles one after the other until the needle pricks of awakening stirred.

Kaldreck offered his arm, and she sat hers atop it as Malic had shown her. Kaldreck tipped his head, entwined their arms and placed hers atop his once more. "This is the proper way to link arms with your future calgent. A way for me to draw you close." He smiled as he led her to a log and motioned for her to sit. She shuddered at the idea of returning to her backside.

"Perhaps a walk to stretch your legs would suit you better?" Kaldreck offered.

Ellianna sighed and nodded her head. "Can you but await a

moment?" She scanned those bustling around her and found Malic not too far off. She lumbered to him on sore, stiff legs.

"My lord?" He stopped and looked up, though he did not meet her gaze. She searched for the proper words. "You said…if I had…need?"

Malic inclined his head, and offered his arm, and led her to the tree line.

After several moments, she returned to the king, dropped her soggy foot coverings on the log, and they walked the edge of the meadow. She saw the guard who had accompanied her before now trailed a short distance behind them.

"What are you thinking, Ellianna?" Kaldreck asked.

"I fear I can think of naught, my lord. My thoughts are quite beset by the great change one rise of the sun as wrought in my life."

"Are the changes pleasing?"

"Aye," she managed. Her rump would not have agreed, but for the most part she could not complain.

"What do you hope for, Ellianna?"

She stopped and looked at him. "I pray to the Divine I do naught to harm you, that I never bring your reign shame or dishonor. I pray I can be of good service to you."

The king frowned, and the hue of his eyes deepened. "I have no fear of these things. You are my One and Only. You can do naught to injure me." His finger brushed her sore cheek. "But is there naught you hope for yourself, Ellianna?"

She turned and started walking again, "No, my lord. I have already received more than I ever dreamed—even in my hopeful youth. If we were to remain here in a tent, I would have more than I could ask for, my lord."

He offered his arm again, "There is so much more, Ellianna, and I aim to give it all to you."

They walked in silence the remainder of the way around the clearing drawn by the crackling fire and the smell of a rich stew.

The mounts stood free of their saddles and harnesses tied to trees deeper in the clearing. The wagon blocked the opening to the road and a bright fire danced. A large black pot hung over it a broth full of vegetables and meat bubbling rapidly.

Ellianna moved to sit beside Kaldreck on the log, but her tenderness forced her to slide off and sit on one hip in the softer grass. As they sat waiting for the others to gather, Kaldreck took a stick and drew in a small patch of dust beside her.

"This is our island, Ellianna." It was a three-pointed large landmass—wide in the south and narrow in the north. "Hearthrop is at the heart of our homeland." He made a small indentation. "Forests thick as night, cover much of the area between Hampel and Illgrove." He scribbled in the areas. "There are large port cities, including Dusk Bay, at intervals all the way around except for the high cliffs of White Tower in the northwest. Fast mounted riders can carry a message from Hearthrop to the furthest point in any direction in a sun rising and a half without sleep."

Kaldreck's gaze rose at the approach of a warrior with a scar disrupting his right brow. He handed Ellianna a wooden bowl full of steaming stew and a small wooden ladle. "Thank you… Alcoff?" she offered tentatively.

He nodded, though his eyes rested on Kaldreck, "Aye, my lady.

You have a good memory. There are many of us."

She settled the bowl in her lap allowing it a moment to cool and relaxed on the firm earth that did not bounce her to pieces.

A movement in the crushed grass to her left caught her attention. She set the bowl aside moving to her knees. When it drew nearer, she snatched the black viper from the thin blades, and rose holding it firmly behind the jaws where it could do her no harm.

The men moved to their knees or leapt to their feet all around her.

"My lady!"

"Lady Ellianna."

"Be careful, my lady. 'Tis a viper."

They all seemed to shout at once.

She took a few steps toward the open space behind them. "Yes, a particularly nasty one. I will snap its neck, and all will be well."

"But Lady Ellianna how did you manage…"

She turned, holding the squirming creature far to the side out of harms reach, to look at the king who stared at her wide-eyed.

"Vipers are harmful to both people and animals. They are easily enough dispatched."

A wide smile shone in the mists of his beard. "You surprise me, Ellianna."

She started to turn, his words settling uneasily in her middle. Did he think her un-ladylike? Did he disapprove? Before she could take another step Malic called after her.

"Hold, my lady queen. That is a tasty treat you hold there."

She crinkled her nose as she held the writhing creature far away from her body.

Malic waved her forward to the stump Alcoff used to chop the ingredients for their meal. "Hold it there, my lady."

Once she had it on the stump, Malic covered her entire hand—and a fair part of her arm—with his massive hand and pulled an ax from behind him. In one quick hack, that skimmed his hand but did no harm, the viper was relieved of his head. He released her hand and she did likewise of the limp flesh. Malic stooped and picked it up, tossing the dismembered head into the fire. "What think you, Alcoff? Can you make something of this treat?"

The warrior set his bowl aside and reached for the dangling thing. "Aye, should only take a few minutes," he said licking his lips.

Movement at the edge of her vision caught her attention. She tried to follow it, but all she saw was a black figure shifting deeper into the shadows.

"Is it not poisonous?" she asked as she returned to her place.

"Not any longer," Alcoff smiled slicing open its belly. "To the skilled huntress goes the first bite."

She struggled to find her appetite both for the viper or even the stew. Fears rattled her insides like a monsuit trying to break free of a cage. Soon the remainder of the tents would be raised, and she would need to go to the king. She knew naught of the ways of men and women. Dread gripped her middle, and she feared she would not be able to keep the delicious stew down.

A few times she had made stew for Villiant, but rarely had she shared in the meal. This was good, thick and well seasoned, but her anxious heart refused to allow her to enjoy it. Long after the others had sopped up the last of their meal with pieces of the bread they shared, she forced down the last bite and prayed to the Comforter it would stay there.

She stood with her bowl and bent to gather the others for cleaning when the warrior with the scruffy yellow hair snatched them from her grasp. "The soon to be Lady High Queen does not wade in the stream to wash dishes," he told her kindly.

"'Tis habit…Net…"

"Nafwin, my lady."

"Yes, thank you, Nafwin."

"'Tis an undesirable habit that will be easily broken." He bowed, took her bowl, and moved toward the river.

Kaldreck stood far off on the other side of the fire talking with some of his men while others worked to raise the last few tents.

Ellianna needed something to distract her mind from her pending encounter and moved through the middle of the meadow savoring the cool soft earth under her feet, now free of the hot leather coverings. She picked a few of the last flowers of the waking time, trying to remember their names as she let them linger under her nose. She turned to see the progress of the tent raising and found the guard still following her a few steps away.

Not as blond as Nafwin, he wore his hair in a low warrior's knot. He was broad about the shoulders with a thick waist.

"Forgive me from keeping you from your other duties, Eton."

"I am your personal guard, m'Lady Queen. 'Tis me duty to keep ye safe while ye go wherever ye so choose." He bowed deep, and she turned back to her rambling.

A personal guard, Elli. How your fate has changed this sun. When you woke not even your own blood gave a thought to your welfare, now you have a man you do not know willing to lay down his life for you. She looked to the heavens and a wealth of jeweled stars blinked their good pleasure. *I pray the Truth knows what He is doing.*

"Perhaps we should move closer to the protection of the torches, m'lady?" Eton offered.

She turned and walked toward him, "Yes, of course." He waited for her to pass and then again fell into step an appropriate distance behind.

As she neared, she watched the king move toward the large center tent. She quickened her steps and met him at the opening as he ducked to enter. Her heart pounded in her ears, and the wilting flowers shuddered in her hands—clasped so tight her fingers lost all color.

His gaze rose slowly from her hem to her eyes, and his brows drew together. "Yes, my lady. Is there something you require?"

Her breath came in shallow puffs, making her dizzy, and her tongue lay like a stone in her parched mouth. How did one go about such things? Her eyes drifted toward the open tent and she moved toward the flap.

The heavy fabric dropped and Kaldreck prevented her from proceeding with his strong arm. He stepped so near his beard brushed her cheek as he bent to her ear. "The rites have not yet been spoken over us thus allowing us the pleasure of union, my sweet."

Air would not enter her aching lungs, and it felt as though her face had been forced into the roaring fire behind her. Her head remained low for she could not look up at him.

"M'Lady Queen, yer tent has been prepared. Would ye come see if there is anythin' more ye might be requirin'?"

She turned abruptly toward Eton's voice and stepped toward the tent almost as large as the king's, seated a few footfalls to the left and facing the back of the clearing.

Kaldreck's hand brushed her elbow, and his voice came tender over her shoulder. "May the Provider keep you in warmth and safety, granting you many pleasant dreams, my lady."

"The same to you, my Lord High King," she stammered without looking at him.

Again, his voice touched her ear, for none other to hear. "I am honored by your willingness and your courage, Ellianna. Thank you."

She nodded and stepped away on quaking legs to look inside the tent meant for her. A raised bed set atop the matted grass. It was heaped high with many colorful pillows and a large monsuit fur.

"Is there anythin' further, m'queen?"

"No… no this is more than enough. Thank you, Eton."

He bowed. "There is a pitcher of water from the stream there," he pointed from outside to the back corner. "and a pot for yer needs there." He pointed to the corner just behind her.

"Then you have thought of everything. The Divine's blessing on you, Eton."

"And on ye, m'queen."

The tent flap dropped leaving her alone. Never had she slept on a raised bed. The memory of nearly falling from her mount earlier came fresh to her mind. She pulled a few of the luscious pillows from the bed and put them and the fur on the ground beside it. This would be more comfort than she had ever known.

As she sank down onto the softness, the weariness of her entire body overwhelmed her. A rustle drew her attention to the opening, and in the shadows created by the torches all around, she saw the shape of Eton. He threw out a bedroll and took his place before her tent. Her mind whirled in wonder.

Other shadows moved about. A tremor raced through her as she tried to convince herself it was Kaldreck's men who prepared for sleep. Fear pricked her heart sending it to thumping in her chest, but her body ached, and her eyes would not remain open.

Chapter 9

The next sun, Kaldreck noted the stiffness in Ellianna's movements. He had pushed her too far for her first time in a saddle. His gaze shifted toward her yet again as she walked toward the fire. She asked for naught—not even a chance to relieve herself. She expected to wait until the men ate their fill, and she took only what was offered and did not ask for more.

His heart fluttered afresh at her attempt to come to him. She would do anything he asked, but he wanted more than a dutiful spouse. He wanted her heart to be filled with the same joy she gave to him. As she moved toward her destrier, he knew she did not wish to mount again. Without hesitation, he made a secret vow to her. He would never take what she did not offer willingly with her whole heart. *I am yours Ellianna, and I truly hope there will soon come a time when you will say you are mine.*

She did not wait as long to request a stop this sun. She stood clinging to him. "How many suns until we reach Hearthrop?"

"At least seven more."

He could barely hear it, but he was sure she groaned. "What if we walked for a time when you return?"

"Yes, my lord."

"Aye!" The men all around him clamored at the idea.

She looked up at him sweetly and a slim smile graced her face. It only made her more beautiful. "It seems I am not the only one with an aching backside."

"It would seem so."

When she returned from the tree line, they walked. They lead their mounts for several degrees of the sun until Farn came back to speak with Kaldreck.

He nodded and called out to his company. "Well, men and Lady Ellianna, Farn says if we ride for the last degrees of the sun we can reach Oracle Ford. What say you?"

All agreed, and they mounted once more. As she sat next to him waiting for Malic to rise into his saddle she looked at him. "Thank you, my lord."

"It is my delight to bring you pleasure."

Ellianna sipped at the evening stew thinking on the king's keen attention to her this sun. The slightest move or jostle, and he would ask after her comfort. They walked for many degrees, and though it did her aching limbs great good, she wondered at the delay it cost him, yet he never spoke of it. This sun had been about her needs. She must do better on the morrow to not complain, for she did not wish to distress him unduly.

A thud and a small yelp pulled her abruptly from her sleep. She sat up and listened. A low snarl and a small cry of pain came to her through the thick fabric of her tent. "Volif!" she cried and sprang from her tent, tripping over Eton as he rose and landing hard on her hands and knees.

"M'lady?"

"Volif," she said again, louder as she caught glints of the green, orange, and golden eyes reflecting in the light of the few torches that remained lit.

Eton shielded her and drew his sword. "Stay behind me, m'lady."

Others emerged from their tents and torches were relit in haste. She struggled to find a place to lay her eyes for they were surrounded by the snarling creatures. Also, many of the men had emerged from their tents naked.

Kaldreck came and stood beside Eton wearing only his short leather breeches. His back was carved with deep muscle that rippled with power as he moved. A long scar danced in the torchlight over his right shoulder blade.

Staring at the half naked king was not helping the situation. She turned and counted their numbers. Two missing—Renwald and Alcoff.

"Alcoff!" she yelled over the growing snarls.

A groan sounded and Malic moved toward it. "I have him, my lady. He lives."

The growing light from the rekindled fire and lit torches glinted off fangs longer than her fingers, bared in narrow snouts. Ellianna yanked the stake free that held up the front of her tent. "Raise the torches," she called out causing Kaldreck to glance over his shoulder at her. "We must find the leader."

"Aye, our lady is right. They will be more likely to give up if we killed the leader," a voice called from somewhere behind her.

A fat volif lunged at Eton and he stepped away from her to

fight it. Goffray appeared standing opposite the king on her other side. A red beast came at the young page who fell back. The snarling animal seized his foot and started to draw him into the darkness. As he cried out in pain, Ellianna used the stick from her tent and smashed it's head near one golden eye of the creature. It released the lad and yelped out of the light.

Fear, like the snapping of a volif's jaw crushed down on her heart stealing her breath. The sight of Kaldreck lying dead on the ground behind her flooded her sight. She turned.

Kaldreck yet stood—unharmed—as he ran a dark streaked beast through.

Though seeing him safe, the pain gripping her would not ease. Another cream-colored volif sprang toward him.

"Kaldreck!" Ellianna screamed as she hurled herself at the beast. She slammed into the king instead, knocking him flat on his back. Ellianna landed on her knees beside him and stared. In the next heartbeat, the cream colored volif she had thought was already on top of him pounced in the space where they had just stood.

"Ellianna?" Kaldreck started to rise.

"I thought that volif had fallen upon—" She whirled to see the beast turn on her. She slashed out with her spike, catching it across the snout with the sharp end, snapping the weapon in half. The volif jerked from her whipping round so its bristle-covered side scrapped against her arm.

Yanked to her feet, she again stared at the king's back.

He ran his blade through the creature as she armed herself with a new tent pole.

"Lord Malic, to your right—the marble-colored one. He is the leader," someone called. All the torches rose pointing in that direction.

She noted Goffray hobbling near to take up a position on her right side. When Ellianna looked back, the leader no longer stood near Malic. She whirled in just enough time to see another beast spring from the shadows. She shoved Goffray aside and rammed the pointed end of her stake into the creature's gaping mouth. The weight and momentum of the animal threw her to the ground and knocked the breath from her lungs.

She lay dazed for a moment in a clamor of shouts, yelps, and cries.

"M'lady?" Eton yelled.

She pointed to his left as another volif sprang from the darkness. She untangled her legs from the dead beast at her feet. Jerking the shaft from the volif's still body, she joined Eton in cornering his attacker.

"There!" someone shouted.

A loud long yelp rang out. A low and mournful howl called beyond the ring of light in the darkness, answered by several others. The rustling of leaves and men's breathing was soon all that could be heard.

"Ellianna!"

The king's sharp cry spun her toward him. "I am fine, my lord it was Gof—"

She was engulfed in a tight embrace. So startled to find herself pressed against the king's bare chest, she lost all thought. Her senses tingled with a life all their own, however. The feel of his muscle-hard arms covering her back reminded her of the steady branches of the yorn trees she climbed as a child. The solid wall of his chest was not unlike the wall of her home. The frantic pounding of his heart in her ear and the damp musky-sweet smell of the sweat drenching his body made her head spin. He kissed the top of her head and her knees threatened to buckle.

He loosened his grip but a little. "My lady, are you harmed?"

She shook her head as much to clear it as to answer his question. "It was Goffray, my lord," she finally managed to stammer.

He turned around still clutching her in his arms. He tightened his grip, crushing her to his chest. "Men, clothe yourselves!" As he continued to hold her, she thought she heard a groan rumble through his chest.

She needed to clear her lungs of his intoxicating scent before she fell into a stupor, and she wiggled from his grasp. She closed her eyes and took a slow calming breath. When she looked around again all the men wore at least their leather trousers.

Goffray sat alone unattended, as Balmson saw to Alcoff. She knelt beside the youth and looked at his leg while Eton held the torch for her.

"Thank you, my lady," the page whispered.

"All praise the Merciful you were not seriously injured." She pulled up his pant leg. "'Tis but a small wound." Her fingers felt the movement of his ankle. "Though I am not the healer, it does not feel broken. Balmson has some salve to put on it, and you should be well healed in a sun or two."

"I will be the judge of that," Balmson quipped as he came to kneel beside the youth.

Ellianna stood to move out of the way and, as she turned, a great shout rose.

"Our brave warrior queen!" Malic shouted first.

"Queen Ellianna," the others shouted back.

Malic came toward her. "You fought as hard as any of us, my lady. Let us acknowledge your skill."

She stared at him, then watched as the men all raised a fist high into the air. Another warrior would come and smash his fist on top of it. She turned back to Malic who stood with his fist raised to about shoulder level. She kicked over an empty crate in front of her, stepped up and tapped the top of his fist with her own. He roared with laughter and the others cheered. "Huzzah!"

Ellianna stepped down, raised her fist, and each man came and bumped hers with great gladness. As the last one passed, Renwald's face caught in a bit of torch light far in front of her. Joy fled, and a shiver trickled down her spine. He vanished into the darkness again.

The men dispersed to different tasks, and Ellianna moved to her sagging tent.

"Let me get ye a new—"

"Not tonight. I do not wish you wandering out in the dark for a useless thing that will have no effect on my sleep. Rest Eton, all is well."

"Aye, m'lady," Eton said with a quick bow.

"Are you sure you are well?"

She turned from where Eton held up the tent to see the king emblazoned in torchlight. If his back had been well cut and fine, it compared not at all to his front. He looked as if he still wore his gold carved armor. Her heart thudded oddly in her chest. She had seen many of Villiant's men work in naught but their trousers, though none like the king. *Guard your heart, fool. Even though he says he promises to love you, a handsome form is not love.*

She tossed her head again. "Very well, my lord king." He started to turn away and the thought finally occur to her. "And you, my lord? You are well also?"

He spoke over his shoulder, "As long as you are hale, my lady, I am well." He moved to his tent and slipped inside.

Kaldreck lay on his pelts trembling. He couldn't sleep for seeing Ellianna battle the volif and the heat she lit in his blood. He thanked the Divine that she had not chosen this night to come to him. Her willingness and the fire her touch stirred in him would have inflamed his flesh's desire for her. He did not think he could resist her in such a state. Well he knew the dangers of contact with his true calgent. Men were taught from their earliest understanding never to dare touch a woman for fear it would ignite the blood, which would then lead to the stirring of lust, and from there bringing her dishonor.

Had the river not lain outside the fire light, he would have jumped in it. Instead, he rose, took the bucket of water from beside his bed, and dumped it over his head. It did naught to cool the fire within.

Chapter 10

Sunwake dawned early after the terror of the night, and it seemed Ellianna was not the only one who struggled to move. As the men staggered from their tents and started the process of breaking camp, she noted many did not choose to don their armor. The king stepped from his tent in a fine brocade doublet, which hugged his well-muscled body reminding her of the sight of his bare chest. He reached his arms high in the air and stretched with a deep yawn.

"Good waking to you, my lady. I hope you slept well after the disruption of the night."

"Yes, quite well, my lord." She looked away focusing her attention on the others trying to hide the memory of lying on her pillows thinking on the king. "However, it looks as though many of us are tired this sunwake."

Goffray limped from his tent, which was pitched near hers.

"How fair you this morning, Goffray?" she asked.

He stared at the ground. "Fine. Thanks to you, my lady." He hobbled off to his morning duties.

"I think you have hurt his pride."

Ellianna stared at the king. "I do not understand?"

"You saved him, but he was unable to assist you. It is what every man in my guard hopes to do—save their queen."

Except perhaps Renwald. It was a mocking thought, though she held no proof of his ill will toward her. "Should I not have stopped the volif?"

The king smiled down at her. "No, his pride will heal only because he still breathes to work the matter out within himself."

"Might I see how Alcoff fairs, my lord?"

He looked at her with intensity but nodded. "I aimed to do the same." He put out his arm to escort her.

Alcoff backed out of his tent coming close to bumping into them. Kaldreck pulled her out of the way. "Alcoff how fair you this sunwake?" the king asked.

The warrior turned around and, seeing her, bowed deep, pain contorted his face for a moment. "I am well, my lord, due entirely to my lady's quick actions. If she had not raised the alarm, I know I would not have seen our glorious sun one more time." He stood and his face relaxed. He stared at the ground near her feet. "I woke to see to my needs and as I entered the trees, I heard a snarl, then the thing was upon me." He raised his bandaged forearm. "I pounded it in the jaw, and it released me for a moment with a small yelp. Leaping up, I ran for the safety of the torchlight, but it fell on me once more." He brushed his side hidden by his baggy untucked tunic. "Then our lady's loud cry called out. It seemed to startle the animal. The men emerged from their tents, the lights flared bright, and the animal slunk away."

"How ever did you hear the attack so far from you, my lady?" Kaldreck asked.

"Many turns around the sun seeing to the care of Villiant's bot. The sound of a hungry volif can wake me out of a dead sleep—which it did."

The king continued to consider her curiously.

"You know enough of the man to imagine what he would do to me if I lost even one of his precious creatures. I hold enough sense in my brain to know it would serve me better to come home injured than without one of his animals."

Kaldreck shifted his gaze back to his warrior, his jaw muscles clenched and loosened, though his voice remained calm. "Alcoff, Brayden can see to the meals for now. And I think it better if you sit the wagon as well."

"Aye, thank you, my lord." Alcoff lumbered off.

Ellianna gazed up at the king.

"What puzzles you, my lady?"

"You care about your men."

"Aye, what do you think of me?"

"No, my Lord High King, you do not understand. I have only seen loyalty through duty or fear of cruelty. But your men follow you because they know they matter to you. You have a good heart, my lord."

"You have my heart, Ellianna."

She turned away from his gaze with a single nod, unease filling her.

They ate in near silence and were mounted to resume their journey as the sun cleared the southern trees. Ellianna noted many sat lower in their saddles than before. After a second man was caught sleeping, Farn called for a forced march. Ellianna was grateful and one of the first to slide from the saddle. As the king promised, each sun saw her ache less, yet walking felt good. Even so, unease plagued her. She looked around. Something threatened them, but she saw naught.

Malic took her mount's lead and holding it in one hand with his own mount's reins, he created a wide space for her to walk between him and the king with their destriers on the outside.

The pace was brusque but good. Ellianna reveled in the fresh air and working of her own limbs. Still disquiet stalked her. There appeared no reason to fret—yet she did. The men remained quiet except for the firm unison footfalls and their heavy breathing. It was only in the quiet she heard it.

Her heart skipped a beat. She stopped, crouched near the ground, and placed her hand on the dirt. The procession behind her came to an abrupt and awkward halt.

"Did you hear it?" she asked as the king drew near.

"Be alert men," Malic ordered, and not a sound could be heard anywhere.

Ellianna thought she must have been mistaken, but then she felt the vibration of the earth under her hand. "Monsuit," she gasped. A roar and crashing through the brush sounded off in the trees behind them to confirm her fears.

In the next heartbeat, Malic threw her in her saddle. She struggled to get her feet in the stirrups as they broke into a frantic gallop. The men in the rear turned to face the threat, but when Ellianna looked behind her, she saw three monsuits emerge from the tree line. The men retreated from their attack, whirling to follow after the others.

"Three," she gasped.

"Monsuit do not hunt or even live in packs." Kaldreck called from his racing mount.

"Unless they have a near grown cub," Malic shouted back on her other side.

"We are extremely blessed, for this one has two cubs," she said. Both men glanced at her. "Two cubs are said to be very rare and an omen of old for good luck."

"I do not feel lucky, my lady," Malic said.

Ellianna followed Malic's gaze behind them. The beasts—thrice the weight of their mounts and traveling on six legs—outdistanced their four-legged destriers closing the gap with alarming speed.

Ellianna's glance caught on Alcoff atop the wagon, as he clutched at his side. She noted fresh blood.

"This isn't working," she stated. She reigned in and swerved her mount behind Kaldreck. Ellianna charged from the procession between the king and in front of the nose of Goffray's mount. She veered her destrier close enough to the page to relieve him of his sword.

"Ellianna!"

"My lady!" the roars went up and the tight procession broke to either turn and stand their ground, or charge after her.

She kicked her mount to greater speed pointing him directly at the tree line to the right of the road. As she hoped, the large mother saw an easy target in the lone rider and charged at Ellianna.

The men bellowed after her.

Near the trees, she whirled her mount back toward the men

coming after her.

The monsuit's thick green fur shifted in waves along her back with each powerful stride.

Ellianna switched back again. The men were nearly upon her —their swords raised shouting a war cry at the charging beast.

The monsuit stumbled struggling to shift her great weight in the new direction.

Ellianna jerked her reluctant mount's head to turn it back again in front of the beast. As she passed, she lashed out with her borrowed sword and sliced open the beast's tender snout. With the power of the destrier under her, Ellianna nearly managed to remove the entire top portion, the length of a forearm, along the monsuit's face.

The beast faltered—its front two legs collapsing under her. She roared, shaking the ground. She reared up on her back two paws and batted at her snout, only to drop back to the earth with a jolt. She roared and tossed her head repeatedly, but Ellianna left her to the men and their larger weapons.

She turned her mount toward the cubs.

"Ellianna!" The king still followed her.

One cub appeared well in hand as a group of the guards surrounded it. The final beast faced off with Malic. In coming to aid their fight, he'd moved from his destrier to totter in the back of the swerving wagon as it bounded behind free-running, frantic mounts in the soft earth beside the road. The cub pressed a paw against the tall side of the wagon and threatened to topple it. Ellianna charged at this cub.

She shouted, and it turned in her direction. It made one more swipe at Malic, who returned the deed, swinging a mighty hammer with a solid metal head the size of her own.

The beast howled at the glancing blow that did no real damage. It lowered its head and charged at her.

Ellianna's mount refused to face the creature straight on and reared up, throwing Ellianna to the ground.

"Ellianna!" Kaldreck's cry roared through the air.

She rolled a few times, rose to her feet, snatched up the lost sword, and charged on foot at the momentarily startled beast. They were within a rod, and the beast rose up batting the air between them. With only a pace between them, it roared. Ellianna coughed at the foul breath. Two strides more and it raised its head to come down over her. It looked as though it intended to swallow her whole.

It was the moment Ellianna hoped for. She dropped to her knees as the creature's throat sailed over her head. She thrust the blade up through the soft spot at the back of its mouth and drove it into its head.

The beast stopped moving and shuddered. A moment longer and Ellianna twisted and yanked on the weapon to dislodge it. The front end of the dead monsuit fell on top of her, trapping her under its weight and knocking the breath from her lungs as it covered her entire body.

Kaldreck watched, in an all-consuming panic unlike anything he had ever known, as Ellianna broke rank with only Goffray's small sword. She succeeded in luring the largest of the monsters toward her and slashed open its face—a tactic he had used on hunts himself—more than once. But she had not stopped there.

She turned her mount toward the next monsuit and drew it from the wagon and Malic.

When she flew from her mount, Kaldreck nearly fell as well. His heart dropped to the pit of his stomach as she rolled. Still it did not stop her. Before he or anyone could reach her, she held the sword and charged the beast on foot. Even in his horror, he thrilled at her bravery. Few men did he know who would do such a fool-hearty thing. Ellianna fell beneath the beast's charge. She thrust up the blade, then she disappeared beneath it.

Kaldreck leapt from his mount, barely able to stand.

"Push it off her!" Malic bellowed as he stomped past him.

They rolled the beast to its side revealing Ellianna flat on her back. The blade laid the length of her from neckline to stomach. Her eyes remained closed.

No one moved.

Only ragged breaths could be heard among the stunned onlookers.

Kaldreck felt his heart stop and his lungs turn to stone.

A soft sigh came from the blood-drenched prone figure. She inhaled a long slow breath and her eyes fluttered open. In the next heartbeat, she pushed herself to a sitting position. "That was far easier with a blade than with a sharpened stone bound to a sturdy stick."

"Huzzah!" the men cheered in a mighty roar causing her to startle.

Kaldreck dropped to one knee, relief falling on him so powerfully he could not stand.

Ellianna turned to Malic. Taking his hand, she rose to her feet with ease. "Are you hale, my warrior queen?" he asked.

Cheers and chants went up at her nod. Fists raised as the men formed a line to acknowledge her victory. She stood with her fist raised high and accepted the reward of a battle well fought.

Kaldreck drew in his returning breath, stood, and moved toward her.

Ellianna put her hands out, crimson palms facing him, and waved him off as she backed away. "Nay, my lord. Stop. I am well." She continued stepping from him. "I am covered in blood. You will foul your fine garments," she protested.

He pressed forward, catching her arm as she stumbled into the beast she had vanquished. "Curse the garments!" He pulled her to him and held her to his pounding heart.

She relented and relaxed into him, though her hands remained barely touching his waist and did not encircle him.

He kissed the top of her head and thought he felt a tremor race through her. "Are you sure you are well, Ellianna?" he spoke into her hair—much of which now flew free of the braid.

She tried to say something, but it was muffled by his tight hold.

He loosed his hold by a small degree.

"I am well and truly fine, my lord." She looked out at the three slain creatures. "There lies good pelts and a huge amount of meat in this field." Her head rested on his chest, and her words hummed over his body.

"Aye, my lady," Malic said from where he stood beside them. His captain turned to the others. "You heard our warrior queen. There is work to be done. See to it men."

As they moved off, she turned in Kaldreck's hold searching for something. "Is Alcoff well? The tossing of the wagon brought the blood again."

"I am sure Balmson is seeing to his needs—whatever they may be." He refused to release her no matter how holding her pained him.

She tried to wiggle an arm free, and she offered Goffray back his weapon.

"Keep it, my queen. You are far more skilled with it than I." He untied the sheath from his waist and handed it to her.

Kaldreck dropped one arm freeing her to accept it.

The young man moped off as she tried to put the sword back inside the leather.

Kaldreck took the blade from her unable to suppress a smile. "Well, if you intend to be a true warrior, you must learn the proper care of your weapon. It may be the only thing between you and death." He waved the tip at the dead beast beside them. "Come I will show you how to clean a sword and inspect it for damage before you don your prize."

They walked toward the wagon resting at a tilt in the grass. Kaldreck's arm encircled her waist, and he instructed her. Once the weapon lay cleaned, and no flaws were found in its fine honed edges, he handed it to her. She tied the sheath about her waist and reached for it.

He held it for a moment longer, allowing their hands to brush. "I fear you will scare me near unto death before the rites are ever said over us."

She released the hilt leaving it in his hand. Her gaze dropped as disquiet churned her insides. "It is as I told you, my Lord High King. I have brought you harm."

He cupped her chin and raised it to capture her gaze. "The fault is my own, Ellianna. I have thought of you as a defenseless girl needing my protection, when in fact you are a woman of strength, bravery, and a power like the best of my warriors."

She pulled from his hold. "How ever am I to be what you need?"

"Be who the Creator made you be, and you will be everything I need, my sweet."

He offered the sword to her again and she slid it into the

sheath adjusting it to rest over her right thigh.

The king smiled shaking his head. "Nay, Warrior Queen. You wield with your right hand, so it must hang from the left." He reached his hands toward her. Slipping his hands between the sheath's cording and the fabric covering her hips, he spun the sheath around her waist until it laid over her other thigh.

"It is easier to draw from across the body than from the same side."

Balmson approached from behind Kaldreck. "Is Alcoff well?" she asked.

"He needed new sewing as the violence tore the old sutures from his flesh." The healer looked the length of her. "Are you hale, my lady?"

She nodded, "Yes, 'tis the monsuit's blood, not my own."

He inclined his head and continued across the field toward the men, his healing pouch tossed over his shoulder.

Ellianna sighed. The heat of the battle over, and the lack of sleep during the night served to make her exceedingly tired.

"Come let us find a place to sit, Ellianna."

She looked out to the earnest work being done all around. "Should we not go and lend our hands—"

"The future High Queen—warrior or no—does not butcher wild game."

She turned to stare at him. "The queen does not prepare meals, wash dishes, help the injured, skin game, or prepare its meat. Whatever does a queen do?"

His gaze caressed her soft and gentle. It made her heart dance. He offered his arm. "The queen accompanies the king, keeps his confidences, raises their children, sees to the education of those children and the squires, and aids the king in being a wise ruler who is good to their people." He held her gaze and heat slithered up her neck.

"My king, here," Farn rushed toward them with an armload of pillows.

"No," Ellianna put her hands out again.

Kaldreck stared at her.

"I have ruined enough fine cloth for one sun," she indicated his doublet and shirt. "A pelt would be better."

Kaldreck nodded. "Put the furs down with the pillows beneath."

"Here," Ellianna said. "I can at least hold those, so you need not make many trips." She took the pillows from him.

Kaldreck continued to scrutinize her.

"You said, my lord, that the queen aids her king. Is not caring for the king's possessions—thus saving his wealth—giving him aid?"

His smile grew, and he nodded, taking one of the pillows about to slip from her fingers. "But you hold the same cushions you feared would be soiled in your blood covered hands, my lady."

A smirk tugged the corner of her mouth. "Yes, but if the stiffness is any indication, the blood on my hands is now well dried."

Farn returned and threw out a large pelt covering the ground before them. She dropped the pillows and Farn added another fur on top. She knelt arranging the lumps and waved for Kaldreck to sit as well.

Before he joined her, he raised his head shielding his eyes from the low sun and called to Farn. "Tell the others there is no haste. We will camp here for sunsleep."

As the king took his place beside her, she moved from her knees to sit, and a huge sigh roared through her.

His hand came to her shoulder and pulled her down on the pillows. "Rest, Ellianna. You are tired."

She did not fight him but curled on her side with the king at her back.

He brushed her untidy hair from her face as she let sleep claim her.

When she woke, she found her tent had been erected over her. The smell of meat roasting pulled her out of the fabric enclosure, and she stretched in the waning light. Men lay about the ground—most asleep, some reclined and talked. She rolled her shoulder and felt a pain. Kaldreck stood leaning against the wagon his back to her as he talked with Malic. The healer stepped from his tent, and she went to him.

He bowed at her approach.

"Balmson, might you have some salve for a cut?"

His eyes went over her shoulder toward the king. "Are you injured, my lady?"

"It is but a small wound. I would not trouble you as it would most likely heal of its own. But if it were caused from a monsuit tooth, the wound is most likely to fester."

"'Tis true. I have many ointments, which could serve you well," he glanced once more from her feet to over her shoulder at King Kaldreck and turned into his tent.

Ellianna followed him inside and knelt on the soft ground near the flap of his short tent.

Balmson bent and rummaged through his pouch, bottles clinking together. With a handful in his arm he turned and gasped when he saw her sitting there. He stumbled back stepping on the side of the tent and almost succeeding in pulling it down on their heads.

"Ellianna!" Kaldreck's bark was sharp.

She brushed the flap aside and he took her by the arm, jerking her to her feet a few steps outside. Both his hands clamped down on her upper arms. His gaze flashed with anger as he searched her face.

Balmson stepped out, trembling so the bottles rattled together in his arms.

"What have you done, Balmson?" the king snarled.

Ellianna trembled in his grasp.

"Salves, my lord. The lady asked for salves—naught more." He raised his full arms and the glass chattered louder.

"I but asked, and went to collect what he offered," she whimpered.

One hand moved to grip her chin, which he raised to stare hard into her eyes. "Do I still have claim to your heart, my lady, or have you given it to another?"

"Nay, my lord. I am for you and you alone."

He lessened his hold on her. "It is forbidden for a woman to ever be alone in the company of a man not her calgent."

Her hand went to his wrist where he still cradled her face. "Forgive me, my Lord High King. I did not know. He is the healer.

I thought of naught more then a bit of ointment."

His hard gaze turned on Balmson.

"Nay, my lord the fault is not his. I came after him not knowing my proper place. Balmson did not invite and knew not that I followed him. Please, the blame is mine alone."

He turned and considered her more. His features softened a little, and he reached back to tuck a few errant hairs behind her ear. "My lady, you not only broke tradition, you lied to me."

"Nay, my lord. I did not know the tradition to honor it as I might, and Balmson did not know I was behind him. Naught happened between us, my lord."

He shook his head. "You suffered an injury, and you did not speak of it to me."

"It was not a lie I spoke. It is but a small cut, and I did not notice it until I woke, my lord. Had I known before, I would have said."

He released her and took one step back. "Where are you injured?"

She pointed to a small cut in the fabric of her garment just left of the bone that circle the throat like a collar.

He moved behind her and unlaced her garment pulling the thong free of the first several holes. "Show us," he directed, as he stood close beside her.

She trembled standing in the open for any to see, though the men all sat with their back to her. She used one hand to secure the neckline of her gown and keep herself covered, while she shrugged down the fabric from her shoulder until the wound appeared.

Balmson sat his bottles on the ground and looked to the king. Kaldreck nodded his permission for his approach, and the man drew near. He looked but did not touch her. He pointed to a spot, and Kaldreck himself pulled the wound open for Balmson to examine it more closely.

"I require something from my pouch, my lord."

Kaldreck sighed and the man scurried away.

Balmson returned with a round bit of thick glass the size of her palm and a tiny set of tongs. The healer indicated that the king should pull open the wound again.

Holding the glass near the wound and looking through it, he pulled several hairs from the opening with the tiny tool. His hands dropped to his sides and he talked only to the king. "The wound is clear of debris, though it should be washed before the creams are applied."

"Give me what is required." Kaldreck instructed, the calm now returned to his voice as stood before her.

Balmson handed him a clean wet bit of cloth, and Kaldreck brought it to her exposed flesh.

"I can return to my tent and tend to the wound in privacy, my lord," she whispered.

"Hold your gown in place, Ellianna. I would see all is done for your full healing." The rag in his hand brushed with a light touch over the cut.

Water ran down under her garment and over her skin. She swallowed at the cacophony of foreign sensations running over her all at once. She moved the fist full of fabric she held to better collect the water, which had slowed.

Kaldreck dipped the rag in the bucket Balmson held for him, and a new wave washed over her hidden flesh.

Her head swam, and the trees danced about her.

The cloth held still on her cut, and Kaldreck's hand encircled her arm steadying her. "Am I hurting you, Ellianna?"

She struggled to move or to grasp a thought in her head as her gaze found his. She shook her head. "The water is cool, my lord." She hoped the lie would explain her trembling.

Light danced in his eyes, and a smile replaced his scowl. He exchanged the wet rag for a dry one and placed it over her injury, sopping the water from her exposed skin. Balmson handed him a bright green salve. He dipped in a finger and spread it in the cut. Next came a foul smelling thinner cream that reminded her of the smell of her leather foot coverings after days of sweating in them. Kaldreck smoothed the second cream over the first, and wide around the edge of the wound. He blew on it to hasten its drying. His breath on her bare flesh felt cool where the cream lay—but searing everywhere else. She bit her lower lip to stifle a gasp. His smile prevented him from blowing for a moment, and she took a quick gulp of air.

When he continued, she thought her knees would give way. The drying cream contracted over her skin drawing the edges of the cut together. As he stood to look at his work, she realized they were standing alone. Balmson had moved near the fire far beyond them.

Kaldreck looked at her again, his gaze holding her unmovable. He brought his hands to rest tenderly on her arms were he had grasped her roughly before. "Forgive my temper. It seems I have become quite captured by you in our few suns together. The thought of you with another, I think, would drive me mad."

"There is no other," she whimpered.

He leaned forward, his breath caressed her cheek, "Aye, I can see that clearly now, my sweet." He lips pressed to her temple—as they had in her dream. Fire seared the spot, and she could not stop the gasp from escaping. He stepped behind her, pulled up her kirtle, and re-laced it.

Coming beside her, he offered his arm. "Shall we go enjoy some of your kill, Ellianna?" His voice was a tender whisper, but the heat of his touch he left on her shoulder and head rendered her unable to move. He placed a hand over the top of hers and drew her to the fire. They sat, and she nibbled at the meat lost in a swirl of memories and new sensations.

A claim of calgent. Days in a stiff saddle. A viper. A volif confrontation. The attack of three monsuit at once. And the bewildering touch of a man on her skin. What more could a new sun possible hold?

Chapter 12

Kaldreck lay on his cushions within his tent relishing the memory of her. This sun held a mix of wild emotions. A warrior from his earliest youth, emotions were drilled out of him. No room for sentimentality on the battlefield. But Ellianna stirred his insides until he no longer recognized himself. From the lowest grip of fear to the height of knowing her safe; from the joy of watching her sleep to the despair and wrath of seeing her with another—the moods swayed in him like a ship tossed on a violent sea. His every thought consumed by her and what she did. Divine, be merciful.

Malic sudden shift of gaze and the stricken look on his face had brought Ellianna's movements to Kaldreck's attention. Kaldreck had watched as she approached Balmson, and his stomach clenched tight.

"She worries over Alcoff. She must seek to know how he fairs," Kaldreck told his friend trying to convince himself.

The healer cast him a glance, and he knew something was wrong. He had started moving toward her. Another glance from Balsom and Kaldreck quickened his steps. But Kaldreck stumbled when he watched her walk boldly into Balmson's tent.

She is not the maiden she claims. She came to my tent the first night, and now she goes to another. His thoughts had warred within him—his heart broke—and at the same moment, he vowed to end her. She claimed innocence, but how could she not know such things?

Now, many degrees of the sun later, lying alone in his own tent, with his thoughts clear, he knew she spoke the truth. Her mother was lost to her while she was still at an innocent age, and Villiant was not a man who would have cared to instruct her on such matters. She did his bidding even if it be without a proper escort around other men.

His eyes closed, and he rested back on his hands entwined behind his head.

The look of innocence as he unlaced her garment, the color of her face, the tightness with which she gripped the cloth to her— she remained a maiden as she promised.

His own breath caught now as he remembered the pounding of the vein in the hollow of her neck at his ministrations. She had swayed, and her breaths became shallow. A smile parted his lips at the gasp she stifled when he blew on her skin. Oh, how his heart longed to dwell in the smoky depths of her eyes so full of passion she did not understand.

Ellianna may be well versed in the ways of wild creatures of the forest, but she knew naught of the ways of men and women. He would enjoy discovering them with her.

Kaldreck exited his tent early the next morning to find Ellianna's tent dismantled and ready to be loaded on the wagon. He looked to the men moving about their duties but saw no sight of her. He approached Malic. "Ellianna?"

Malic smiled, "She is at the river cleaning. She wanted to wait to ask your permission, but it was quite obvious she was uncomfortable in her gown grown stiff from its layer of blood."

Kaldreck looked toward the sound of a river off to the east.

"I sent Eton to guard over her, and a handful of men to stand watch at a distance. She will be safe."

Kaldreck's gaze shifted back to Malic, and he slapped him on the shoulder. "Thank you, my friend." With many of the others off seeing to his calgent's safety, Kaldreck stored of his own equipment and was saddling Ellianna's horse when she returned. Her garment hung heavy with water as she approached him.

She stared at the ground, "Good sunwake to you, my Lord High King." Her voice was a tentative whisper.

"The Divine bless you, Ellianna."

A breath of air slid between her lips, and her shoulders dropped as her head rose. Her eyes searched his face.

She feared him. Kaldreck brush her cheek, and his heart broke at the cringe she fought to hide. "Forgive me my anger at sunsleep, Ellianna. I did not mean to frighten you so."

""T'was naught you did, my lord. The fault was entirely mine. I did not know my proper place."

"I will never hurt you, Ellianna."

She pushed a smile to her lips. "Of course not, my lord. I trust you." She took his arm, and they moved toward the fire where the morning meal awaited them.

"Where is Farn, my lord?"

"There is little you miss, my lady," Kaldreck said as he ate.

Her cheeks flushed bright as her gaze fled from him. "There is a great deal I miss, my lord, much to my shame."

He had not meant to remind her of the indiscretion. "I spoke only a compliment, my lady." She would not look at him as they finished their meal and moved to the horses. "Farn has gone ahead to alert Lord Santon of our intentions to stay at his home in Hampel this sunsleep."

She said no more and again fell into a contemplative silence.

Some degrees past the sun's zenith, Farn returned. "Lord Santon awaits the arrival of his Lord High King and our future Lady Queen. He prepares a great feast for the occasion, my lord."

"Thank you, Farn."

Farn pulled a parcel from his pouch and handed it to him. "I thought this might be needed? Please forgive me if I've overstepped in presuming to get something for our lady."

Assuming what lay inside the package he nodded. "You are ever attentive, Farn. I thank you once more."

Kaldreck helped Ellianna from her mount and offered her the bundle. She drew a new gown and slippers from it. The garment loose with billowing sleeves was much like her own, lacking in any real shape or form, but it was of a finer cloth and a deep purple like the evening sky. The simple black slippers were embroidered with yellow night starflowers.

She looked at them for a moment and then up into his face.

"Farn thought you might make a better impression on your future subjects if their queen was not covered in monsuit blood."

"'Tis true," she looked around them. "Where might I change without bringing you shame, my lord?"

How he regretted his actions of the previous sun.

"Brayden, fetch a tent. Eton a bucket of water," Malic ordered.

Soon, there in the middle of the road, his men held a circle of tent fabric high in the air for her to be concealed within. She handed her sword to him, "You best keep this as well. It would not appear welcoming."

She disappeared within the screen and the men held it closed, their eyes shut as well, should something go amiss. Ellianna emerged a short time later fussing with her hair, her old garment tossed over her shoulder.

The men took the tent and her old dress and to put them in the wagon as she worked nimbly to straighten the braid. Her hair fell to below her knees in crinkled waves. She brushed her fingers through it and began to rework the braid.

Kaldreck stepped forward. The blue fabric brought even more warmth to her skin and tinting the color of her eyes. Her sleek hair lay filled with an endless array of brown hued strands from light like the fruit of a jahala tree to dark tinged with red like the sonnet bird. Every time he looked at her, he found her more beautiful.

She glanced up at his approach. "I will only be a moment longer, my lord."

He rested his hand on hers. "Will you leave your hair down?"

Her brows crinkled together in the most endearing way. "Is it not inappropriate for a woman to leave her unbound?"

"'Tis beautiful."

She let her hands drop at her side with a puzzled shrug, and he, reaching up to run his fingers through it, released it from the braid she had begun.

They approached the walled city of Hampcl, and Kaldreck

noticed her wide-eyed stare. *I have never seen a city*, she had told him. "What do you think, my lady?"

She did not speak for a moment. When her words did come they were guarded and seemed to be chosen with great care. "It is very large. The walls are tall. How can one see the beauty of the Creator's work with such high walls, my lord?"

"They go for walks, I suppose."

They left their mounts with a stable hand, and Kaldreck drew her aside before they entered the fine brick hall of Lord Santon. "My lady, Lord Santon is one of our oldest lords. He is of the old time and does not do things like most of the others of our land. He has been a trustworthy lord and a good supporter."

She nodded and waited.

"Lord Santon is of a mind that men and women should not socialize together. When we enter, you will be escorted by a female servant to the women's chambers where you will dine with Santon's second spouse—the first died in childbirth."

Again, she looked confused, "But she is not a mate—a true calgent—a One and Only?"

"This was a union, not of love but, of practicality. Santon needed heirs to his holdings so he sought a woman who would join with him."

"Without love," she stated with a deep frown.

"It is done."

She took only one step before the meaning of his words took hold of her, and she seized his arm with both her hands. "My Lord High King, I am not to be with you this evening?" The terror in her face was startling.

"I shall dine with the men and sleep in a chamber Santon has reserved for me. You will dine with the women—"

"Nay, my lord. Do not leave me," she begged. "I know not the ways I am supposed to behave. I will say or do the wrong thing. Please, my lord, do not allow me to bring you dishonor by my simple ways." Her fingers bore into his arm until he feared she might draw blood.

"Ellianna, calm yourself. You have faced down volif in the middle of the night and charged on foot at monsuit with naught but a small blade—this is merely a meal."

"I have never dined with a group of women… and never done anything with noble women."

He pried her fingers from him and entwined her arm around his. She remained reluctant, and he needed to pull her with him. "The Comforter grant you peace, my lady. It is only a meal. You will be fine, and I will see you at sunwake."

"Please," she whimpered as they walked through the door.

"Eton will go with you as far as he is allowed."

He pulled from her hold, and her eyes—white with fear— pleaded with him. "All is well, my sweet." His heart broke for her pain, but he could not bring her with him without offending his supporter.

Chapter 13

"Arrgghh". The dark figure bellowed. Crash. His earthenware bowl shattered against the wall carved from the granite.

"Hush, my love. We will find a way."

The dark-hooded man whirled and seized the woman by the hair, holding her near his face as words raked over his teeth. "Her gift wakes faster than I feared. I must stop her if I am to save Windmere. But the luck of the ancients shields her."

"Yet you are far more powerful, my love. And you know the throne is rightfully yours."

He tossed her aside and slammed his fist onto the table rocking the candles upon it and causing shadows to dance on the rough walls. "Had not my father feared his enemies' threat against me, and my mother hidden me away, all would know I am the rightful high king. But none knew of me. Now that hopeless weakling Kaldreck sits in my place, and the kingdom teeters on the brink of falling to our enemies across the sea. He is blissfully unaware they, even now, build ships and amass their army to invade."

His fist smashed down again, this time hard enough to upset a candle. She caught it, placing it back in its holder as he continued to rant. "He is enamored with this ancient idea of a true mate who will bind with him heart and soul and continue his inept rule. He is besot by her and knows not the danger to befall us all."

"Still you are more powerful than she," she stroked his arm.

"I lured the viper. I stirred the hungry heart of the volif. I alerted the monsuit to a great threat." He threw his fists into the air and shouted at the ceiling hidden beyond a blanket of black. "She defeated each one of my attempts." His hands dropped to his sides. "And her report with not just the imbecilic king, but with the best fighting men of Windmere, grows—as do her powers."

"There is still time, my love. She goes now to the house of Santon—"

"Yes, I have worked long on my pet Zorgot. Her jealous heart will not take much prodding to do her future queen harm."

She brushed a long strand of black hair from his face. "And should Zorgot fail, I have been assigned to attend our new queen as one of her maids. She will not escape me, my love." She pressed a kiss to his cheek.

He smiled at the woman he used so effectively, grabbed her hair, pulled her close, and drank of her willing lips.

⚭

Ellianna trembled as she followed the slender plainly-dressed servant girl down a long corridor lit by many torches. Eton followed for a time but remained without when they passed through ornately carved doors marking the boundary of the women's chambers. Dark chamber led to dark chamber with no windows to bring her the comfort of the sun. She shuffled along to keep her slippers on her feet.

The endless darkness brought to mind the time Ellianna went

into a cave after a young bot. She could hear it lowing in the darkness but became lost. When she found her way out at last—filthy, hungry, and weak from thirst—Villiant said she had been gone for the better part of three suns. She shivered at the memories, and her stomach grumbled at the phantom hunger of so long ago.

At last, the servant stopped at another chamber door and pushed it open for her to enter but did not follow. The brightness of the room, lined on one wall with windows and painted in bold yellow, hurt her eyes. Before she could see clearly, the murmuring of many women assailed her.

"Well, here she is—at last," a voice much like the elder's wife from Illgrove when she talked to a dirty child in her path, greeted her. "It is our future Lady Queen, Lady Ellianna."

Her vision cleared, and she found herself among many women dressed in an array of elegant shimmering gowns. Jewels covered their fingers, necks, and arms. They sparkled like the stars at deep sunsleep. A lady reclining at the top of four steps at one end of the room, lounged upon many colored pillows, a servant behind her waved a large fan. The lady, draped in a bejeweled purple gown, inspected her.

She did not rise. She did not offer observance to her future queen. Fear wrapped around Ellianna's heart. If she thought she could have found her way, she would have run to the king's side, or at least Eton's. *You have faced down volif in the middle of the night and charged on foot at monsuit with naught but a simple blade—this is merely a meal.* Kaldreck's words came bringing her strength. She stood unmoving, staring at the woman.

"Please find a seat," the lady offered.

Ellianna did not move. She was soon to be queen and Ellianna knew enough to understand the disrespect this woman gave her. If it had only been the two of them she may not have bothered, but the others in the room were following her poor example.

The lady, who had a face like one of Kaldreck's destriers, looked down her nose disapprovingly at her. Her small, barely visible mouth, held in a condemning pinch, contorted into a force smile. "Make yourself welcome, Ellianna."

"A queen is not to make *herself* welcome in a subject's home, my lady," she said dryly, and prayed no one could see how she trembled.

A woman with auburn hair, arrayed in many braids pinned up with sparkling jewels, stood and curtsied to the ground, most of the others rose and did likewise. "You are most welcome, my lady and soon to be queen. The Divine bless your union to our Lord High King with love, and many strong sons," the first said.

Ellianna inclined her head toward them, "I thank you. Your kindness will not be forgotten." She slipped a glance at the lady still lounging on her cushions. "The Lord High King will know of the favor you have bestowed upon me. May the Giver visit blessings upon blessings on your homes."

Though she knew she should be sitting with the lady on the stairs—if not in her place—Ellianna looked to those who greeted her with warmth. "May I have the pleasure of your company, my ladies?"

They looked to the stern woman, but Ellianna did not wait for permission. She walked as calm and smooth as she could, gripping her slippers with her toes, toward them. She did not want to appear haughty like her hostess but smiled and inclined her head to the women who reshuffled the cushions to make room for her. She lowered herself down with as much grace as she could manage and leaned back on her elbow, as she had seen them doing. She placed herself a short distance from the lady with the auburn hair.

"I have never seen Lady Zorgot so displeased with anyone. Well done, my queen," the woman whispered with a giddy chuckle.

Ellianna glanced from Zorgot to the lady beside her who shielded a mischievous grin with a small hand-held fan.

Zorgot clapped her hands for the food to be brought, and the woman next to her introduced herself. "My queen, I am Glenda, my calgent is a successful merchant of silk in Hampel, pleased I am to meet you." She leaned in and whispered, "And even more pleased to have you as queen and not Zorgot's sour daughter." She indicated a woman just below the steps who was a mirror of Zorgot though less gray entwined her head. "If Zorgot is insufferable now, I cannot imagine how intolerable she would have become as the queen's mother."

Ellianna wondered what her own mother would have thought of her new status. Mother would have been happy for her knowing she would be well provided for and that she'd escaped Villiant's hold. She could not image Mother taking pride or lording her daughter's position over others, however.

Glenda went around the circle of women introducing them and informing her of each of their men's status. They respectively greeted her with a pleasantry and many of the women joined her in congenial conversation as they waited for the meal. Ellianna remained quiet listening to their manner unless asked a question.

Soon, maids flooded into the room with an array of breads, fruits, cheeses, and meats. There was a momentary pause.

"Provider of all good, Creator of all bounty. We give Thee thanks for all we receive from Thy hand."

Ellianna had heard the blessing of the meal said on occasion when dining in another's home. But never had she heard it with such dead and meaningless words as all these women had just spoken. A pain pricked Ellianna's heart, but she did not have time to consider it as a large bowl of purple mush was sat before her.

"Ellianna, you must try the koii. It is a specialty of my home," Zorgot called with a smug grin.

Ellianna noted the grimaces and crinkled noses of those around her. To refuse would offer insult. To accept would mean falling into her trap. *Divine, let me not bring dishonor to King Kaldreck.*

She looked at it closely and returned it to the tray. "Alas, I must decline your kind offer Zorgot. I am a simple maid raised on a farm, and I would never wish to bring dishonor to your home by telling the king my delicate stomach was beset by some sweet delicacy it did not know. I could not shame you so, Zorgot. The Lord High King thinks well of Lord Santon." She smiled at the woman. "I regret I am forced to enjoy only the familiar breads and cheeses."

A murmur stirred around her, and she caught Glenda smiling. "Never has Zorgot been put in her place with more grace," she snickered behind her fan. "I must remember your kind words in the future, for I will never eat that vile gruel again."

"What is in it?"

"Blood, animal innards, and inferior grain."

Ellianna's nervous stomach almost rejected the dark bread she nibbled as the vile mixture was passed among the other women.

They lounged in pleasant conversation past the last degrees of the sun. Zorgot's daughter rose and went to the harpsichord and plunked out a grating tune. Zorgot cheered her with great fanfare, and everyone was obliged to clap.

The feasting concluded, the ladies bid their farewells, and bestowed their blessings one by one until only Zorgot remained with Ellianna. "You are to take my bed," Zorgot said, looking down her long nose.

"It is kind of you, Zorgot, but unnecessary. A few pillows would suit me."

"My lord demands I come to his bed this night, so you are to have mine," she waved a hand beyond where she'd reclined for the meal. "My girl will attend you." She strolled from the room, her chin tipped high and her back straight. "Sleep well, Ellianna." Her mocking farewell sent tiny cold footfalls of apprehension down her spine.

Shaking free of the woman's open dislike from her, Ellianna climbed the steps toward the waiting maid.

The girl fell in a deep curtsy. "May I help you with your garment, my queen?"

"What is your name?"

The girl startled, "Selna, my queen."

"Selna, I have naught else to wear, I will be fine in my garment for tonight."

"The lady said I was to offer you one of hers."

"I cannot imagine she would wish such a thing," Ellianna said with a dry smirk.

Selna trembled, "Truly, my queen, the lady wished it most earnestly."

Ellianna considered her, "What will happen if I choose not to accept her kindness, Selna?"

The girl trembled and dropped at her feet, "Please, my queen."

The sight softened Ellianna's fearful heart. "She will punish you if I refuse, then. Well, I will not see harm come to you on my account. Let us do as Zorgot wishes."

Selna rose and with quaking hands began to loosen the laces of Ellianna's new gown.

Ellianna enjoyed the rare treat of assistance with her garment. She was forever donning her dress backwards to work the laces to some tightness before twisting it around her and struggling to pull them tight and tie them at her neck.

Selna pulled the gown to the floor, and she stepped from it. Still covered from the waist to her feet in men's breeches, she drew the sheer chemise lying on the end of the bed over her head. Selna stared at the breeches for a moment more, and Ellianna saw the girl would not leave without them as well.

Ellianna slipped them off. "Modesty required me to don them while astride my Lord High King's large destrier."

"Yes, I would imagine many things are required for the Lord High King," Selna breathed with a winsome air. "What is he like?" she asked.

"King Kaldreck?"

Selna nodded.

Ellianna paused a moment finding her words. "He is caring of both his men and me. He is kind, but he has a fearsome anger if provoked. He has always remained gentle with me even though I bring him a good amount of consternation in my ignorant ways."

"Is he as handsome as the ladies all say?"

Ellianna smiled with new understanding. "Oh, yes. The Creator has cut King Kaldreck a fine form—tall, broad of shoulder, and adorned with many muscles under rich warm skin."

Selna sighed, "Oh, I do hope the calgent the Giver has chosen for me is as fine." She floated down the steps to lay Ellianna's garment over a long stool. She busied herself with tasks as Ellianna turned to the bed.

Tonight, she would have to find a way to sleep atop a bed without falling. The pillows lay heaped down the middle of the wide straw mattress on the raised platform. They looked odd to her. Eton spread her pillows out in a consistent layer over her bed. Ellianna removed several and tossed them to the floor. There were far more than the bed required.

"May I help you, my queen?" Selna asked, her head tilted to the side.

"I am fine Selna, but I do not require so many pillows." Ellianna chose one last mist green one to remove and a biting-tail appeared snapping its claws at being revealed.

"Eeek!" Selna shrieked and fell back against the wall of the sleeping chamber. Her hands clutched tight to her chest. Her face drained of all color, and she remained still as if turned to stone.

Ellianna considered the creature with interest. The multi-legged vermin spun around in the light. It was about the size of her hand with claws the length of her longest finger. Its tale whipped in all directions, the poison-filled barb on the tip looking for a target. What if she had not removed the pillows? If the biting-tail remained concealed she would have been stung. Did Zorgot still have hopes for her daughter?

The creature raised its tail and skittered for the cover of another pillow. Ellianna snatched it up as she had the viper the first night in camp with Kaldreck. This beast she seized by the tail, just below the barb.

Selna squealed and jumped farther from her, almost tumbling backwards down the steps.

Ellianna gave a sharp flip of her wrist breaking the creature's spine and threw the thing against the far wall for good measure. "That will need to be removed," Ellianna said. Taking care as she went, she removed all the pillows and searched both the bed and its platform. No more danger could be found, and she turned to replace some of the comfort to the bed.

Selna stood where Ellianna last saw her.

"I require a robe, Selna."

The girl nodded and shimmied down the wall never taking her eyes from the biting-tail's lifeless form.

Once covered in one of Zorgot's heavy fur trimmed robes, Ellianna snatched up the carcass and moved toward the girl.

Selna fell back with a gasp.

"You will lead me to where my guard waits, please, Selna.

The girl scurried out ahead of her.

Eton stood from the chair in the corner as she appeared. "M'lady?"

"I require your assistance, Eton," she held out the dead vermin to him.

"M'lady!"

"I found it in my bed before it could do me harm."

"Aye m'queen, if ye are well, I will see the thing disposed of immediately." He looked toward the doors with a twist of his lips and shifted his weight between his feet. "Are ye safe…"

"I have made a thorough search of the bedchamber. No more danger should present itself this sunsleep."

He nodded, and she returned to the borrowed chambers.

As she lay nestled safely between two long rows of pillows in the center of the bed, sleep would not visit her. Selna's soft snores drifted from the foot of the stairs, and her mind wondered over many things.

Why was Zorgot so insistent she relinquish her garments? What more awaited her at the jealous woman's hands? She remembered Airamena's rage at the king's refusal to speak with her. Zorgot welded far more power than a young distraught maiden. She prayed her Protector would keep her vigilant to danger.

As she rolled to her side, her mind drifted to what her own chamber would look like in Kaldreck's palace. Would it be forged from mighty stones so solid the breeze or the gentle rain on the roof could no longer be heard? She fought to inhale a hot breath. Would the polished stones of the floors cause her feet to slide in her slippers or send shards of ice through her soles when her feet were bare? The mere thought brought a freezing, stabbing pain up through her feet until she wrapped the blanket more tightly around them. Would there be naught but a rainbow of pillows to sit upon? She squeezed her eyes closed, willing images of the orange fields and many colors of the trees from her youth back into her mind. Would gossamer fabric be draped in every direction and color from the ceiling? But never a star or a cloud?

Can I find contentment so far removed from the Creator's works?

Chapter 14

Hands with long slender fingers worked with adept skill sewing sparkling jewels into the embroidery. A chill filled the woman and she shivered, but it came from a black heart and not the dying fire beside her.

"My girl will be found worthy when *you* are accused and put to shame."

Ellianna rose in the still, cool chamber before sunwake. She braided her hair and wondered if she would always wake so early. She moved down the stairs passed where Selna slept and collected her clothes that had been laundered and returned.

As she stepped beyond the servant again, Selna startled and leapt to her feet. "My queen, you are awake?"

"Forgive me, Selna I did not mean to disturb you."

"I must help you with your gown."

"It is not necessary."

"No, I must," she snatched the clothing from Ellianna's arm and held it tight to her chest.

Ellianna narrowed her gaze on the odd girl. "You may tell Zorgot you assisted me, but I will dress myself. My garments?"

Selna placed them in her outstretched hand.

"You may go, Selna. If it would not get you into trouble, I would like a bit of cheese and bread before I leave."

Selna quavered, curtsied, and dashed from the room.

Ellianna took her gown and breeches and sat on the end of the bed examining them with great care. The dream had felt so real. And the embroidered gown matched the one before her. As her hands skimmed along the hem something sharp scratched the base of her finger. Upon a closer inspection she found the large jewel in an intricate gold setting she expected. Ellianna unbound it and laid the ring in her hand. "So, if you could not kill me, you thought to accuse me the thief." Setting the ring on the toe of her waiting slipper, she continued her search.

Two bejeweled earrings were worked into a flourish of embroidery at the waist, but she found naught more. She jerked the chemise of the traitorous woman off, tossed it on the bed, and slipped into the breeches first. She took the slippers and tucked them into each leg of the garment so she would have better footing if she needed it. Selna returned as she settled the soft kirtle on her shoulders. She allowed her hands to run over the woven fabric, her fingers tracing the embroidery remembering the images of the dream, as Selna tightened the laces.

Ellianna moved to the tray of food and decided not to eat it in case it was poisoned. She strolled to the door. "My queen, your food?"

"I have lost my appetite," she crushed the jewelry tight in her hand. "Please lead me to my guard; the king will be preparing to leave."

"The manor is quiet, my queen. All still sleep."

"Then I will request my guard to accompany me on a tour of your city," she flung open the doors forcing the girl to go with her.

"Thank you, Selna. I no longer require your service. I will be sure to tell the king of your kind treatment." Ellianna dismissed the servant and waited for her to disappear through another door before she spoke in hushed tones. "Eton, I require a boon."

He snapped to attention as an eager smile came to his lips, "Aye m'lady."

"I wish to have both Lord Santon and Lady Zorgot present as we depart. It is imperative they do not know I requested it, nor do I wish for them to know the other will be present. Is such a thing possible?"

Eton's smile turned to a straight hard look of concern. "M'lady?"

"I merely wish to thank my hosts, Eton. I will do naught to shame the king. This I swear!"

"Aye, it will be done as you asked." His features softened, and he waved for her to precede him.

"I do not know where I am going, Eton," she whispered with a small smile.

"Straight ahead, m'lady. At the great hall, turn left and you will see the doors leading out to the ward." He followed her until she stood in the faint light of the waking sun.

A few of the king's guards stood about as provisions were loaded into the wagon and their mounts saddled by Santon's servants. They bowed to her and blessed her morning and she noticed over her mount now lay a new white sash—free of monsuit blood.

Ellianna moved out of the way as Eton spoke to Brayden and Naton before returning to stand near her. "Eton, would it be appropriate to walk around the city without the king?"

"A proper escort could be arranged for such a venture, if you wish it."

"I would welcome the walk before we mount again, if it will not take the men from any needed task."

Soon Eton stood behind her elbow and three fully-armored guards waited behind him. Eton nodded and she moved toward the homes, which also served as shops. The smell of baking bread drew her to one shop. As she neared, the porch awning lifted to reveal a row of breads cooling on the shelf at the window. The unshapely baker placed the awning poles in their niches and turned to greet her customers. She wore a rough garment much like Ellianna's old one.

At seeing Ellianna, the woman curtsied as low as her aging form would allow. "M'queen, honored I is to have ye visit me humble bakery."

"The wonderful smell drew me."

"Thank ye, m'queen."

"I do not wish you to give away secrets, ma'dam, but there is a tangy sent mixing with the warm grain and sour hint of yeast. May I inquire?"

The woman threw back her shoulders and entwined her fingers over her belly. "Thank ye for noticin', m'queen. 'Tis me best seller. I mixes in a little rosemary and mindome into the dough. 'Tis a spiced bread."

"It smells quite grand." Ellianna turned to leave.

"Do ye nay care to be tryin' any, m'queen?" The woman's lower lip pooched out as she spoke.

"I would love to, but alas I did not bring any coin with me this sun."

"Ye're soon to be our new queen, I gives it to ye. As a gift." She picked up a loaf in her stocky fingers and offered it to Ellianna.

Eton took it before she could reply. He tore off a bit and ate it before handing it to Ellianna.

She too took a piece and allowed the warm tangy bread to linger on her tongue. "Oh, that is the finest thing I have ever tasted, ma'dam. You have a wonderful gift from the Giver to creature such a treat."

The woman gave another observance, "I thank ye, m'queen." She hesitated for a moment, then cleared her throat. "Might I solicit yer favor on me shop?"

Ellianna looked to Eton for help.

"The queen's seal has yet to be created. But, Queen Ellianna will see her favor is visited upon your bakery when it is so."

"Thank ye, m'queen. Oh, thank ye, indeed. And may the Divine bless yer union to our Lord High King with love and many strong sons."

Ellianna continued down the street looking at wares and speaking to the people. She nibbled on the bread and offered some to the guards shadowing her, and they took it eagerly.

By the time they returned, the king stood among his warriors in the ward. He looked up at her approach and smiled. "Good sunwake to you, my lady."

She curtsied, "Good sunwake to you, my Lord High King. I hope you experienced good sleep."

He nodded as Zorgot stepped from the manor. The woman startled to see her husband standing on the lower step but as her gaze was already held by Ellianna, she could not retreat within her home.

Ellianna stepped close to the king and rose on her toes to gain his ear. "Would it be proper to approach Lord Santon with a concern and also speak with Lady Zorgot?" She slipped to her heels and gazed up at him.

His smile was broad and approving. "If I am in company, the queen may address any male she so chooses." He led the way to their hosts.

Ellianna noted the worry in Zorgot's flickering gaze. She inclined her head toward the short lord whose thin hair was full of gray. He must have been many turns of the sun older than Zorgot. "My Lord Santon, I wished to personally thank you for your generous hospitality. *Never* I have been treated so."

Santon stood a little taller, "It is I who am honored to be first to host our queen."

Zorgot looked to the ground and quaked.

"I wished to speak with you for I have a great concern for your Lady Zorgot, my lord."

The lady jerked, and her eyes went wide.

"My lord, I do not know where the nest lies, but a biting tail found its way into your lady's bed. I searched the room finding naught, but it must be close for it to find its way so deep beneath the pillows since Lady Zorgot last slept. I know you do not wish harm to come to your spouse, so a charmer should be called to uncover the vermin before they overtake the entire women's chambers. Your daughter could be at risk, as well."

Ellianna spoke with earnest concern as Santon turned a deep shade of red. Though he did not turn to her, the icy gaze he afforded Zorgot from the corner of his eye made even Ellianna tremble.

"I will see to the matter at once, my queen," he groaned. "I thank the Merciful, no harm came to you. May I ask how you dealt with the creature?"

"Our queen has quite a way with wild beasts. On our journey thus far, she has captured a viper at her feet, fought volif in the night, and single handedly taken down a monsuit," Kaldreck reported with a straight back and puffed up chest.

Santon's eyes went wide, "Truly?"

"Aye, my men have taken to calling her their warrior queen."

"Well, again I am much relieved you were not hurt, my queen." His gaze strayed to Zorgot. "I cannot imagine the shame to come upon my house if anything had happened to you during your stay with us," his words ground between his teeth.

Ellianna inclined her head once more and started to turn to leave. She swung around to face Zorgot once more. "I almost forgot, Lady Zorgot, I found this." She held up the ring between thumb and finger, as the color drained from the woman's face. "If my calgent offered me such a priceless treasure, I would take more care in where I left it."

Zotgot put out her trembling hand.

"These earrings are also exquisite, but I cannot take them from your home, my lady. Though I do thank you for thinking of me." Ellianna closed the lady's hand around the jewels and looked at her in a sweet calm. "I will not soon forget the kindness you have shown, Lady Zorgot. I look forward to returning the favor when you visit my home."

The trembling turned to a visible shudder.

"Lord Santon, I fear Lady Zorgot may be taking a chill. Perhaps she needs to return to her chambers," Ellianna said with a kind smile to the lord. She turned and raised her hand waiting for Kaldreck to lead her to the mounts.

As they drew near the destriers he leaned into her, "May I ask what that was really about, Ellianna?"

She shook her head with a shudder as her nerves released the tremble she had been hiding, "I think this is one of those times you are better not knowing all, my lord."

Malic offered his hands to assist her.

She placed her hand on his shoulder for balance, "I need but a moment, my lord. I am not wearing my slippers," she muttered so not everyone would hear. She slipped the first out of the leg of her breeches, dropping it the ground before moving to retrieve the other.

"My lady?" Kaldreck asked.

She slipped them on her feet. "I walk out of them and they were extremely slippery on the lord's polished floors," she told him and mounted.

Kaldreck looked up at her with a bemused smile and slight shake of his head.

Ellianna thrilled at the rolling hills beyond the gate and sighed with contentment as the air brushed her face.

"I would care to hear the tale, my lady," Kaldreck said with a raised brow.

"My lord, you need not trouble yourself over the antics of a jealous woman."

"Jealous?"

"Yes, she hoped you would choose her daughter as your calgent."

The king's fine face twisted as if he ate an onga root. "Zilina? Have you seen that sour-faced girl?" Kaldreck shuddered, and it made Ellianna laugh.

"She is the image of her mother," Ellianna continued to be tickled by his reactions.

He turned to her as she laughed, awe filling his face and tenderness flooding his eyes.

Chapter 15

Kaldreck marveled at Ellianna. She was keen and intelligent, and he wondered if there would be anything she could not learn if she so wished it. Though she did not know what to expect, she'd handled herself with poise under Zorgot's ploys, and as with the monsuit, came out the victor.

He laughed to himself at the thoughts going through Zorgot's head now knowing she would soon be in Ellianna's new home for the saying of the rites. Ellianna had finally relented and told him of all that occurred hidden so far from his protection. His anger ignited at the woman, though he sat in awe at the way Ellianna handled the situation with such cunning. Her way was the far better course. Any punishment he could have cast on the woman would have been fleeting. But Ellianna's veiled threat would haunt Zorgot every time the two women met. He could not keep the smile from his face.

She may be innocent of a great many things, but if naught else, Villiant taught her a shrewdness, which could make her a formidable foe. She reminded him of the opening petals of a tossel bud. Each moved petal released a sweet fragrance revealing a deeper hued petal beneath and creating the greater beauty of the full bloom. But he knew he would never see anything so beautiful as Ellianna when she laughed. Then the sun dawned new, and he found her more beautiful still.

Ellianna squirmed in her saddle under Kaldreck's long stares. *Does he regret his decision? Does he wish he had chosen another?* His smile spoke of approval, and his kindness remained without limits, but surely he looked on her for many degrees of the sun for some reason. The possibilities rattled in her head, tightened her grip on the reigns, and churned her stomach. *What does he wish of me?*

Early the next sun, they came to another of the cities of their realm. The first building, which came into view, was made of stone with a steep pitched roof of thinly sliced stones. Weeds covered the path to its entrance. The door,though faded and peeling,looked as though it had once been ornately painted. It was more than a league from the next city, but it sat out here all alone.

"That is an odd little hut. Was it once someone's home?"

Kaldreck turned from his inspection of her to the dwelling. "No, no one ever lived there. It's a Sanctorum—a holy place. Our land is dotted with them."

"What were they used for?"

His gaze fell on her once more. "It is said that in the days of our five and six-fathers, our people would meet with the Divine in them."

Ellianna gasped and almost stopped her mount. "Meet with the Divine? Is such a thing possible?" An excitement like the first time her mother took her to collect healing herbs bubbled in her until it left no room for breath.

"The Divine wasn't there for them to see, but it is said His presence could be felt as the faithful came to sing and worship."

Closing her eyes, she thought she could hear the long silent songs of those blessed souls. An ache pierced her heart, and a longing more powerful than anything she had ever experienced overwhelmed her. A whispered plea slid from her lips. "Oh, to again open the doors of each Sanctorum and praise the One—to sing Him songs, and worship Him as He meets with His people. Could there be any higher honor?" She stole one last glance at the neglected building.

"We still honor the Divine everywhere in Windmere," Kaldreck said with brows drawn tight together considering her. "We do not need buildings set aside for just that single purpose."

Ellianna nodded, though the hunger in her soul only grew.

As they approached the city beyond the Sanctorum that had so enthralled Ellianna, Kaldreck took note of the early degree of the sun and knew they would not stay. Ellianna's eyes caught at the sight of the bazaar outside the city gate. The way her eyes danced at seeing it made Kaldreck halt their journey for a few degrees to allow her to explore.

"Truly, my lord? We may visit for a short time?"

"If it pleases you, my lady."

She clapped her hands like a young child and bounded from the saddle. She took three quick steps before she left her slipper behind and stopped to retrieve it—and the guards she forgot she needed to accompany her.

She walked back passed the men coming to his side, radiating joy. "Would you accompany me, my lord?"

It was an earnest request of innocence and Kaldreck's heart fluttered. He lifted his arm for her to wrap hers around and she jumped with a squeal. Such a child and yet fully a woman. She made him dizzy.

"Now I tell you, true, my lord," she said as she skipped along beside him. "I do not want a thing. I merely wish to look." She turned and gazed up at him for a moment, the seriousness returning to her countenance. "I have all I require, my king."

His heart filled to bursting. She was all he needed as well.

Once between the many booths of the bazaar she released his arm to flitter like a bright winged bristlemite from trinket to treasure to delicacy. He watched her realizing this is what she was —a small clumsy crawling centerworm transforming into a beautiful fluttering bristlemite who drew every eye by her grace and beauty.

Peasants and merchants all around them looked to him, then her, and back again. Word of the king strolling among them, with his newfound calgent, spread like a fire in a dry field at the end of the growing time. Throngs swarmed around them. She accepted each blessing, brushed her hand over children's heads, and smiled at all. Graceful and regal, she comported herself as a proper queen.

From queenly regal, she transformed again. She moved to a booth, asked permission of the merchant, and snatched up a gossamer length of fabric, draped it over her head and shoulders, and danced around in circles as she laughed. She folded it neatly before returning it and floated off to the next booth. She gave her admiration to the jeweler for his fine work and picked a pearl-incrusted stick burette. She held it up to the back of her head and turned to get his approval. She returned it and danced off only to come up short with her mouth open.

She turned and waved frantically for him to join her. She took hold of his arm and he watched her marvel at marionettes on long strings acting out a grand tale. She stood clinging to him, gasping as the tale unfolded, laughing and sneering with the rest of the young audience. She clapped as the small curtain fell, and her attention flittered to the next bobble. Kaldreck loved her all the more for her expression of uninhibited joy and followed her to see what next would catch her fancy.

She stopped at the end of a long row of booths her face filled with a contented smile. "Thank you, my lord." She glanced at the sun and back at him, trying to contain her smile. "We should be on our way. The sun is passed its highest. Thank you for indulging my whim."

He stepped to her and brushed his finger over her cheek—how he wanted to taste of her lips. "Never apologize to me for expressing such joy. I would have you spend every sun this happy."

Her smile faded, and her gaze sobered. The spell broke, and she was again the timid girl going off to join with a man she hardly knew to be his queen. Uncertainty washed over her countenance, and once again, she hid her heart from him.

Kaldreck mourned the loss as they strolled back to the waiting mounts, but he had seen it. She allowed him a few degrees of the sun to experience and revel in her. He knew it would take time and care, but he believed she would give him her heart when she was ready. He began counting the suns until that time.

Ellianna sat her mount still awash in the memories of the sights and sounds of the bazaar as they mixed with the hunger the Sanctorum had stirred. She could not have imagined ever having so much fun or being so moved. Her gaze slid to the king riding beside her. *He enjoyed seeing me this sun as much as I enjoyed experiencing those wonders. He said he always wanted me to be so happy.* What would it be like to live in such an emotion? She turned to the tall mountains surrounding the valley they rode through. There would not be a valley save the jagged mountains. One cannot know joy if not for sorrow. The one must be suffered in order to appreciate the other.

Her musing wove around her like a heavy blanket. Kaldreck called her name, and she realized they had stopped as the sun sat low on the horizon.

He helped her down as the men set up the camp. He offered his arm and led her to a spot in the middle of the road. "Your new home, Ellianna." He pointed to a gray blotch jammed between two peaks of a many-peaked pale green mountain range. It made her shiver.

He smiled, "We should arrive by evening meal next sun." He waited for a response.

"Is it large?"

"Hearthrop is the largest of all Windmere's cities. The Lord High King rules from there with his Lady Queen, and many warriors make their homes within the city walls. There are also a great number of merchants and their families and others who make their home in the shadow of ours."

She nodded, and he led her back to the fire, where she ate little in silence and retired early to her tent.

There was a hum of excitement in the men the next morning. They knew they would be with their calgents by sunsleep. But Ellianna's heart filled with trepidation, and she could not share their joy. Could she bare gray walls and many people? She looked to Kaldreck arrayed in a fine maroon doublet over a cream shimmering shirt and glanced down at her own garments. The gown she wore, though lightly embroidered and finer than her own, was plain compared to his. Her drab brown hair was naught as fine as the king's curled locks. His friendly way and easy smile were so unlike her trembling fearful heart. She did not fit with him. How long would he claim love and affection for her until his clouded eyes saw clear? How long before those he trusted pointed out her many flaws and he decided he no longer wanted her? Would he capture her heart only to crush it?

She could not shake the growing fear as they rode toward what felt like her doom.

The men pulled to a stop and rearranged themselves. Kaldreck drew his mount close. "It is time, my lady." His voice was calm, but it only served to make her heart race. He pulled the white sash from her mount's neck and held it in his hands. "The calgent of the high king is not to be seen by Hearthrop until the sun the rites are spoken. I will drape this over you—"

"But how will I see?"

He put a calming hand on her forearm. Her heart pounded all the louder threatening to burst through her ribs. "Eton will lead your mount. He will assure no harm comes to you."

Eton pulled his destrier forward and took the reins from her trembling hands. He eased forward and looked at her with a nod.

Kaldreck drew her attention again. "I will lead the way into the city. You will probably hear a great many things you will not be able to understand. We have a very busy city. Goffray will ride beside me with my banner, and Eton will lead you directly behind. Do not become afraid, it will take a long time to wind through the city." He smiled. "They will want to congratulate me for finding my One and Only and they will call out welcome. They will not speak to you yet, and you should not try to speak with them. That time will come later."

The king gave her arm a squeeze. "I will assist you down, as I always have, and lead you up the steps to our home. There are eight steps."

She nodded.

"I will leave you without a word as is tradition. Calla, a servant in my home, will lead you to your chambers where the drape may be removed."

Again, she only nodded her understanding.

His smile was kind and tender. "You will remain within your chambers with your servants for five suns as all is prepared for the rites. At midpoint on the fifth sun, you will be given a different drape and brought to me where we will stand on the balcony over the wide square. There, all our people who wish, may witness the ceremony, which unites us as one."

He leaned back more at ease and his smile grew, "Then we will go to the great hall and I will place the crown on your head, and we will dine together in great merriment with our people."

She glanced around her. Only Goffray and Eton were before her, the king sat at her side, and all the others were in pairs behind.

"Are you ready, Ellianna?"

She took a deep breath and gave a single nod.

"I will pin this to your gown. Be careful so you are not poked. We cannot have the drape blow away and reveal you. It is said to be a bad omen."

She turned to look at him as he arranged the cloth behind her.

Kaldreck shook his head. "I do not believe in such things, but it would upset the people for tradition to be broken." He raised the fabric to her head. "I will see you in five suns, my sweet." Then there was naught but the sun's blue glow through the rippling, white fabric. She felt it brush over her hands and a few tugs as he positioned it properly. He pinned it in place, and she heard his mount plod away.

The air was hot and moist under her shroud. Her heart pounded, and her breath came quick and sharp. She wanted to jump down and run.

If I choose to take you with me, would you try to flee? he had asked her their first sun together. She told him she would do her duty. She took a deep breath to calm herself. She would do as he wished. He was the Lord High King, and she belonged to him. He treated her with kindness. Surely whatever awaited her would prove far better than what lay behind.

She would do all he asked.

Chapter 16

Draped in her cloth cocoon, they moved along for some time with naught more than the sway of her mount and the clop of hooves to tell Ellianna of their progress. In the distance a horn blew, followed by another and another.

"They announce the king's return," Eton whispered.

She thanked the Comforter for providing Eton and filling the man with kindness.

"Hail High King Kaldreck. Peace and grace to you, majesty." Voices called out greeting from many different directions.

"The Divine's blessings be upon your union," others called.

"'Tis the farmers outside the city walls who greeted the king." Eton's words were a balm.

Ellianna fought the idea of ripping the shroud from her head as the mounts' hooves took on a hollow clomp. She managed to catch a glimpse of a wooden bridge as the edge of the cloth rippled in a small breeze. Horns trumpeted overhead, the progress slowed to a crawl. By the noise there were many and in the jostling to be near the king some bumped against her legs, and her heart stuttered. Hands brushed over the cloth touching her. Men and women called welcome and blessings to the king. The heat of so many added to the warmth beneath the shimmering fabric and dizziness stirred.

She wanted to throw off the hateful covering and breathe of the air until she caught a whiff of it. Stale with unwashed bodies and sour sweat, baking bread and dung, she fought the bitter spurts washing over her tongue. The hooves clapped over stones creating a cacophony the people shouted over, and soon the ringing of a blacksmith's hammer added to the din. Her ears ached, her head spun, her lungs burned, and her heart lodged in her constricted throat.

They moved forward and into more noise, more smells, and more heat. She gripped the mane of her mount sure she would tumble to the ground any moment—the vague memory of the rocking and swaying sensation of a ship in a turbulent river overwhelmed her. Something changed as the voices fell away. Only deep male voices with a small smattering of women's cheers came now. Smells died away too. They climbed for a few moments before stopping.

"The stairs are a pace away," Eton whispered.

Kaldreck's hands arranged the shroud over her waist before he pulled her from the mount. The tightness of the cloth against her raised the heat further and she wavered, unable to cling to him for support. He released his grasp and a wisp of cool air entered from below the edges. He took her hand and placed it around his arm.

She felt him step forward and moved with him. She tried to mark off a pace in her mind, but her foot hit the first step and she almost fell. He did not grab for her or try to steady her. Other than where her hand lay over his arm, Ellianna would not have known

Kaldreck accompanied her.

She lifted her hem and stepped up. One-two-three-her slipper came off and remained on the last step. Her mind startled. She couldn't retrieve the wayward footwear and it would be long before the trail of shroud pulling back on her head revealed it to anyone following. She kept moving. Four—or was it five? She tried to keep count, but fear made it impossible. Seven, maybe. Eight? No, she stumbled again.

The creak filled the silence. The coolness of smooth stone on her bare foot and the stillness fell as a comfort, until Kaldreck pulled from her and she heard his steps stride away without speaking to her as promised. She stood alone, no sounds told her if anyone remained near. She jumped with a yelp as the doors banged closed and echoed around her. Ellianna brought her trembling fingers to cover her mouth. Torchlight now her only veiled light, as tears burned her eyes. *Why did I ever agree to this?*

A warm, soft hand took hers,. It wrapped her arm around another arm like when Kaldreck led her. But instead of her hand resting atop the back of the other hand as she did with the king, both hands gripped hers with a tight assurance. "Come, m'lady," a tender voice beckoned.

They walked for double the length it took to reach Santon's women's chambers, she was sure. The arm leading her paused. "Stairs, m'lady." Ellianna collected her hem and climbed.

"There, only another short walk now."

They pause for a moment as a latch clicked and she was led into a cool dim room. There was another similar sound behind her and they stopped.

The voice sighed with satisfaction, "Now, here we are. Let us free you," she said in a pleasant volume. The pins were drawn out and the fabric lifted from her face. Ellianna closed her eyes and drew in the sweet air. She swayed on her feet at her rapid breathing and dropped to her knees, landing on a pillow.

"Avery, wine for our queen," the voice called. The clink of metal against metal danced behind her. A gust of cool air caressed her face, then another and another. Ellianna settled back onto her heels and relished it.

The breeze stilled and something pressed to her lips. "Here, m'lady, drink."

Sweet wine skipped over her tongue and cascaded down her parched throat. She placed her hands over the hands holding the cup and raised it to drink faster.

The holder would not allow it. "Slowly, m'lady. It will help you little if you choke on it."

The cup drained, Ellianna opened her eyes. A kind face framed in short white hair sat before her. The woman smiled and revealed a few lines now visible near her eyes in her otherwise smooth skin. The woman raised a finger to pull some of the soaked stray strands of hair from Ellianna's cheek.

Another servant with a fan woven of fronds stirred the air once again. Ellianna closed her eyes, tipped back her head, and relished the blessed coolness caressing her neck as well as her face.

"Here, m'lady," the white-haired woman offered her a filled cup.

Ellianna drank slowly but deeply.

"That's over, m'lady. You're safe here in your chambers, and I will see to your needs until such a time you no longer wish it so. I am Calla."

"Thank you, Calla."

Calla rose to her feet, and the fan fell still. She was a slim shapely woman; only her hair spoke of her many turns, yet she moved as one much younger. "Let's get you out of that drenched garment. A scented bath has been prepared for you, m'lady." Calla placed a hand under Ellianna's elbow and helped her to her feet. "This way m'lady."

Ellianna scanned the room as she turned to follow. It was a small square stone room, two long lengths of heavy fabric hung on one wall—possibly over windows as light leaked around the edges gave the space huge height. The fabric may have been blue or gray, it was hard to tell with the few candles.

"The curtains will not be drawn until after the rites, m'lady," Calla explained.

Other than the window wall, every direction held a closed door set in dead stone. Surrounding each of these openings, whimsical paintings covered the walls. Fairy folk dancing, one-horned steeds, and legends she heard as a child laughed and frolicked. A long dark table with a single chair sat before the windows; two pairs of simple wooden chairs sat on either side of the door where Ellianna must have entered. The pillow she collapsed upon was long and narrow and the only one in the room.

"This is where women come to seek an audience with their queen." Calla pushed open the door to the right of the desk.

Ellianna stepped into a room full of clusters of padded chairs, couches, divans, and pillows upon the floor. Small ornately carved tables set in groupings, and a heavy cloth covered the floor. A large hearth sat on the opposite wall, whic it glowed with heated coals. Three more covered windows lay along the left stonewall. All these walls were painted in the deep blue of the waning sun and embellished with silver leaf patterns.

"This is where you will entertain the ladies of your favor," Calla said as she continued to the right. She pointed at a small door down from the hearth nearer the windows. "Your guests are to use that privy."

Privy? What is that?

A pace into the room, they entered a narrow stone hallway that turned again to the left. Sconces in the wall lit their way. Three doors stood to their left. Calla identified each as they passed. "Your private seating room, your bedchamber." They walked for almost another pace before coming to the last door. "And this is your private privy and bathing chamber."

Ellianna turned to the stairs on her right that appeared to be cut from a great rock as Calla opened this last door.

"The maids entrance, m'lady. It leads directly down to the kitchens and pantries."

Ellianna turned her back on the stairs and stepped into the long room. The fragrance of flowers filled the space.

Two covered windows greeted her. To her left, a small closet with an open curtain held a bench with a hole in it. Ellianna stared.

"'Tis your privy, m'lady."

Ellianna looked at her.

Calla smiled. "When you have need, you come in here, draw the drape, lift your skirts, and sit upon the hole. When you are done. Simply collect yourself and return to your task." Calla lifted the bench seat to reveal the pot within. "The maids will see it is cleaned regularly."

Ellianna turned to the right of the door and found cut stones surrounding an enormous pool. The smooth petal-covered surface invited her.

Calla motioned for her to sit on the stool beside it and began to unlace her garment. "When the palace was built near seven hundred turns ago, this part was cut from the mountain itself. The master mason, knowing these rooms would serve as the women's quarters, cut the pool especially for this purpose. Don't let the height of the side fool though, m'lady."

The side came to the level of her knees as she sat beside it.

"It is deep enough to submerge yourself, if you wish it." Calla motioned for her to rise and, before she realized what she intended, Calla pulled the gown over her head.

Ellianna crossed her arms over her exposed skin. Calla's gaze fell to the breeches and her one slipper. She wanted to hide as heat warmed her checks. Calla pulled everything off her leaving her naked and trembling, but made no remark, and her face showed no expression. Calla stepped to the side and pointed inside the pool. "There are three steps until you reach the bottom, and a shelf lies over there to sit upon."

Ellianna entered cautiously, but the warm, sweet-smelling water welcomed her, and she slipped to the seat, water coming to her chin. She herded the petals over her naked body attempting to hide among the floating veil. The water was neither too warm nor too cool, and her tight muscles unwound as her frayed nerves were soothed.

Calla let her soak in peace for a time before she returned with a small soft cloth and a large jar of smashed soapwort.

"Thank you, Calla. I welcome washing my hair and skin."

Calla sat the jar on the floor and wet her hands in the water. "'Tis my pleasure to see to m'queen's needs"

"I can wash myself."

She shook her head. "It is my honor to aid you."

Ellianna wrapped her arms about her. "Please, Calla."

"I will see to it all m'lady." Her words were firm but not harsh.

"Please," Ellianna moaned.

Calla mashed some of the soapwort paste and spread it between her hands. She started at Ellianna's shoulders above the water and worked down managing to wash Ellianna completely despite her continued protests.

As the woman's hands ran over every bit of her, Ellianna tried to recall the last time her mother had bathed her. Searing heat in her cheeks told the tale of her embarrassment, but Calla would not be dissuaded.

Once her body received a good scrubbing, Calla moved to her hair. She unwound it, cleansed it with the soapwort, rinsed it, and anointed it with perfumed oils.

Calla had her step from the water, and after wrapping a towel around Ellianna's hair, Calla proceeded to dry her entire body before placing a gossamer chemise over Ellianna's head pulling her hair free. She directed Ellianna to the door on the same wall as the privy. It opened into a colossal chamber wider and longer than any she had been in thus far—larger than the entire of Villiant's hut.

Six-curtained windows lay along the right wall and a small seating area by the main double doors on the left. A small desk and chair sat in the corner nearest her. Ellianna stopped with a gasp and her mouth hung open at the main feature of the chamber. Enormous carved posts, the size of tree trunks, held a rail covered in embroidered velvet curtains surrounding the bedstead. A stool made of two steps set beside it, for the bulbous feet on each post raised the bed high off the ground.

Calla directed her passed the monstrous piece of furniture, which seemed larger than the entire room she had slept in all her life. They moved on to the fire and a three-legged stool on the far side. Ellianna noted the pillows on the bulging mattress covered in brocade fabric. She sat on the stool and picked at the bread and fruit on the table beside her as Calla combed out her hair before the fire. Once it was dry, Calla braided it again and helped her into the soft bed.

"Rest, m'lady. There is much to do and learn in the next four suns. I will be there on my bed if you have need of anything." She pointed to a small room within her chamber nestled between the bathing chamber wall and the door to the hall. Calla blew out all but one of the candles and disappeared within.

When all was quiet, Ellianna rolled to her side and cried herself to sleep.

Chapter 17

"I have been forbidden to attend our queen as yet, my love."

The dark figure stepped from the shadows. "The fates may yet work for us. I have other ones to send her way. And, my pet," he stroked her cheek with a finger. "a disturbance grows in her own soul. I will feed it until it consumes her. You will see. She will never make it to the rites."

The two cackled together.

The woman leaned in and pressed her lips to his. She withdrew and smiled. "Then, my love, you can rid our land of that inept king and bring this land to bare under your strong hands."

Candles flared to life, as Calla called, though in truth she lay awake for at least two degrees of the sun. She saw no point in rising when she would not be allowed to go anywhere. Calla ushered her back into the bathing chamber's clear steaming water.

"I do not need another bath. How dirty could I become in silk sheets?"

"Every morning we will wash off the perfumes and rinse your hair of the oil from the bath the prior night." Calla explained as Ellianna huddled in the water trying to cover herself.

Two baths every sun? By the time of the rites, she would receive wash more than in two turns around the sun.

As she set by the fire, Calla combing her hair until it lay dry, she nibbled bread and fruit. "Calla, may I have a little cheese?"

"There will be cheeses and meats aplenty at the feast, m'lady."

Her hair dry, Calla knelt beside her and worked a heavy cream into the skin of her hands paying close attention to the area around her nails. Then she sat upon the floor with a stone and a grainy cream and worked on her feet.

Ellianna watched serving girls come and go. None spoke to her or even looked her way. Calla would answer questions in the most efficient manner, but she did not converse. Ellianna trembled.

No sunlight shone in this place, little more food than in Villiant's home. Stone, tapestries, and dead wood surrounded her. No one spoke to her. *My Helper how will I survive this place?* How could she find contentment when she was so alone? She had more friends among the bot. A tear trailed down her cheek at the thought of Old Man, the bot who always gave her the most grief —and the most affection.

"I do not understand why there is no light and so little food."

"The clagents prepare with a time of lacking. They are deprived of contact, offered only what will sustain them, as a time of reflection before they are joined in union."

A knock sounded on the door and Ellianna looked up hopefully. A maid opened the door and Calla went to greet the tall wisp of a woman who entered. She was so thin she reminded Ellianna of a branch from a weeping tree.

They approached Ellianna together and Calla motioned for her to stand though neither woman spoke to her.

"She will need the yellow gown for the rites, of course, and I think it best to begin with three festive gowns and only two simple over dresses." Calla said.

A cold pricking gray cloud wrapped around Ellianna's heart like an ill wind off the sea.

The needlewoman nodded with a scowl appraising Ellianna through her thin chemise. "What of other sundries?" Her voice whined as though she pinched her nose closed when she spoke.

"Everything."

Again, the woman nodded. "I will need to take proper measurements and fit the stays and braies."

Calla stepped toward Ellianna and, without speaking, reached for the hem of Ellianna's chemise bringing it up to remove it.

Ellianna held her hands on her thighs to prevent the garment from rising. Calla looked at her and shook her head. Forced to stand naked before the needlewoman and her assistant, Ellianna fought to hold back hot tears.

Calla walked away leaving Ellianna alone with women who would not speak to her. The needlewoman pulled a long slender length of leather marked at regular intervals from the pouch the assistant held. Ellianna held out her arms and the length of leather marked her dimensions. The squeaky woman called out her measurements, which were recorded by the assistant kneeling over a bit of parchment with a thin reed of coal. Arms, legs, waist to chin, and toes to waist were each recorded for their length. The needlewoman moved to mark her breadth too—around her shoulders, breasts, hips. Naught was forgotten in the measurement or record.

The first task completed, the assistant, a drably dressed girl only a few turns younger than Ellianna, knelt and helped her into braies of fine tight woven fabric. She tied them around Ellianna's waist and the needlewoman pulled, tugged, and twisted, barking instructions to the assistant recording for shorter length, less girth and a few things Ellianna could not understand.

A stiff, lightly padded item appeared next from the pouch. Laces filled one side, but Ellianna couldn't contemplate what manner of garment the small shell could be. The assistant took it, spun Ellianna so her back turned to the needlewoman and placed it against her ribs. She worked the odd thing until it sat under her bosom and pushed up. Her breasts rose uncomfortably high bulging out for all to see.

While the assistant held the garment in place, the needlewoman laced the back. The two sides pulled together, and her bosom rose all the more. The woman put one hand at Ellianna's shoulder blades and pulled with the other hand to tighten the laces more. She worked to where the garment ended at Ellianna's shoulder blades and repeated the process two more times.

Ellianna was turned to face her as she struggled to take even a puff of air in her constricted chest. Her heart pounded in her ears, and she feared it had been forced out of her chest into her head. The room spun, and heat brought drops of sweat to her body.

"Calla," she gasped and her legs giving way.

She woke a moment later as air flooded her lungs now freed from their binding. She laid on the fabric-covered floor her—

shoulder and her head throbbing.

Calla knelt behind her waving the blade she'd used to free Ellianna at the needlewoman. "What fool thing are you about, Clovis? The Divine has blessed the lady with a fine figure. The stays are only needed to support her womanhood. There is no good reason to bind her so. You are saved the fires now only because she lives. Hurry and be done with your tasks and be gone. If any further harm comes to your queen at your hand, I will alert the Lord High King."

Clovis snorted, "Everyone knows a slim waist is most desired by men."

"Men do not care about the waist but what lies above it. And then it is only best when uncovered," Calla quipped back as she helped Ellianna stand. She tossed the stays back at Clovis and threw Ellianna's chemise over her head.

Ellianna trembled and looked to the chairs longingly.

She remained in place, however, as bit after bit of different colored fabrics were placed under her chin. Clovis called out the colors, which could and could not be used for her gowns as the assistant continued to write them down.

Another knock sounded, and a small woman scurried into the room. Messy brown hair, heavily intertwined with gray, flew about her head. She wore a dirty leather apron over her brown undertunic, her toes black in her sandals. Her head never rose as she moved to kneel where Ellianna now sat on the stool. Clovis glided from the room with the assistant hurrying behind. Ellianna released a slow breath and relaxed as the new woman raised her feet to place them on a large scrap of poor leather.

The gentle, kneeling figure pulled a lump of coal from her apron and traced Ellianna's feet. The feathery motion of the woman's hand tickled, and Ellianna fought to remain still.

"Measure the height heel to knee as well," Calla instructed as more bread and fruit was placed beside her. "The king wishes boots made as well." The tone in Calla's voice spoke of her disapproval.

"Yes, ma'am."

This woman left too. Ellianna sat alone in her large room with Calla hovering near. "You must eat," she said.

Ellianna lost her appetite as her insides still felt mashed about, but she nibbled at what was before her due to Calla's insistence.

The afternoon passed in the reciting of Ellianna's portion of the rites. She was made to say them over and over. Then she was bathed, her hair oiled and dried, and she went to bed. It was a pampered, lonely, boring existence and once more Ellianna filled the pillow with her sobs.

The next sun preceded much the same as the last, though no more strangers came to see her undressed. Calla also instructed her on the movements required during the saying of the rites. Calla spoke to her even less—if that were possible—and a dark humor settled on Ellianna's spirit. One she could not shake.

"Please may the curtains be opened just a little? I will not go and look out, I swear by the Divine, I will not. Please?"

"It is not done," came the quiet, firm reply.

Ellianna despaired.

Chapter 18

Stepping from her bed, Ellianna was again faced with a room devoid of the sun's blue light or any sign of the natural world. The cold left by its absence filled the growing hollow space in her middle. The hard tiles beneath her feet sent pinpricks up her legs. And the floor covering was harsh and bristly under her feet—naught like the sweet wind-blown, orange grass that had always cushioned her steps.

Ellianna bit down on her lower lip to stifle the groan as she slid down into her sixth washing. Surrounded by unbending, unforgiving stone, she begged the Divine to feel the squish of silt in the rivers bottom. Sitting by the fire, she fought away tears—her heart crying out for wind stirred by the Creators hand brushing against her cheeks. She stamped down the desire to charge from her chamber into the nearest field.

Now, long after the dawning of the unseen sun, Ellianna stood draped in the gown she was to wear for the saying of the rites. Yellow, the color of salted and churned bot milk, and covered with small red flowers. Ellianna, however, could only see her bosom pushed high and hovering until she feared they would of spill over —leaving her exposed before all the world.

She spoke her displeasure first to Calla. "This is not right." When she would not heed her words she tried Clovis, the needlewoman. "Ma'dam, I cannot wear this." But no one would heed her words. In a desperate fit she screamed. "I will not wear this! I will not be on display to be ogled over like a wanton woman. No! I will not!" She took hold of one sleeve and began to tear it from her arm. She pulled at the waist. Stitches popped filling her with a wild joy. Encouraged by the renting, she gripped the offending neckline in her hands and pulled downward.

"M'lady," Calla scolded. She held Ellianna's hands still. "I will remove it." The laces loosened, and Ellianna squirmed from the hateful thing as if it were a squeezing viper and trampled it with her feet.

She clawed at the laces of the stay until Calla helped her. She threw it down on top of the crumpled gown and yanked her chemise over her head. She circled her bed pulling all the curtains closed and threw herself upon the mattress overcome by tears.

That is right. You can't do this. You will never make a good queen.

The menacing voice, haunting her waking dreams, mocked her louder each degree of the sun.

You are not strong enough for this responsibility. You have failed before you have even begun. King Kaldreck will despise you for your failings.

Ellianna pressed her face into a pillow. "I should run away. I would be better off anywhere but here." She moaned and let the tears consume her.

Yes. Run away. Far, far away.

As sleep teased to release her from her staggering fears, Ellianna sensed a shadowy figure rubbing his hands together talking to a dark-haired woman.

"She is near to breaking. It won't be long now," he promised.

Calla's cajoling filtered through her curtain wall. "M'lady, please come. Your bath awaits." She returned later. "Now m'lady, you are not behaving as a proper queen. Come and eat something. You cannot continue to behave this way.

Ellianna would not be moved, no matter what tactic Calla tried. She would not eat. She would not bathe. She would not recite the words or practice the movements. She simply cried until sleep claimed her.

Kaldreck was supposed to be isolated in his chamber as Ellianna was within hers, but he stood with his cook discussing the items to be included in the feast yet again. Servants worked all about him. Some laid new rushes on the rough stones, others polished the many dishes required for such an important celebration, and still others carried armload after armload of supplies into the kitchen.

A new arrival caught his attention. Eton stood in the doorway. The firm set of his jaw and grim line of his mouth, together with his arms locked at his sides, created a tightness about the queen's guard. Concern grew in Kaldreck. There was to be no contact between Ellianna and Kaldreck until the rites. Eton should not need to seek him on her behalf.

"Calla insists she must speak with ye, m'lord. She said if I did not come to bring ye back, she would come after ye her own self."

"What's wrong?" Kaldreck's feet were already in motion.

"She would not speak of it to me, m'lord."

Calla stood at the top of the second-floor landing outside Eton's chamber ringing her hands. She paced from side to side in the hallway, and Kaldreck's pulse increased. He chose Calla personally to see to his calgent's needs long before he left in search of his One and Only. Of all those who worked in his home, she was by far the least excitable. No matter the need or the crisis, she never failed to perform with grace and calm. To see her in such a state told him something seriously amiss lay beyond her in the woman's chambers.

"You wished to see me?"

She looked at him, opened her mouth to speak and snapped it closed. She made one more circuit the width of the hall and back then stopped before him. She closed her eyes and inhaled a deep breath. She released it with slow purpose and looked at him yet again. "I know it is not proper, m'Lord High King, but 'tis your lady."

"If she is ill, Balmsom's calgent could easily be summoned," Eton said with a frown.

Calla ignored him, "M'lord, she does not suffer an illness of her flesh." She looked at Kaldreck with intent eyes, which begged him to help. "She has fallen under a dark humor. It is a deep sickness of her spirit, m'lord."

Kaldreck stared at her.

"She cries herself to sleep with great sobs torn from her small body."

Kaldreck looked to Eton.

He shook his head. "I slept at the opening to her tent every night, m'lord. I heard no tears, and she woke with cheer and a blessing each morning.”

“M'lord, she refuses to eat. I know tradition dictates few attend her and none speak to her. Thus when she sees you again on the sun she is united to you, her heart will bind to yours with great rejoicing. I fear she will not make this joyous event, m'lord.”

Calla sighed and wrung her hands again. “When Clovis came last sun to fit the dress to her. The lady became distraught over the cut of it upon her person. When no one would discuss the matter with her, she set about rending it from her body with her bare hands. She discarded it on the floor and flew into her bed. I have been unable to get her to do anything since.”

Calla took another long breath and rose up to her full height, her gaze searing into him. “M'lord I fear she will do naught more. She will not eat. She will not get out of her bed. M'lord she will not even speak. She only cries, and cries.”

Kaldreck raked his hands through his hair. “'Tis tradition…” He looked to Eton and back to Calla. “Has she asked for anything? Something we might offer as a comfort?”

Calla shook her head but stopped with a raised brow. “She asked if the curtains might be opened, even a little. She promised she would not try to look out. She merely wished to see the sunlight.”

“Do it, Calla. I have known her only a short time, but she is a woman of her word. Allow the sun in and perhaps it will sooth her.” Calla curtsied and started to turn away. Kaldreck called after her. “Calla… do what you can to help her, within tradition. I do not wish her to come to the rites hating me.”

She bowed again and disappeared behind the door through

which he had never passed.

Ellianna heard Calla call. She rolled to her other side covering her ears.

"M'lady you must come from your bed this sun. There is much to do before the rites are said over you on the morrow. M'lady, please."

Her voice—though soft and pleading—raised the hairs on the back of Ellianna's neck. She would not be moved now—or ever again if her wish were granted.

Good for you. Don't bend to their will. They'll only break you and reform you to their desires. The voice—now her constant companion—cheered her on. *Show them you are a woman of your own mind.*

She wondered if her mind was still truly her own, but just then something drew her attention. The curtains parted from around her massive bed, and light filled the darkness within. Not flickering candlelight but a bright blue glow. Ellianna turned her head to see shafts of sunlight streaming in through the windows beside her bed. She slid from the heavy coverings. The beams of blue light came from the top half of the windows where the curtains opened about twice the length of her foot. They were still bound closed further down, so she could not see out, but the Creator's true light entered her world.

Ellianna moved to where the nearest glorious rays caressed the floor and dropped to her knees in it. The warmth and splendor of it washed over her. It seeped through her skin and into her bones until it reached deep into her aching soul chasing the dark voice far from her hearing. A breath—deep and rich—filled her for the first time in four suns. She sank until her backside touched the floor covering, and tipped back her head with her eyes closed.

Sun, glorious sun, her heart sang. Her muscles relaxed under the warmth allowing her shoulders to slip far from her ears. She breathed again, and the knot in her stomach relented to unfurl. Calm eased through every part of her body.

"M'lady, will you eat?" Calla asked.

She did not open her eyes for she knew the bread and simple fruit would again be prepared for her. She did not turn her head, but raised her hand and held it open toward the voice. A portion of a loaf landed in her palm and she nibbled content in her spot of natural light.

Chapter 19

"M'lady, will you rise so we can see to your gown again?"

Ellianna looked over her shoulder passed Calla to where Clovis stood scowling, her assistant a step behind with the gown draped over her arms. Ellianna glanced about the room finding the stool where she sat to have her hair brushed and dried. She rose to her feet, calmer than she had felt in several suns, strolled passed her visitors, snatched up the three-legged seat, and carried it to the brightest rays now flooding her room. She set the stool within the stream, ripped off her chemise, and stepped up on the seat. Facing the window, eyes closed, she threw out her arms allowing the sun's warmth to caress her bare skin not caring who saw her or what they thought.

The braisers came first, and Ellianna stepped into the soft cloth, which covered her from knees to waist. A new stay covered her bosom, the fabric softer, and the stiff beams now replaced with strips of quilted fabric. Ellianna sighed at the new gentleness as the laces were drawn—though not tight. Next, Calla asked her to step into a slip. At last, the gown slid over her head covering all her flesh except her neck and face—shielding most of her body from the direct caress of the sun.

As the laces were drawn, Ellianna glanced down noting the valley between her breasts could be seen but not as before. The garment—now altered—lay more modest about her form. The sleeves rained down at her sides with an expanse of fabric at the back of her arms all the way to the floor, revealing only the tips of her fingers.

Clovis's assistant fluttered about her pinning the front of the sleeves so her whole hand lay uncovered. She cinched in the waist and shortened the hem over her toes. Satisfied with the garment's fit, the assistant removed the gown from Ellianna once more. Two more gowns, one a simple kirtle and the other more fashionable, were tried on her next. Then she was stripped of all and allowed to again don her chemise and robe.

The rays no longer flooded her bedchamber, but Ellianna sat where she could look out at the violet sky and watch the clouds float by to be framed first by one window, then another. Slippers of fine satin were placed on her feet, and Calla made her practice the movements and the words she would say on the next sun.

Ellianna could only manage a few steps before she left her slipper behind. Calla replaced it only to have the other one fall off two steps later. So distracting did the footwear become, Calla took them both off and set them aside.

The degrees of the sun slipped away like one falling into a dream, and the sky faded to deeper hues until it lay like a black blanket embellished with twinkling jewels. Ellianna sat once more on the stool as Calla brushed her hair. She pulled her feet up to hook her heels next to her rump on the seat and wrapped her arms tight around her legs. She set her chin upon her knees and sighed.

"Does something trouble you, m'lady?"

"Calla, I know naught of the ways of men and women."

Calla did not speak as she continued to stroke the brush through her hair.

"I am to go to the Lord High King at the next sunsleep, but I know naught of what I am supposed to do to please him or at the very least fulfill my duty as his calgent."

Calla's voice trembled. "Did your mother not discuss such matters with you?"

"Mother died when I was but seven turns. I am sure she did not believe so young a girl needed to know such things. When the bleeding came upon me, Villiant sent me to an old neighbor woman."

Calla came to sit upon the floor before her. She took Ellianna's hands in her own and talked in tender tones. Calla spent many degrees of the passing Little Moon, explaining the wonders of union. As Calla led her to bed, Ellianna could not say the pending event seemed so desirable to her. She had seen the coupling of bot in the fields, but what Calla described sounded much more complicated and involved. She shuddered as the covers were pulled to encase her in their warmth. *Divine, let me be what the Lord High King needs.* Comfort surrounded her, and sleep claimed her—even as the dark voice tried to whisper.

❤

Sunlight drew Ellianna once more from her bed, and she sat in its rays from the time it cleared the closed portion until it rose half way up the window before Calla emerged from her small chamber.

"No other servants will enter this sun. I will be the only one to attend you until the rites begin."

Ellianna bathed with oils and perfumes and creams were massaged into her skin. The under garments were placed on her body but the gown would not be donned until the last moments so she could sit or do as she pleased without creasing or soiling it.

Calla brought her slippers with an addition. A narrow length of ribbon was sewn to each side. Once her feet slipped inside Calla tied the ribbons together over the top of her foot assuring she would not loose them.

"Thank you, Calla. I now have one less thing to worry about."

"It is my pleasure, m'lady." Calla moved a large padded footstool from the seating area near the main doors and set it in a ray of sun. Ellianna rested in the blue warmth trying her best not to tremble at her racing thoughts while the older woman arranged her hair.

She started by weaving the locks near her face in many tiny braids and connected them to one another on the top of her head. Calla also braided the length of her hair in a myriad of tiny strands. Some she pulled up and looped or draped about her head while others she let cascade down her back.

When her hair lay arranged fitting her new station, Calla brought the gown. "The yellow represents a precious and sacred flower so rare, only the Fathers are allowed to harvest it," Calla explained. "The tiny red flowers are from a popular spice only grown in Windmere. Therefore, the gown represents the best of what your kingdom offers its people."

The gown lay about her, hugging her curves, and draping from her waist in a waterfall of fabric. Calla brought another length of silk. This one, only half as long as the white one draped over her as she entered the city, was a vibrant red. "It represents your maidenhood, m'lady."

Ellianna's trembling could no longer be contained. She chewed on the corner of her lip.

The drape lay over her head blocking the light all around her, trapping her beneath. Calla reached beneath the cloth and wrapped Ellianna's arm around her own.

"M'lady, your ordeal is almost over. In a few moments, you will say the rites and from that moment forward you will be queen. You may go where you wish, and you may speak to all who please you. Of course, you may see the Lord High King as oft as you wish. Naught will be forbidden you ever again."

Ellianna took some comfort from those words as she was led through her chambers to where the rites would be preformed. Calla positioned her and slipped from her side. A light breeze ruffled the concealing drape. All else lay quiet. Again, she did not know if anyone stood near. Ellianna waited. She knew what was to come and her part in it. Now she waited for it to begin—and for it to end.

Chapter 20

As Ellianna stood waiting, the dark voice battered her once more rattling her already frayed nerves.

This is your last chance to escape. You will never make a good queen. Kaldreck will never love you. You know where you are. The balcony over the ward. Step forward. Fling yourself over the side and end this insanity.

Ellianna shifted her weight and her right arm brushed something. Fear made her heart leap into her throat, and she sputtered against it.

Kaldreck had taken his place beside her, as Calla had when they practiced. They were not permitted to speak until the elder began the ritual, but he pressed his arm against hers. Her quaking stopped, and her heart slipped back in place, though it pounded yet.

Be quick before you are trapped forever.

The warmth of the man who claimed her as calgent seeped into her and muffled the malevolent voice within.

Ellianna startled as a deep voice boomed. She could only conclude it was the elder who spoke to the murmuring crowd gathered below. "Men and women of Windmere," he called. "We come here this sun, before the Divine with many names, to see our

Lord High King Kaldreck, united to his One and Only—the woman of his heart—Lady Ellianna of Illgrove, Daughter of the Most High."

Ellianna knew he was supposed to say she was the daughter of Villiant, but her heart thrilled at being called the daughter of the Holy One. Yet at the same time, she despaired, for she believed herself unworthy of such a claim. Oh, but how she wanted it to be undeniable truth.

The crowd erupted into cheers of joy. Ellianna stepped back from the noise. Kaldreck's hand brushed hers. Still blinded by the fluttering fabric, she trembled beneath it. "This sun, they will bind their lives together forever more," the elder called.

Kaldreck raised his right arm, and Ellianna did the same. Bent at the elbow they pressed their forearms together, her fingers at his elbow and his at her elbow. As their arms touched Ellianna marveled at the calming his warmth and strength afforded.

The elder wound a cord around their forearms literally binding them together. She felt his fingers brush and hold her elbow as they stood facing opposite directions. The trembling abated all the more and the voice fell silent. A new calm swept over her as Kaldreck's presence reassured her.

The elder spoke again. "We join in union one to another because the Divine has created us for relationship. The Divine is holy. The Divine is all."

Kaldreck and Ellianna each took a step to the right as they recited the words which all said at their joinings. Ellianna could not see where she stepped, but the strength of her bond to him as their arms touched guided her. Because of Calla's careful instruction she now knew faced the south and he the north, and they said the words they practiced repeatedly for the last suns.

"The Divine is solid. He is immutable, unchanging. The same from the beginning of all until the unending forever."

They took another step and spoke as one again. Their voices mixed in harmony with the deep richness of a melody. Ellianna heard, even in their intertwining words, how matched they were for one another. A melodic chord rang out within her spirit. "The Divine is fluid. He is cleansing, quenches the soul's thirst, and is essential to all life."

Another step, "The Divine is vapor. He is invisible, seeping into the soul, changing all who He indwells.

One last step, and they were back where they started. "The Divine is holy. The Divine is one."

The elder spoke again. "Uniting one with another is not easy. It is a meshing of thoughts, traditions, behaviors, and hearts. Union should not be entered into lightly, for in the joining of two lives, both must make the effort."

Kaldreck had seen her trembling when he joined her on the balcony and felt her flinch when he brushed against her. But the tune rising in his heart as she said the words of the rites with power and conviction, made him anxious beyond all reason to unbind them and free her from the drape hiding her. He needed to look upon her and draw her into his arms.

Ellianna stepped forward and Kaldreck back so they stood against the railing. Tradition held that the longer a couple took to work the knots loose from their arms the more conflict their union would suffer.

Kaldreck clawed at it franticly, cursing the tradition, which forbade him cutting them free.

Ellianna's hand covered his and held it still. Heat, more powerful than before, surged up his arm stealing his breath. She moved his hand aside and gripped one length of the first knot between her thumb and forefinger. She tapped the opposing length with her third finger. Kaldreck gripped it in a similar manner and they pulled against each other.

The knot pulled apart with ease.

She felt again for the next knot, and repeating the movements, it too fell away. In moments, their arms were free.

He turned toward the crowd below and held up the dangling blue-purple cord as the elder covered his hand. "Our Peace has blessed this union with His favor," he declared and those below cheered.

Ellianna still draped in red silk, now stood facing Kaldreck. He knelt before her and proclaimed his promises to her as he rolled the cloth from her. "This sun, I, Kaldreck, Lord High King of Windmere, freely join my life with you, Ellianna of Illgrove. I make this vow to you before all gathered. I promise to love you and you alone."

He rolled the fabric and rose as he went. His eyes caught on the curve of her hip and the slimness of her waist in her fitted gown.

"My eyes will look on no other. My mind will think of no other." The back of his hand brushed her bosom and he almost lost all thought. He paused, cleared his throat, and continued. "My heart will be given to no other."

The cloth covered only her face now, and his heart pounded so hard it threatened to drown out his words. The shapeless, loose garments she wore earlier had hidden a great deal, and his flesh burned with a passion he did not believe he could survive.

The Elder cleared his throat now, for Kaldreck stood silent and unmoving admiring the beauty of the one the Giver chose for him.

"I give my life to share with you. Two lives—one future. Two hearts—one beat. United in purpose and goal, I bind my life to yours."

Ellianna squinted in the bright light, blinked and looked up into his face.

It took all his warrior's discipline not to seize her in a tight embrace and kiss her soundly. The clouds in her eyes barely moved betraying her fear. Her hair lay tight to her head in a bewildering array of braids. It was not unpleasant, but he preferred it soft about her oval face, free to be caught by the breeze. He gazed at her willing his body to quiet lest he frighten her further.

Kaldreck stepped behind her to finish removing the shroud. When he returned to again stand before her, she spoke her promises.

"I, Ellianna of Illgrove, do willingly accept the offer of the Lord High King of Windmere, Kaldreck, to become his calgent. I will serve at his side in anyway he finds me of use. I will not give my council until it is sought, and I will defend the Lord High King with my life. I will care for his children. I will love no other. My eyes will look at no other. My mind will think of no other. My heart will be given to no other. I give my life to share with you. Two lives—one future. Two hearts—one beat. United in purpose and goal, I bind my life to yours."

"'Til death does part us," they said as one.

The elder called over the balcony in conclusion. "The Divine has ordained the holy union of one man to one woman. What the One has brought together, no mortal can break asunder."

He gave Kaldreck a nod of consent and Kaldreck bent to touch his lips to Ellianna's. She stiffened, but she tasted as sweet as the sticky jahala fruit. She shied from him far quicker than he wished. Her gaze was long in returning to his. Kaldreck turned her toward the waiting crowd and a cheer, loud enough to shake the ground, roared below them.

He smiled and waved to their people. Ellianna grabbed the stone railing to steady herself. Kaldreck turned to look at her more directly. The color drained from her face. She did not look well, and he feared she did not breathe.

Chapter 21

The events of their joining rites rattled in Ellianna's skull as she fought to control her raging emotions. She had said every word as Calla taught her. She remembered every step. Kaldreck at last freed her from the sweat tent, and she breathed of the fresh air perched on the palace balcony. When he kissed her lips, and it felt as though a hot coal were placed there. As she swayed from the heat, within and without, he turned her to look out over their people.

Then her world shuttered. She fought for breath. Fear crawled her insides. Despair choked her heart and stole her life. All Ellianna saw was undulating waves of faces surrounded by cold stonewalls. No breeze carried over the vast height of those barriers. No tree or growing thing could be seen beyond nor within. An inner wall separated the town from her new home, and another outer wall lay beyond, trapping her in the unnatural world.

Her vision blurred while images around her swirled. She panted for breath. The world swam before her. She remembered the feeling of falling from a few suns past when bound in the too-tight stay. A strong arm encircled her, and she soon stood in the cooler interior of the palace with the balcony behind her.

"Ellianna?" his voice floated from somewhere far off.

"Ellianna? Are you well?"

She reached out a hand to touch the stonewall beside her. The coolness seeped into her hand and up her arm. She slid from Kaldreck's grasped and pressed her entire back against the refreshing relief. She looked at him trying to open her mouth to speak, but her parched tongue stuck in place.

"Wine!" Kaldreck snapped and his voice reverberated off the flat surfaces surrounding her.

Gazing into his chestnut brown eyes, she saw it again. As when he removed the drape, she was locked in his gaze, and she saw into his heart. There within him lay a deep care for his people and his land. But what terrified her was the gigantic power of the love he carried for her. As mighty as a monsuit protecting her cub, his love threatened to crush the life from her. She turned and lowered her eyes as the servant returned with the cup.

Kaldreck held the vessel to her lips and helped her drink cradling her head in his hand.

She took a steadying breath as he used his ruffled shirt cuff to wipe the perspiration from her face.

"Ellianna, are you well?" he asked again, concern marring his fine face.

She nodded. "'Twas the heat, my lord."

"You will return to your chambers at once and rest."

She gripped his shirtsleeves. "No, please, my lord. Do not lock me away again."

"But if you are ill…"

She shook her head. "The people will think you have chosen unwisely if I am unable to celebrate with you after being confined so long. I will not have your people view you poorly on my account." She took an unsteady step, and he pulled her closer offering his unwavering form as her strength.

"It matters not what our people think of me, Ellianna. For truly, if you are not—"

She took another surer step. "The wine has served me well. The shade of the hall and more refreshment will do me far better than cowering in my chambers." She shook her head muttering. "I wish it a long time before I am confined within those walls again."

He stopped her from proceeding and turned her chin to him. "I am sorry your time has been so unpleasant, Ellianna. You are now queen, and no one can tell you where you can or cannot venture."

"Expect my calgent. I belong to you."

He stammered his next hushed words. "I have given you my heart and my love. I will never do anything to cause you pain. You are free to go anytime you wish. I will not stop you."

The thought of racing from his side, out the massive gates, and into the many-hued orange fields beyond tugged at her heart. She forced her longing soul to be silent. She looked at him again. "There is a feast waiting, my lord. I am sure, with something of greater substance than fruit and bread and a cool drink with people who will speak to me, I will revive completely. Please… let us go."

He helped her down the stairs, and she summoned all her remaining strength to walk with confidence beside him. They entered the hall full to bursting with more people than lived in Illgrove in all its history combined.

Kaldreck led her to the high dais where she knelt before the table. She rested comfortably on her knees and swayed less. When she bowed her head before him, a hush fell over the crowd.

Kaldreck held a small circlet of gold above her head. "Lady Ellianna of Illgrove, do you swear and promise to rule with King Kaldreck the people of Windmere according to their laws and traditions?"

"I do so swear and promise."

"Will you use your position of authority to rule in justice and mercy for all Windmerians?"

"I do so swear and promise."

"Will you uphold the teaching and instruction of the Truth? Will you see to the instruction of our sons and daughters and all the squires who come to our home in these teachings?"

"I do so swear and promise."

The crown was placed on her head and Kaldreck took her hand to help her to her feet. He stepped a little from her and announced with puffed chest. "My good people, I present your queen, Queen Ellianna."

Fists thumped on tabletops, and a ruckus cheer went up filling the room and threatening to unhinge the doors.

She inclined her head and followed Kaldreck around the table to sit in a carved high-backed chair identical to his. He set a full cup of wine before her, and she drank easing the discomfort of her parched throat if not the ache in her ears.

She looked out over the crowd seeing familiar faces, like Malic, Nafwin, Alcoff, Balmson, and Goffray. They were seated directly below them. As Kaldreck's personal guard, they took the seats of greatest honor. All but Goffray sat beside a finely dressed woman. These men she had traveled with hoisted their cups to her. She managed a smile.

"Arrayed at long trestle tables sitting perpendicular to our guards, are the lords of Windmere," Kaldreck explained. "and farther away from the center, the wealthy merchants, and finally the villein and servants, far against the walls."

As they ate of rich meats and sharp cheeses, he pointed out individuals and told her who they were and what they did.

Flooded with relief at her freedom from her confinements and seeing the full sunlight wash in at the end of the long hall, she paid him little attention. Ahe noted Santon and Zorgot, who sat on the outer edges of the lords. "Did you place them there?" she asked.

"Who?" Kaldreck scanned the room.

"Lord Santon and Lady Zorgot?"

He smiled at seeing them. "No, my sweet. They chose those seats for themselves. I believe Santon feared your vengeance."

"But he is a strong supporter. If I have alienated him, I should make amends."

His hand covered hers, and a tingle fluttered over her skin. "You did far less than I would have. You will not apologize. If Santon is offended, he can discuss it with me."

"Does he not disapprove of this combined festivity?"

"It is a joining celebration, my sweet. We must celebrate together. It is the whole point of the rites."

She nodded and nibbled as she continued to scan the room. "Have you seen Renwald?"

"No, why do you ask after him?"

"I noticed he left your guards after the monsuit attacked. I wondered if he'd reappeared while I was locked away."

"No. In truth I have not seen him either, now that you mention it. Brayden told me he turned aside to meet with a coven of seers. I expected him to arrive by now."

Ellianna shuddered, though she did not know why. Fear tickled her awareness while a darkened image danced at the edge of her thoughts. She shook it off as a band of minstrels moved to a small open spot on the floor and performed for them.

The festivities stretched long into the evening. Ellianna had slipped away to her chambers some time ago, and Kaldreck finally extracted himself from the hall and the last of his well-wishers to climb the stairs to his chamber. His personal servant, Gwidus, greeted him at the door pushing it open and followed him within.

"Good sunsleep to you, my lord."

"Good sunsleep Gwidus," he sighed.

"I would have thought you would be more energized on your union night." A soft chuckle teased his ears as Gwidus took his doublet.

"It has been a very many degrees of the sun, my friend, and I fear Ellianna is not well. She looked quite stricken after the rites."

Gwidus was a long-time confidant and considered him closely. "I have attended you much of your life, my lord."

Kaldreck stripped off the ruffled shirt and tossed it at him. "Get out of my head, old man."

"I can still take you, my lord, if you require a schooling."

Kaldreck raised a brow and saw the smirk on the man's lined face. "You have never seen me like this, I will warrant."

"Twisted in knots by a love more powerful than you can comprehend?"

Kaldreck nodded and dropped to the sofa in the middle of his outer chamber.

"I have not seen it in you, to be true, but I know well the feeling that burns in you—yet I also see you have no intentions of calling her to your bed this night to quench those flames."

Kaldreck's head dropped back to the padded sofa and he groaned. "She is unsure, Gwidus. She would—"

A soft tap sounded at his door causing his head to rise curiously. "Come."

Ellianna slipped through the slender crack she made in pushing the heavy door open. The Mericful help him, for she stood in his chamber barely covered in a sheer sleeping garment and a bit of cloth that could hardly be considered a robe. The shapely silhouette of her body clearly visible in the dancing candlelight sent his entire body to aching for her.

Kaldreck shot to his feet as Gwidus chuckled. "Not so unsure as you might think." He bowed to each of them and pulled the door closed behind him.

She stood near the door eyes searching for…direction perhaps.

"Ellianna, are you in need of something?" He dared not go near her for fear he could not resist the pull of his flesh.

Her head tipped, and her gaze dropped to the floor. Her arms came up and closed the robe over her and folded beneath her bosom—Divine be merciful—outlining their curves and making them the more noticeable.

"The rites have been completed…" she whispered. She shifted

her weight from slender foot to slender foot drawing his eyes to the swinging action of her hips and the line of her legs he could see clearly through her garment.

He swallowed the need strangling him.

She trembled. "I have displeased you again, my lord?"

With slow, methodical steps he closed the distance between them and dared touch her with a single finger to raise her chin. "Never, Ellianna." He wiped a tear from her cheek. Fear stilled the swirl of her eyes. "You have overwhelmed me with your willingness and your boldness."

Her brows drew together. "Was I not to come? Calla instructed me last sunsleep…" She trembled more.

"It is usually the king's pleasure to call his love to him. That you should come of your own, touches my heart." *And my very flesh.* He struggled to keep the need from tainting his words. "Do you love me, Ellianna?"

"I am for you, my lord," confusion distorted her face.

A soft chuckle released some of the tension in his chest. "Clearly the answer is no since you cannot yet speak my name. We are alone, Ellianna. I am your calgent in the sight of the One and our people. Say my name."

"I am for you—Kaldreck. I have come to provide you sons."

He closed his eyes and breathed deep at the sound of his name on her enticing lips. He looked at her again as they stood with only an arms-length of air between them. "I require more than sons, Ellianna."

Her gaze slipped to the floor.

He raised his arm to her. "Here, let me escort you back to your chambers, my sweet."

"My lor—Kaldreck?"

"Be at peace. We have known each other for but a scant number of suns. Let us get better acquainted so you can willingly give your heart to me.

She looked up and searched his face. "I have come…"

"Willingly. Yes, I know, but you still hide your heart and your passion."

He took her hand and steeled himself against the torment. He entwined it around his bare arm and turned her toward the door. "I will be patient, Ellianna. I have made a vow to never take from you what you have not offered. I will wait, and you will see I am for you. I can be trusted to love you and no other."

Near the bottom of the stairs as they approached the hall to the women's chambers, a shriek tore through the still night air. They raced toward her chambers and collided with Eton as he burst from his room to see to the trouble.

"Your Majesties," he stammered, bowing awkwardly.

The doors to the women's chamber flew open, and Calla charged through them. She ran for the guard but seeing Ellianna standing beside him, she pulled up short. She staggered forward and fell at her feet. "Oh, thank the Protector you are safe, my queen. Thank the Merciful," she sobbed onto Ellianna's feet.

Ellianna knelt beside her and pulled her into an embrace—and though not the picture of a proper queen's actions, it showed Ellianna's kind and tender heart. Kaldreck loved her all the more for it. "I am most well. What has happened, Calla?" she whispered stroking the woman's hair.

"A fire, my lady."

"Fire?" Kaldreck barked.

"Yes, my lord king, the curtains of the lady's bed where engulfed in flames.

"All of them?" Ellianna asked, and her worried gaze shifted up to look at Kaldreck.

"Yes, they all caught and I thought you lay within."

Ellianna pulled from Calla and looked down on her. "Call for the healer," she groaned.

Kaldreck stepped around Ellianna and saw the charred, blistered flesh of Calla's forearms. Eton was already on the ground floor before Kaldreck could direct him further. More of the maids came from the women's chambers. "The fire?" he asked.

The one nearest him dipped a quick curtsy. "'Tis out, my lord. The bedding and mattress were lost, but all else in the room was saved.

Ellianna cradled Calla to her chest as the older woman shuddered. Ellianna's eyes were on the maids, and the swirl of her smoke eyes stilled. The dark center grew and her breaths came in rapid pants.

"Ellianna?" he stroked her arm.

She blinked, and her gaze shifted to his—though it seemed a moment before she saw him. The movement of her eyes resumed, and her breathing calmed. "It would seem someone wishes me dead."

Chapter 22

Footsteps sounded below them. Kaldreck popped to his feet and started barking orders. "Ellianna, go to your chambers."

She opened her mouth to protest, when he grabbed a maid by the arm.

"Tend to Calla. Ellianna now." He pulled her to her feet and pushed her toward the door. Her hurt must have been evident for he huffed and muttered. "You are not dressed, my love." He shoved her inside and closed the door behind her. She stood there for a moment with a few of her maids.

The door latched, and she looked down at her thin chemise—possibly appropriate for meeting one's calgent—certainly not for anyone else in the palace. Unable to do much about her situation, she turned toward the maids who curtsied. Staring at the floor they waited for her directions.

There were four standing with her. One caught her eye. One who stirred a darkness within her. Ellianna could not understand her reservations, but she cared not at all for the dark-haired woman. "You three come with me." She stood before the fourth and stared at her for a long moment. There was something unsettling about her, and it had naught to do with her appearance.

"You are dismissed."

"Aye, my lady. I will return in the morning with your meal."

Ellianna shuddered. "No. I wish you to leave the palace."

The woman's deep brown eyes—so dark it was hard to distinguish the black centers—narrowed on her. "My lady? Have I done something?"

"I have no need for so many. You may find work anywhere within the city that suits you. Good sunsleep to you."

Ellianna left the audience room and moved to the guest sitting room. She closed the door on the threat crawling across her skin and leaned back against the cool wood. The other three maids trembled before her. Never had she been so cruel. She shook the foreboding from her spirit and moved to her private chambers, which reeked of smoke and burnt fabrics.

She turned to the three women. "We have work to do before we slumber this night."

"What do you require of us, m'lady?" the blonde in the middle asked with quiet reverence.

Ellianna moved toward the charred remnants of her bed. "Throw open all the windows, remove the burnt items, and I would like some pillows for tonight if they can be found."

She moved to help them, but they stopped her. "No, my lady you will soil your fine bed clothes."

She stepped toward a window and the shortest woman shooed her away. "My lady someone may see you in your state of undress."

She huffed her frustration and went into her private sitting room. The space lay dark and full of shadows barely touched by the candles in her bedchamber. She turned, retrieved a candle from a nearby table in her bedchamber and entered the sitting area again.

The square room nearly half the size of her huge bedchamber was filled with furniture. Carved chairs with satin cushions, two divans, a spinning wheel, a loom, and a harpsichord made the room feel crowded. She moved to one divan, set the candle on a table, and reclined.

A dark figure stood in the shadows. "She was not summoned, but she was with the king. Now, I am not allowed in the palace." The voice of the new comer felt familiar floating in a place between vision and dream but Ellianna could not see the woman who lurked in the darkness appearing only as a silhouette.

"She is a lucky thing," the shadow answered in a sinister male voice. "Truly her latent gift is waking more quickly than expected, and if I cannot stop her, she could be a problem to my plans."

"My lady."

The gentle whisper startled Ellianna awake, and she jerked upright almost colliding with the maid standing beside her.

"Forgive me, m'lady. The king has asked you to join him for the morning meal and a walk if you are agreeable?"

She nodded and rubbed the sleep from her eyes. As she moved back into the larger chamber she noted the bed frame stood washed and prepared to receive a new mattress and the walls lay clean of soot as well.

She sighed deeply.

"Does something displease you, m'lady queen?"

"I only meant to have the room cleaned of the worst to fight the stench. I never intended for you to work all night without sleep in order to see the whole place cleaned. Forgive me for not making myself more clear."

The woman shuddered unable to speak.

"I'm sorry, but I do not know your name."

"Avery, my lady."

Ellianna smiled. "You brought me sweet wine when I first arrived."

"Aye, my lady."

"Avery, if you would take one more moment to help me dress, so I do not keep the king waiting any longer, you and the other women who helped restore this chamber with such haste are to spend the rest of the morning—as long as you need—sleeping."

"M'lady, but—"

"It is my earnest wish, Avery. You will not refuse your queen, will you?" she asked with a playful smile as Avery stared at the floor.

"No, of course not, m'lady."

Dressed in a green well-fitting simple linen gown, Ellianna raced from the women's chambers and to the stairs.

"M'queen!"

Eton stepped from his chambers startling her so she almost tumbled down the stairs. Her hand went to her chest as she tried to coax air back into her lungs. She leaned against the wall and stared at him.

"M'queen ye are not to leave—"

She stood straight, hands on her hips. "But the rites have been said. King Kaldreck promised me I could go wherever I wished."

He put up a hand to stay her triad. "As long as I accompany ye."

Her hands dropped to her sides and she exhaled her fury. "Yes, forgive me. I did not realize you were required to protect me even in the walls of the king's home."

"It does not appear ye're safe even in yer own chambers. As ye said last sunsleep, m'lady, someone wishes ye ill."

"So it would seem."

"When ye are in the women's chambers me door remains open. I will come anytime ye wish to be leavin'. Please don't go anywhere without tellin' me, m'queen. 'Tis me honor if somethin' should happen to ye."

"I will remember."

He closed his door, waved her forward, and fell into step behind her.

Kaldreck stood from talking with Malic at the entrance to the hall. He smiled as she approached, and his captain bowed. "The Divine bless you this sunwake, my queen."

"And may He bless you as well, Lord Malic." She turned a degree and curtsied to Kaldreck "The Divine's blessing to you, my lord."

His smile slipped by a degree, but he offered his arm and they entered the hall. "Most of our guests have already eaten as they sought to begin their journey home at the first opportunity. We should be afforded a quiet meal this sun."

She looked to him as they neared their chairs.

He spoke before she could ask. "Calla is resting comfortably. Her One and Only sits with her and sooths her. Balmson says if infection does not befall her, she should heal in time."

"I feel responsible."

He handed her the tray of cheeses to select from. "Why ever would you think such a thing?"

"I did not tell Calla I left. If she had known where I was, she would not have injured herself seeking to save me."

"But if Calla knew, then so could the one who set the fire. They may have tried another night when you would not have been safe with me."

She chewed on a spicy bread and looked at Kaldreck. "This tastes like a bread I tried in Santon's city."

He smiled. "Yes, Santon heard of your favor for the bread and brought several loaves with him. I think he hoped to make amends for Zorgot." He put his food down and considered her. "You spoke before of someone wishing you harm? What can you tell me of this?"

"A viper is not likely to be found where men and mounts have trampled for a degree. Volif do not usually attack so many and with so great a number of lit torches. Monsuit do not attack without provocation, and biting tails rarely find their way into beds. Candles are known to start careless fires—but around all the curtains of a bed—at once? One of these things would seem plausible, but all of them together speak of a direct attack."

He nodded thoughtfully. "I will increase your guard."

She smiled at him. "Unless you have trained female guards, I will still be unprotected within the expansive women's chambers."

Kaldreck nodded with a huffed grunt.

"We must pray it is the Shield's will for me to live."

Their meal concluded, Kaldreck stood and offered her is arm. "I wish to show you our city, Ellianna."

She took a deep breath to prepare herself, rose, and went with him.

Chapter 23

They stepped out into the ward and Ellianna shuddered, but the warmth of Kaldreck's constant gaze comforted her as he pointed out the features of their home. The kitchens at the north of the palace, fine stone houses of his captain and officials nestled against the north wall, the armory, the huts for the hunting fowl, and those for the hounds. Pride dripped from his lips and puffed his chest. The state of his home, and those who lived in his city, filled him with joy. He saw it all as a polished gem and boasted it was the finest city of their lands.

Ellianna looked an eerie stillness filling her spirit. She swallowed down her needs. Not a growing thing lay anywhere within her sight. Not even dirt to trod upon. Everything that surrounded her was man-made or cut from stone.

Kaldreck turned her toward the homes on the south wall. "This is where many of our servants have their private homes. Though not as many are filled as once were, my sweet. I took your advice and released them from their bond status. All who serve us now, do so because they wish it."

She relaxed by a small measure, and a brief smile danced on her lips. "You are a kind man, Kaldreck."

She dared to shift her gaze to the man who claimed her calgent—the man she had willingly bound her life to only the previous sun. His shoulders were thrown back, and his chin high. He had a wide stance as he swept out a strong arm to all that surrounded him. Ellianna fought the tremor raging up her spine.

They moved toward the inner gate, and he pointed out Balmson's large home. They stepped inside and found Calla resting in one of the healing chambers on the lower floor. Ellianna offered apologies and comfort before she rejoined Kaldreck. She stood facing him in the doorway.

Her lungs would not allow a full breath to enter. She agreed to join her life with this man. She left her home without thought of where she would go or what she would do when she arrived. Only a few suns had passed, and those spent with the king were pleasant. His kindness and gentleness acted as a balm to her battered soul. But now here in this crowded, unnatural place… She bit her lower lip. *Can I find happiness here—locked so far away from the Divine's creation?*

He told Ellianna she could go anywhere. Eton said he would travel with her no matter the location. As they neared the inner wall dividing the palace and its surrounding buildings from the city that lay beyond, she again stole a glimpse of Kaldreck. His curly locks shimmered in the blue glow of the sunwake.

She had made her promise to him, and she did not wish to disappoint him. He would never mistreat her. She knew this as she knew the two moons would rise this sunsleep. A cacophony outside the gate battered at her, driving her back a step. *Peace, quiet my soul. Comforter, sooth my anxious heart. Creator, create in me contentment and fashion me into the woman he needs.*

"Most of the un-joined men-at-arms and squires live here," Kaldreck pointed to the two large towers surrounding the gate and the space hanging over them as they stepped through into the city beyond.

Her glance barely graced where he directed, but she stared with wide eyes at the bustle beyond in the city. Her head swiveled in every direction as she tried to take it in all at once.

Kaldreck proceeded with slow purposeful steps as their people approached, covered their faces with their hands, and gave observance and blessings.

Ellianna pulled close to him and clung tighter to his arm with both her hands. As they moved among the shops, she did not flitter about as at the bazaar. The deeper they strolled into the city the more she trembled. Her nose crinkled, and she cringed at the loud noises.

Kaldreck moved her toward a tower in the east wall. They entered and, in the stillness, she calmed, loosening her fierce grip on his arm. He led the way up the narrow winding stairs, pushed open the door to the battlements, and she slipped past him.

She stepped out of the tower and inhaled the cool air wafting over the top of the wall. Her shoulders dropped, and she hurried to the far side of the battlements a half a pace away. Resting her forearms on the stone surface she leaned over until her toes came off the ground and she could see the earth below. She perched there looking out, her feet swinging like a child's.

Bits of their conversations came back to him. *I have never seen a city. I have walked all over the distant hills beyond Illgrove. If we lived here in this tent it would be enough.* But one comment pulled at his heart most, *How ever are they supposed to enjoy the Divine's creation within such high walls?*

Kaldreck drew alongside her, and she looked up at him with a radiant smile. His heart sored at the sight and a notion started to take form in his head. He worked at its details as he led her around the battlements pointing out the city below and the great expanse of nature without.

Over the next several suns, Kaldreck put his plan into motion. As others worked at his bidding, he spent time with Ellianna. They walked the battlements and took rides out in the country. Ellianna smiled more, and he even heard her laugh on occasion. She opened her heart to him a little more each sun.

"Ellianna, I have a present for you," he told her as they left the midsun meal.

"A present, my lord? But I have all I require and more. And I have been unable to do anything for you." The sadness in her eyes pricked his heart.

"It is my greatest pleasure to provide for you, my sweet." He kissed her on the temple and again felt her shudder. He stamped down his frustration and offered his arm. He led her out of the palace to the place where the servants' huts had stood. As they approached, five men were pummeling the last three honel huts nearest them with large hammers.

"The servants' quarters, my lord?"

"I have made other arrangements for the few who still lived here. They have better quarters in a nearby tower. You need this space."

"I need it?"

He only smiled at her.

As the last of the mud walls fell, a large pool carved into the rocky ground came into view. Beside it a gnarled man with wild gray hair and a tattered, soiled tunic stood waiting. Kaldreck walked Ellianna a few steps closer and waved for the man to proceed.

The man raised his hand with a bit of purple cloth to another man higher on the mountainside behind the palace. He in turn waved a cloth to another man higher yet. Kaldreck watched as Ellianna's gaze rise following the waving flags halfway up the steep slope before the last man waved his for a long time and then it dropped. The man below him waved for a moment before his dropped and down the signals came until the lowest man on the slope dropped his.

Ellianna gasped and stepped back as a torrent of water burst over the edge of the mountainside and cascaded into the hole carved in the ground where the old man stood.

"Do you like it?"

"You have given me a—a waterfall." She gasped with awe. She looked up at him, light dancing in her eyes, smoke within swirling with such speed it made him dizzy. "'Tis beautiful."

"It would have been better on the north side so you could have heard it from your balcony, but having it there would have required moving the kitchens and Malic's home."

"'Tis perfect, Kaldreck. Thank you." She skirted the rubble and put her hand in the falling water. She stood and looked at him with such wonder. This was enough for her.

He smiled, for there was a great deal more to what he planned. "It will make a good centerpiece I think."

"Centerpiece?"

"Aye." He stood quiet, playing with her confusion. "The waterfall is only the first piece of the present."

Her head tipped to the side and she considered him, a smile playing on her lips.

"This whole space is yours, Ellianna."

She looked around at the empty ground scattered with rubble. "What am I to use it for?"

"The queen's garden." He waved out his hand to the wagons standing behind him full of rich soil. "This is Wilfarm. He is touted as one very good at growing things. He is here to help you."

She didn't move as she stared wide-eyed at him. "A garden…?" she stammered.

He nodded.

She raced to him and flung herself into his embrace. Wrapping her arms around his neck she said, "Oh Kaldreck, thank you. Thank you so very much."

"This makes you happy then?"

She slid from his embrace, regret hiding her heart once more. "I have not been unhappy, my lord. Forgive me if I have appeared ungrateful or discontent."

Kaldreck hated the change and determined to see the joy again. He turned her toward the empty space, stepped close to her until her back touched his chest, and wrapped his arms around her waist. He leaned down and whispered, "Can you see it, my sweet? What does your garden look like?"

She rested back into him with a sigh and started pointing. "A tree needs to be there to the left of the waterfall near the palace wall. And benches—there need to be benches around the pool. There is a blacksmith in the city who makes fine twisted art pieces in metal. Benches from his hand would be beautiful. There should be paths of uncut stone and mounds of flowers and grass. Flowers of every kind that can grow here—those that open with the end of the sleeping season, and those that open in the wakeful season and the growing season. Trees that sleep and those that do not. Bushes of every hue. It will be a beautiful peaceful place."

"And will you share your peaceful place with me?"

She turned in his arms, and he saw the full light of her heart in her eyes. They shone like the waning sun surrounded in beautiful bright clouds stirred by a strong breeze. Her arms encircled him, and her head rested over his heart. "You above all others will always be welcome. I would wish no other."

He kissed her head and she quivered still. He was closer to her heart, but he still did not possess it.

"Excuse me, my lord. The sketches of the queen's seal have been finished."

Kaldreck relinquished his hold on his love and turned to the man. "Yes, Halfort." He took the parchment and held it out before Ellianna.

The seven teardrop-shaped petals of the starflower formed a circle, the center of which held the brilliant star of the Divine. In the center of the star lay a dagger. Kaldreck held out the sketch for Ellianna to see. "I do not favor the placement of the blade. Our lady may be powerful and brave, but her heart is kind and tender—

not that of a ruthless warrior."

"Yes, my lord. I will instruct Scribbler to remove it."

Kaldreck shook his head. "No, the strength of the blade is a part of our queen, just not the at her heart. Perhaps if it sat on a petal of the flower?"

"Understood."

"The words are not quite right either," he looked to Ellianna for an opinion.

She rose on her toes and whispered in his ear. "I cannot read, my lord."

He gave no reaction not wishing to embarrass her. "Bold, Fierce, Kind." He shook his head again as she searched his face. "Our lady queen is these things, but this is not her essence." He looked at her, his gaze washing over her whole face. "Queen Ellianna is—faithfully devoted to me and our people. She is compassionate in her concern for others over herself." His hand brushed her cheek, but her heart fled from him slipping a little further inside of her. "Queen Ellianna is an endearing treasure for all of Windmere."

Her gaze fell to his feet. "Thank you, my lord. You are too kind."

"And our queen is humble." He turned and handed the scrap back to his steward. "Any of these would describe our queen better than the words Scribbler has chosen, Halfort."

"Yes, my lord. I will inform him at once."

As Halfort left, Kaldreck turned toward the ward, and his eyes caught on another wagon waiting. "And there lays the last of your present, Ellianna."

She looked up, a mix of emotions coloring and swirling her eyes. "Kaldreck, you honor me too much. I do not deserve…" A tear rolled down her cheek.

"Love—true love—is not given based on merit. It is unconditional, full, deep, and above all—unchanging."

She stood at his side and slipped her arms around him, again resting her head on his chest.

He walked with her to the wagon full of pots of various size and shape. "I thought you might also wish to bring your precious plants into your chambers."

Her smile pulled at the fabric of his doublet, and she squeezed him a little tighter.

"Do you see any you could use?"

She slipped from his grasp and touched a deep blue vessel wider than her slender frame and nearly reaching her waist. "This one would be perfect," she breathed.

"Perfect for what?"

She took his hand and led him to the front of the castle pointing up at her balcony. "For there. It could be filled with flowers and—if there are artisans with the skill—metal posts could be pushed deep into the soil and a large circle of glass placed on top of them to form a table suspended above the flowers."

"It will be done as you wish, though you may need to explain it to the craftsmen for I have never seen the like."

"The calgent of the wealthiest wool merchant in Illgrove has one. I have long admired it."

Kaldreck sighed and turned taking up her other hand too. "Well, there are more pots for your choosing too. Take as many or as few as you wish. I hope the overseeing of the construction of your gardens will bring you great joy in the suns to come—while I am away. I will also speak with Scribbler. He has seen to the instructing of the squires in their letters. It is a task for the queen, but he will instruct you in private first. You will be reading by the time I return, I warrant."

Her grip tightened, and she took a small step toward him. "You are leaving?"

"A sadesman came this morning reporting attacks at our northern ports. I have called the army and they should be ready before the next sunsleep. I will leave my guard here and a third of the men."

She shook her head. "No Kaldreck. Your guard should be with you for your protection, so many need not be left behind. The walls around our home are strong and formidable. Leave only enough to secure and well guard both gates. If trouble comes, they can be shut tight and the warriors can move to secure the palace."

"I would see you safe, Ellianna. We know there is danger within these walls for you."

"The greater danger is for you fighting a formidable enemy. Take your guard and a goodly number of your men so you return safe."

She wanted him to return. Concern stilled her eyes. She cared what happened to him, and his heart thrilled at the knowledge.

"How long might you be gone, my lord?"

My lord. She sat so close to giving him her heart, but still some unknown fear kept it hidden. He must learn what troubled her so, it prevented her from giving him that part of her he wanted most.

"If the enemy is still present, and we engage in battle with them, it could be as much as both moon cycles—though I hope it far less."

"A whole season," she sighed.

He smiled. "Will you miss me, my sweet?"

"Most assuredly," she slipped into his arms again, and his flesh and blood cried out in his need for her.

Chapter 24

Kaldreck pulled from her grasp with what sounded like a groan. His next words were husky and low. "I must go to prepare, my sweet. I leave you to the pleasure of your garden." His steps were stiff as he walked away. She watched him for a moment as her heart and head wrestled within her.

He deserves your love, her heart scolded.

Her mind was quick to counter. *Men speak conveniently of love when it suits their purposes, but they should not be trusted to love forever. Men do not possess a steadfast heart—it is not in their nature.*

Kaldreck will be different.

Fool!

She shook her head and turned back toward the raging waterfall and Wilfarm. She walked to the pool carved in the stone gathering the falling torrent and looked into its depths.

"There are many underground chambers beneath the palace," Eton told her coming near now that Kaldreck was gone. "The king had the water routed to join the one feeding the well."

Ellianna followed his pointing finger to the small brick structure near the inner wall. Turning back to the chasm below her, she watched the deluge of water pound against the boulders within. She grasped for Eton's steady arm as her head spun. "It is so deep."

"This is why I begged the king to place a high wall around it."

She stepped back and looked at the opening. "A small stone wall could be stacked around it, but I would not want it higher than a few footsteps."

"Such a wee wall wouldn't detract from the beauty o' the water, ta be true," Wilfarm said from behind her.

She turned, and he covered his face and bowed low. "Where should we begin, Wilfarm?"

"I 'eard some of them ideas m'lady had 'or this corner of land. Best we should walk it together and a list be made o' the supplies for harvestin' and gatherin'."

They spent the next two degrees of the sun mapping out the garden on a scrap of vellum. Ellianna would make a suggestion, and Wilfarm would refine and record it. He made careful notes of the quantity and manner of materials she required.

Eton and three additional guards trailed silently behind.

As they came back to the waterfall, Wilfarm pointed to the corner where she wished the tree. "A weeper would do there, though the ground 'tis so hard a great quantity of earth will be needed to anchor it."

Turning to the wagons Kaldreck pointed out earlier, Ellianna smiled. "The king has provided almost a dozen wagons-full. Will that not be enough?"

The old, bent man considered them. "Not 'or the whole of the garden, but 'twill make a goodly start."

"Then shall we be about it?" She moved toward the nearest

wagon. Eton stepped in her path drawing her up short. She frowned at him.

"The queen can nay be workin' in the dirt."

"The king gave me this garden for my enjoyment, and I will get the most pleasure in working it with my own hands."

"Again, m'lady, the queen cannot go about in soil stained gowns and dirt deep beneath her nails."

She crossed her arms and tapped her foot at him. She could order him to allow her—but in truth he only sought her best. She could go to Kaldreck and get the boon from him—but he had already given as much. A smile came to her lips and her hands moved to her sides. "I wish to go to the tanner's shop, Eton." She did not wait for his response as she marched toward the city. He came close to her elbow and the other guards encircled her.

The one on her right called out, "Make way for the Lady High Queen," as she passed within the city so those meandering the streets gave her a wide path.

They approached the mud hut nestled near the outer gate, and Ellianna glanced at Eton. His eyes scanned everywhere around them, alert for danger. "Eton, what is the tanner's name?"

He did not speak to her for a moment, but consulted with the guards around him. When none of them knew, a guard—the same one calling out—stepped within the hut, only to return a moment later.

He bowed. "The tanner is Sole, my lady. He comes out to meet with you."

A dark-skinned man with sinewy arms stepped out with a limp, covered his face, and bowed awkwardly on his stiff leg. "Me queen, thank ya for visitin' me humble shop. Are ye displeased with the slippers, me queen?"

"Oh no, Sole. They are the finest things I have ever worn. Thank you."

"Me pleasure."

"I have a new order, if you are agreeable?"

"Me honor to serve, me queen."

"I believe it was your calgent who came to measure my feet?"

"Cami is the one who came to ye, me queen." His constant use of her title and his continued hunched bow grated on her.

"Sole, she wore a leather apron—"

"Da ya wish her ta remove it?"

Ellianna suppressed a smile. "No, I wish you to make me one similar to it."

"Cami, come," the man shouted over his shoulder. "Give the queen yer apron," he ordered when the woman appeared.

"No. I will not take from your One and Only. I wish one made for me. If you are unwilling?"

"Nay, me queen." He put his hand out for the apron and passed it to one of the guards.

"Sole, I—"

"Be donnin' it for but a moment so I can make measurements of your requirements, me queen."

The guard handed it to her, and she slipped the wide leather strap over her neck. Sole waved at Cami and she took up a bit of leather and a piece of chalk.

She lifted it higher over her bosom. "Perhaps a little shorter strap?"

Eton held her unbound hair aside as Sole measured the length and reported it to Cami.

She looked at the width now. "I wish to work in the garden the king has provided me, and I do not want my gowns soiled. I think it should be wider and longer for the protection so I might kneel on it without strangling myself."

Sole took a knee before her, his stiff leg stretched out beside him. He measured off and reported again.

She removed the apron and handed it back to him and he struggled to stand. "Might I also have a couple of large pockets for my tools?"

He glanced back to Cami who recorded it and he nodded. "Aye, me queen."

"There is one more order, Sole. Can you fashion me a pair of gloves?"

Sole stood a little straighter and his chin rose. "I make fine gloves, me queen."

She smiled at him. "I thought you would."

He snapped at Cami who disappeared within the hut only to emerge with a soft expanse of leather on a slender wood box. She handed it to Eton who held the box while Ellianna placed her hands on it fingers spread and Cami traced them.

"When might ya be needin' these items?" Sole said.

"Wilfarm says it will take almost six suns before our materials begin to arrive. It would be nice to start when they are here, but I do not wish to rush your artistry."

"Have 'em done 'fore the end of the sun two from now. Anythin' else I might be doin' for me queen?"

"You have done more than enough. Thank you Sole, and Cami."

Cami dipped a quick curtsy before Sole shoved her through the door with a grumble.

Ellianna turned to Eton. "There is a blacksmith on the far side of town who works with twisted iron. We will go there next."

Eton waved out his arm in the direction for them to travel.

The blacksmith, Ironwrin, a short solid man with a toothless grin was ecstatic to fashion four benches for her. He made several quick sketches in the dirt near his forge and allowed her to pick her favorite shape. She liked two different ones, so he promised to make a pair of each.

As they returned to the inner ward, Ellianna's eyes caught on the waterfall as it fell away from the mountain above the palace. The sun's rays peeking out from between the peeks above lit the water and a rainbow shone in its mist. Her heart fluttered wildly in her chest. *What a loving gift Kaldreck had made for me. He deserves your love too.* She stood for a moment and let the wonder of Kaldreck's love wash over her.

As her gaze shifted toward the front of the palace she gasped. "By all the Truth holds holy, what are they doing?"

Eton drew near and followed her finger as she pointed to men teetering on the roof above her balcony.

"It looks as if they are lowering the large pot in place where ye wanted it, m'lady."

"If they fall or are injured, I will never forgive myself for making such a foolish request. It would have been safer to carry it in the doors."

"No man is allowed in the women's chambers, m'lady."

"Then they should have brought it to the door and allowed us to roll it or drag it inside. There are plenty enough maids for us to have seen to it." One man wobbled as the pot swayed, and Ellianna turned toward Eton's shoulder clenching her eyes closed. No scream rent the air and she dared ask. "Did he fall?"

"No, m'lady," Eton chuckled. "All is well. The pot is set and the men are entering a window near the king's chamber in safety."

"Thank the Divine. Tell everyone, I forbid them to be out on the roof for such foolishness ever again."

Eaton bowed and nodded his understanding with a smile.

She stood on the front steps two sunwakes later as Kaldreck prepared to leave. Her heart hurt, and fear gripped her. She waved Malic over. "Lord Malic, stay close to him and do not leave his side. He will have need of your strong arm, my lord."

Malic bowed. "I will stick to him like vermin on a hound, my queen. I swear on my life I will do everything to return him to you hale."

Her gaze shifted from the undefined foreboding stirring in her, to consider his face. "And that goes for you as well, my lord Malic. I expect both of you to come back hale. If anything were to happen to you, your Lady Palma will be quite cross with me for making you see to his safety, and I fear she would never forgive either of us."

Malic laughed and waved his calgent over—a tall and solid woman who was all curves. She was a good match in size and temperament for the mighty captain. "My Palma knows well the trials when man set off to battle. May she bring you comfort and encouragement, my queen, as she always does for me."

Palma curtsied and Ellianna looped her arm through hers as she straightened. Ellianna pulled the woman to stand beside her on the step. Palma almost matched Kaldreck in height and Ellianna felt small next to her. "I welcome Palma's company, and we will care for one another as you two watch over each other."

"Be brave, my love. Fight with the might of the Strong-arm and bring Him, your king, and me the glory of your victory," Palma charged her husband.

"The Comforter be with you both until we return," he answered and kissed Palma deeply.

A strange longing tore at Ellianna's heart, and she turned her gaze to find Kaldreck among his many men. As though he knew she searched for him, he pulled from among the others and walked toward her.

She left Palma on the bottom stair and moved to perch one step up. She looked into his eyes and drowned in the love pooled there. He took her hand and squeezed it, a smile forced to his lips. She spoke first. "You have chosen me and set my world on end, Kaldreck Lord High King of Windmere. I charge you to take all care to fight well for your people, but to return to me hale." The fear she could not understand threatened to strangle the words from her throat. She fought to contain her tears. "I will sorely miss our walks and your calm strength beside me. Come back to me, Kaldreck. We still have much to experience together." The tears would not be held, and one slid down her cheek.

"I love you Ellianna, with all my heart. I leave it here with you to care for, and as a man cannot live long without his heart, you can be assured I will return to you."

He leaned in to brush her cheek with a kiss, but she turned her head and pressed her lips against his. The searing pain caused her to pull from him more quickly than she wished. But he smiled at her with a joy that sent her heart to somersault.

"The Strong Tower go before you, the Shield beside you, until you return."

"And the Peace remain with you, my sweet."

Chapter 25

Ellianna's suns fell into a quiet routine with Kaldreck gone, but a longing grew in her heart to the point of breaking in his absence. She spent the cool mornings laying stones for paths and digging holes for the arriving plants. Her midsun passed in her seating room with the balcony doors open wide while Palma taught her how to work a loom. Each evening before sunsleep, she would walk the battlements thinking of Kaldreck and searching the horizons for his return. Following the final meal, she would sit in the king's empty council chamber with Scribbler and Eton for her reading lesson.

This sun she laid the last stone for the walkways and knelt in the dirt. Her hands were soaked with sweat inside the thick leather gloves as she held a large purple leafed bush in one hand and scooped dirt around its roots with the other. She filled the hole and packed in the soil like Wilfarm taught her.

"Well, you are a sight as always, girl."

Breath caught in her lungs, and her heart skidded to a stop at the menacing familiar voice. *Where is Eton?*

"So, this is what the high queen of the land occupies her day with, or has the high king come to his senses and relegated you to a common slave where you belong."

Ellianna sat back on her heels and raised her gaze. She swallowed the quaking of her voice as she addressed him. "Villiant. Is there something you require?"

He drew back his hand as if to backhand her but never let it fly. Sweat appeared above his upper lip, and his gaze flickered about. "You worthless girl." The words were almost a growl through his tightly lock jaw. "You will repay me for what you have stolen, or I shall be forced to tell the king the truth about your uselessness."

Her stomach clenched for a moment, but reason flashed in her brain. She forced her lungs to draw in a deep needed breath as she rose to her feet. She considered him, and her shoulders squared. "I am no longer the vermin under your boot, Villiant. The king has claimed me as calgent and the rites have been preformed."

Her father snorted his distain.

"I did not cost you your wealth or your precious bot. Lord High King Kaldreck deemed it just punishment for your mistreatment of me. Where you saw expense, he has seen value. Where you strove everyday to break me down, he has raised me up. I am Lady High Queen. I owe you naught. And there is naught I have ever done, or you could ever accuse me of doing, that would turn the king's heart from me. Eton!"

Her guards came quickly to the spot hidden by some of the larger plants where Villiant had tried to conceal himself. Swords rang from their sheaths.

Villiant's eyes grew wide, his hand dropped to his side, and he took a large step back.

Ellianna raised a hand to stay Eton and his men. "See he gets a meal and provisions for the return journey. Then make sure every guard at the gate learns his face before he is escorted out." Her voice was calm and level as she looked to her father and gave Eton the final instruction. "See to it they know his life will be forfeit should he try to visit again."

Villiant opened his mouth to protest.

She stepped near him, her voice low and tight. "Would you prefer I have you bound in chains and held in the dungeon until Lord High King Kaldreck returns, and I tell him of your threat against me?"

His lips clamped shut and he went willingly with the guards who led him by the arms passed her.

"Goodbye, Father. May the Forgiver of Men's Souls show mercy on your hard heart."

"M'lady, forgive me, I do not know——"

She put up her hand silencing Eton's words and smiled. "Peace, my friend. Villiant is ever the wily one. If there was a way, he would find it. 'Tis not your fault. I am well. Better than I have been after any confrontation with him."

"Truly, m'lady?"

"Aye, I am well."

Eton scowled at Villiant's back as they moved toward the kitchens. "Are you sure you wish to feed and release him?"

"Most assuredly. My kindness in the face of all his hatred and abuse will burn like a coal in him. He expected me to cower, and if not, then to lash out at him and end his destitute life. I have spared him that he may know kindness when none is deserved. Mayhaps the Merciful can yet capture his stubborn heart."

Eton looked at her with a look she could only describe as awe. He bowed deep. "I am honored to serve one who is wise, compassionate, and ever merciful."

Ellianna rested her hand on his forearm. "We have all been shown much mercy by the Giver of all. Can we not spare a little for another?"

He inclined his head and smiled.

A movement caught their attention as Ironwrin arrived with the benches. He placed them where she wished and started to leave.

"Ironwrin, you did a beautiful job on the benches. I shall think fondly of you each time I take my rest. Thank you."

He bowed low—his grin revealing his many missing teeth. "Glad I'm ya're pleased, my queen."

"Ironwrin, there is more, if you are agreeable?"

He rubbed his plump hands together with an eager nod.

She walked to the center of the ward and looked back on the growing garden. Ironwrin stood beside her, with Eton always close at hand. "The waterfall the king commissioned is lovely, but I think it needs a frame to draw one's eye to it. Also, Eton informs me I must wall-in the natural beauty—especially after a very unwanted visit this sun. But I do not favor any more stone walls."

Ironwrin smiled and took a knee to draw in the dirt. "My queen, a tall wide arch made of latticed metal rods would frame the fall without blocking any o' the view. The same pa'ern could be applied to a railin' to close the space. I could make it simple like, so ya can train creepin' plants to grows on it. In no time, it'd not look like metal or stone, but a growin' hedge."

She sighed deeply. "I can see it, Ironwrin, and it will be perfect. Wilfarm sent men out in search of a flowering vine that grows on the far side of our mountain. It will hug your fine frame with color."

Ironwrin bowed and hurried off to start his new project.

Palma sent regrets as she tended a sick son, and Ellianna chose to walk the battlements early this sun. She searched the road, but there was still no sign of Kaldreck, or anyone else, traveling its path. She moved along the high wall and turned to look down on the city. She gasped, and Eton stepped to her side.

"Eton look," she pointed below them.

"What concerns ye, m'lady?"

"No, look at the homes."

"Aye, m'lady?"

"Do you not see the windows on that home, and that one over there, and another over there?"

Eton did not respond.

"They have flowers growing in boxes and baskets around the windows."

His shoulders slipped down, and his hand came off the hilt of his sword. "They follow their queen's example, m'lady."

"Oh, but is it not beautiful to see so much color against the drab stone?"

"If it pleases ye, m'lady, it is a fine thing."

She looked at him with a critical eye.

"I must confess, flowers do not stir me as they do ye, m'queen." Merriment toyed on his lips and she laughed.

"The Creator's work should stir every heart, Eton," she said as she started walking again. She marveled at the number of homes and businesses that were now adorned in all manner of plants.

"I will endeavor to be more appreciative, m'lady."

She smiled at his mirth.

Chapter 26

Seven suns after Villiant left, when she ran out of new plants to place in the ground, Ellianna stood and brushed off her gloves before removing them and stuffing them into a pocket of her apron. She strolled in quiet peace through the hard work of her hands. She drew near the cascading water, put her hands in it, and ran them around her neck. The beads of sweat mingled with the cool water to arrest the climbing heat of the sun. She sat on a bench until a man approached through the newly erected gate.

"My lady," he bowed.

Ellianna considered him, unsettled by his presence. He was one of Kaldreck's guards but not one who served her. None of the king's men approached her unless through Eton.

"Where is Eton?" she asked, concern making her heart flutter.

"Forgive the disruption, but I bring word from the Lord High King."

Something in the way her calgent's title slithered across his lips made her shiver. "And you could not give this message to Eton?"

"Such was part of the message, my lady. Eton has been called to serve the king in a different capacity for a time, and I have been asked to see to your training with the sword, my lady."

"The sword?" Ellianna eased to her feet, fear tightening around her like a constricting viper. "The king wants me to train as a warrior?"

The guard grinned, but it sent a shudder down her spine. "The Lord High King would see you protected—even if by your own hand—in these difficult times."

A new pang strummed her heartstrings. "The fighting does not go well? Is the king hale?"

"Aye, quite hale and whole, my lady. There are more enemy on our shores than he realized, and he fears much over you. He spoke of threats to your person even within the walls of the home you share."

"Surely there is another solution to my safety than me training with arms…Warrior—I cannot remember your name," she groaned in frustration.

"Brayden, my lady."

"Yes, of course, Brayden, there must be another course of action."

"Our Lord High King was quite explicit. He sent me to see to your training as I train all the squires when they first arrive. They complete their training with Lord Malic, but they start with me."

Ellianna hesitated. Her heart beat out an odd rhythm at the words that rang as true in her ears but as lies in her mind. Her stomach rolled with unease at the conflict.

"My lady, you know the king's harshness when you behave contrary to custom. How much more would you inflame his wrath by refusing his direct command?"

"But he did not command me, Brayden."

"He sent me with the words." He narrowed his gaze though it still did not meet her eyes directly. "Do you call one of King Kaldreck's personal guards a liar, my lady?"

"No, Brayden. I… Mayhaps I should speak to Eton on the matter before I proceed?"

"As I have said, my lady, Eton is not here for you. He has been sent on business of the kingdom."

"Should not Eton have told me of these changes?"

Brayden shrugged his narrow shoulders with an uncaring sigh. "I will return to the king and tell him of your refusal. It seems you refuse him a great many things. Perhaps the One has chosen badly for our Lord High King in order to seek his downfall in favor of another. Good sun to you, my lady." He spun on one heel and stalked away on hurried steps.

"Brayden?" she ran after him. "I will do as you say."

He turned and bowed with a smirk. "Pleased I am to hear it, my lady." He looked to the sky. "The sun is declining and overly warm. Meet me here in the ward on the next sunwake, and we will begin. I will go to the armory and see all is prepared for us."

He left and Ellianna shuddered again. *Something is wrong,* her spirit warned. She could not find any of her guards. Had they all been called to the king's side?

As sleep struggled to claim her, she thought of Eton. He warned her never to go anywhere without him, and it felt contrary to his protective nature for him to leave her in another's care without speaking with her on the matter. Maybe he was needed urgently in the battle. Were things truly well with Kaldreck? Her heart skipped a beat at the thought of him being injured, but it near froze in her chest to think she could be used by the Sovereign to bring Kaldreck harm.

Coldness surrounded her. She heard water dripping and cool moisture stuck to her skin like a wet blanket. Her nose curled at a reek most foul. A prone figure lay in shadow on the rotting reeds. It moaned and Ellianna felt her spirit cry out.

Chapter 27

The next sunwake, Brayden met Ellianna with a shield and a short sword. He placed the heavy shield on her left arm and proceeded to wrap the sheathed sword around her waist.

She stepped from him. His words of the Divine using her to bring harm to Kaldreck became the only thing to keep her feet planted, but her entire body trembled at his nearness and familiarity with her. Her thoughts jumped between her desires to flee and seeing the disapproval on Kaldreck's face. She would not be the cause of his downfall—but everything in her screamed this was wrong. Eton should be here. Did he abandon her? Did Kaldreck send Brayden to test her? Should she return to her chambers and hide there until the king—or Eton—returned? She fought for an even breath as her questions piled up like dung outside the stables.

"Shall we begin, Ellianna?"

He did not address her by her title. Again, part of her screamed of the wrongness of everything Brayden said. He lied. She knew it deep in spirit. "I am your queen, soldier." She could not keep the tremor out of her voice.

He smirked, bowed exaggeratedly, "Of course, my lady. How

thoughtless of me."

Again, he lied. She knew it—as assuredly as she knew her own name.

He drew his weapon, waving the tip at her.

She should go inside. Naught good could come of this.

"Do you refuse the order of your king?" He asked waving the sword toward her again. Then he added more quietly, "Fie, but you are an obstinate woman."

Once more his earlier words rattled her insides, *Perhaps the One has chosen badly for our Lord High King in order to seek his downfall in favor of another.* She inhaled a ragged breath and closed her eyes in a quick prayer. *Please, Compassionate One, do not led me bring harm to the Lord High King.* Her plea dropped as a dead weight in her soul.

She pulled her sword from its home and took an unsteady step away as the shield's weight anchored her arm, leaving it useless at her side.

Brayden raised his weapon and threw his sheath aside. Like lightening from the heavens, he slashed at her and pushed her back in retreat from his fearsome attack. She used the sword and— when she could hoist it—the shield to protect herself. His movements were wild and careless as he still refused to look at her.

"Stop!" Ellianna gasped. The shield fell off her aching arm as Brayden drew to his full height. She met him near eye to eye though his gaze lay far to her left.

"You are doing well, my lady. The One has gifted you with a natural skill. It will not be long before you could best Lord Malic himself."

Ellianna fought to capture breath in her searing lungs. She bent using her blade for support. "I do not wish to best anyone."

"If you are beset by an enemy and should die, think what it would do to our king. He needs heirs and only heirs of a true calgent can inherit the throne. Would you deprive the Lord High King of such a legacy?"

"Of course not," she panted. "But I say truly, the only one who threatens me now, is you, Brayden."

He staggered back, and his hand came to his chest with a gasp. The mail, which lay hidden beneath his clothes, rattled in the stillness. He offered her no such protection. "My lady, I am here only to assist you. I would never…"

"If you speak truth… If indeed King Kaldreck sent you to train me and if you wish only my protection… then you will look at me when we meet in these mock battles." She quaked at the insincerity of his words.

"I could never break tradition and so dishonor my Lord High King by looking on his One and Only as if she were mine."

"If you do not look upon me, your wild swings will remove my head."

His head hung low and he groaned. "But I could not, my lady."

"You must. I will not be trained by someone who cares so little for my welfare. It would be the ultimate dishonor to kill your king's calgent."

He shifted the weight between his feet, then paced before her. He rubbed his chin. He turned his back on her and looked to the sky as if expecting the Divine to aid him. At last his shoulders slumped, and he nodded his consent. "As you wish, my lady. I must obey my king to train you, even if I am punished for my irreverence for my queen."

He raised his gaze to meet hers, and his eyes smoldered with a dark malice. She regretted her insistence at once. Cold fear seized her entire body, and a vision of the sinister presence within him swallowed her whole stealing her breath. A smile parted his lips revealing his teeth. His sword rose to her chin.

"Defend yourself," his tone mocked her as he refused to release her from the clutches of his hard stare.

She gulped, hoping he would not boldly strike her down with so many witnesses as palace workers ventured about on their various tasks. Ellianna pushed the tip of his weapon aside with her own sword and bent to retrieve the burdensome shield. She barely straightened before he came at her once more. His sword whistling through the air as it smashed into hers. She fought to keep her short blade in her hand as he pressed her, harder and harder, blow after blow. Several times the only thing to save her was the protection of the mighty shield she cowered behind.

He battled against her as she struggled to protect herself. Their eyes met, and she lashed out in the moment he sought a breath. He stepped from her and his gaze drifted passed her.

"Ellianna!" a voice boomed behind her.

Chapter 28

Kaldreck left his army and raced, with only a handful of men, for a sun and a half to see Ellianna. His heart cried for her. His blood burned at the thought of her. His body ached for her. He laughed at his excitement and his guards' teasing. He charged into the gate and passed all his subjects without even a wave, only to race through the inner gate and find his love with another. They looked boldly at one another. She paraded her betrayal before everyone as she sparred with Brayden.

The dark-haired man dropped at his feet as Kaldreck dismounted. "Forgive me, my Lord High King. I did only as our Lady Queen requested. I never wanted to dishonor you."

Though Kaldreck could not see his face as he knelt before him, the man turned his head toward Ellianna and she gasped.

"Leave us," Kaldreck ordered the warrior and he stomped passed Ellianna. He could not speak with her now for the rage burning in his belly. The image of his hands wrapped around her slender neck and choking the life out of her, thrilled him.

"My lord, 'tis not true. I did as you bid me," she stammered as she raced after him.

"I bid you to give your heart to another?" he roared climbing the palace steps two at a time.

"Nay, I have not. You sent word you wanted me to train with the sword."

He whirled on her as he smashed through the double doors, causing her to almost collide with him. "I gave no such order. Why would I wish such a thing?"

"Brayden said—"

"Brayden? Where is Eton? No other should ever speak to you."

"Brayden said you called him away," she whimpered, tears pooling in her eyes. Her tears and her pleas would be the undoing of his rage. He could not learn the truth from her lips.

"Halfort!" His bellow echoed off the smooth stone of his home.

A moment later, the man came racing to him with a bow. "Aye, my lord?"

"Where is Eton?"

"I know not, my lord. A sadesmen came in early last sunwake. Before I could meet with him, Brayden sent him off, and I have not seen Eton since. Is he not with our queen?" Halfort turned to follow Kaldreck's gaze as it shifted toward her.

"Oh," Halfort gasped.

Kaldreck could not bear to look on her trembling form. "Search for him at once," he ordered Halfort. "And bring Brayden into my council chamber. I will speak to him." He turned and moved deeper into the palace muttering to himself. "I sent no message. I would never remove Eton from her care. I did not wish she learn the sword."

"I only did as I was instructed. I wished only to be obedient to your word. My desire was only to please you…"

"And again I say, you thought it would please me to give your heart to another."

"I am for you alone," she vowed again.

He whirled on her at the second-floor landing, noting Eton's closed door as he turned. She remained on the steps appearing even smaller as he towered high above her. "Do you know why none are allowed to look upon you? Why all must avert their gaze from yours?"

"So they will not loose their heart to one not their calgent," she whispered.

"No!"

She jumped at his outburst.

"I want all my people to give their love, affection, honor, and respect to my queen. They hide from you so you will not give your heart to any other."

Her head raised, and her wet cheeks glistened in the dancing torchlight. "I belong to you, my lord. I will give myself to no other."

"Are incapable of giving yourself—you mean to say." The sound of his hard footfalls bounced off the walls as he climbed away from her to his chamber. He crashed through the door and stormed inside.

"I belong to you. I am yours, my lord. I only sought to make Brayden look at me to save myself."

He staggered back from her. He thought she would enter her own chambers, not follow him. He did not want to see her, but she stood trembling in his outer chamber pleading her case. Tears running down her face with the force of the waterfall outside, left dark splashes on the front of her light gown.

He waved her off in disgust and turned to flop in a chair. "How could his heated stares of desire save you—unless you wished to be saved from my affection?"

She moved to kneel before him, her smoky eyes still and dark. "He insisted you wanted me trained with the sword. He assured me if I did not obey your wishes, the One would seek another for the throne of Windmere. I could never knowingly cause you harm, my lord. I agreed, thinking it was your wish and it would be for your good alone. Brayden came at me with a fierceness that made my blood run cold. He would not look at me and his sword flew wild." She turned her head, tucked her hair behind her ear, and revealed a line of blood below her ear the length of his longest finger.

Kaldreck sat up.

She turned her right shoulder to him and spread the fabric until he could see the slice within it.

"I only wished not to die at his hand. I thought if he looked at me he would be more careful. I was mistaken. His eyes were dark and his heart full of hate. Looking at me only gave him a better target. If you had not returned…"

A bucket of fear extinguished much of his fury.

"My lord?" Halfort entered through the open door. "We have found Eton."

Kaldreck turned to give his steward his full attention anger sparking bright once more.

"My lord, he suffered in the dungeons beaten and bloody."

Ellianna gasped bringing her hands tight over her mouth. "I had a dream of a human form in a dark place," she muttered.

"He has been taken to Balmson, who reports he will recover."

Kaldreck looked at Ellianna once more. "Did Eton speak of who beat him?"

"My lord, he said he thought Brayden the villain, until he woke in a cell with the very man. Brayden's injuries are older than his and Balmson fears he may not recover."

"What of our queen's other guards? Were not Coby, Dane, and Free also charged with her care?"

"All have been found in the dungeon, my lord—though it seems as if they were drugged and not beaten. And the man we thought was Brayden has disappeared. We cannot find him anywhere within your walls."

"Thank you, Halfort."

The man bowed and left the room closing the door behind him as Kaldreck stared at Ellianna. Fear cooling the sweat of his body until he shivered. "Another veiled attack?"

"Veiled, my lord?"

"Was the intent to kill you in a mock battle or to raise my ire enough to…" He could not speak the words to describe the hate-filled images that overwhelmed him moments ago.

"I belong to you, my lord. You can do with me as you see fit."

Kaldreck frowned. "You are not my belonging or possession, Ellianna. I do not own you. You asked me when we met that I not treat you like a mindless thing."

Her head fell. "But clearly, my lord, I do not think. I should have not listened to Bray—if he was not Brayden, who was that man?"

Kaldreck raked a hand through is hair. "A question I wish I had the answer to. You knew Brayden from the journey here. Yet the man fooled you."

"I never spoke to him and only saw him at a distance. Of all your guards, I know least of him."

"Probably the reason he was chosen to impersonate. Someone only vaguely familiar but who you would trust."

"I was wrong to trust him. I knew Eton would not leave me without speaking, but…"

"He used your concern for me against you." Kaldreck sighed. "I cannot fault you that, Ellianna."

"But you can find much fault in me."

He leaned forward cupping her chin, and his blood roared. "Forgive me, Ellianna. I should have known you would not betray me. 'Tis not in you."

Her eyes swirled at his kind words as her body relaxed into his simple touch. "May I stay?"

"You are still not ready to give me your heart, Ellianna. I have told you—"

She pulled from him and shook her head, "I…I have missed talking with you, my lord."

He frowned at her continued use of his title.

"Kaldreck, I want to know of your struggles and victories. How fairs the borders and your men? May I stay so you might tell me all that has transpired in your absence? Might I be allowed to remain in your presence?"

He could not refuse her desire to be with him. He stood and offered his hand bringing her to her feet. They moved to a monsuit skin he threw in front of the closed balcony doors.

She sat facing him as her right arm rested on the low table, her legs curled beside her. As the last rays of sun waned, she listened attentively asking questions when he ran out of words.

Kaldreck sat with his legs out toward the balcony doors as he leaned back against a short sofa. His heart beat a contented rhythm. His anger, now forgotten, left only the burning of his blood and the need of his flesh prodding at him as they passed the last degrees of the sun. Yet the song of his heart strummed loudly.

He reached out to take her arm to go to the evening meal, and she recoiled from him with a stifled yelp. Taking her hand gently, he pushed up her sleeve revealing several wide bruises and flaming red welts. He looked at her.

"The shield Brayden supplied me was large and heavy," she told him quietly.

He closed his eyes and remembered coming into the ward and seeing her battle the man they thought was Brayden. "He gave you Malic's practice shield. Even I would have difficulty wielding the heavy defense. You were not meant to walk away from your time of sparring, I think. I will have to give extra thanks to the Preserver of Life this night."

Gwidus entered then with a tray and placed it on the table she leaned against. "I thought, mayhaps, you would prefer to dine here tonight."

"Thank you. If Balmson can be spared, would you send him to me?"

Gwidus bowed.

After they ate, the healer entered, and Ellianna turned pressing her back against Kaldreck's chest as her arm was inspected. With naught broken, Balmson gave Kaldreck a jar of ointment for the welts and the cut before leaving.

Ellianna did not move as she lay her cheek on his chest, and he was forced to wrap her in his arms to apply the thick cream. When he was done she yawned.

He should send her to her own bed. He needed to meet with his men farther down the coast on the next sunwake, but she nestled back into him. He clamped his jaw shut and stamped down the need screaming inside his flesh. Kaldreck stretched out with his back to the balcony and pulled Ellianna to her side next to him.

He bunched up the fur to make her a pillow, but she slid back against his chest. She lay pressed to him from shoulders to knees, and he could not breathe for the pain at her nearness. She intertwined the fingers of her right hand with his left and laid her head on his outstretched arm.

He put his right hand on her upturned hip to push back from her—if only a little—but the furniture blocked any escape.

She turned on her back and looked up at him, the light of a nearby candle reflecting in her eyes. His hand now lay on her flat belly and burned as it rose and fell with her gentle breathing. "I am hurting you."

He shook his head as every part of him burned.

"I am causing you pain." She moved to sit up, concern twisting her fine features. "I should leave."

He held her firm. "Sleep, Ellianna."

"You are in pain."

"My blood burns for my love—as it should. And my flesh aches for union with you as it does with every man for his One and Only. I will endure."

She lay still, and a small tremor shuddered under his hand. "I am for you," she whispered.

"All but your heart, Ellianna. I will wait—now sleep."

She tried to move away again, but he slid his hand around her waist and pulled her onto her side, then pressed her back against his chest. He couldn't stifle a groan.

She raised his palm to her lips and kissed it.

Chapter 29

Ellianna stirred as Kaldreck's warmth pulled from her. She turned and looked up as he stood above her.

"I must rejoin the army. We were successful in repelling the enemy, but I hope I have truly defeated them and not but sent them to another port." He stared down at her with tightness in his gentle face. "Ellianna, you ask me to trust your promise not to give your heart to another."

She nodded. "I am for you."

"Why is your promise more trustworthy than mine?"

She looked at him as her heart flipped in her chest.

"I have promised to love no other but you. I am yours, Ellianna, and I cannot give my heart to another because I have already given it to you. Why can you not trust me?"

She sat up and pulled her knees to her chest, her arms wrapped tight around them. "I have seen men claim love and tenderness only to be cruel when the rites have died away."

"I am not Villiant." He growled with a huff.

"No, you are not. But he is not the only one. Lord Kanton has no love for Lady Zorgot nor she for him. Many in Illgrove do not love the one they have bound in calgent ribbons. They care not at all for those they bind. Even here, the tanner Sole, does not love his mate Cami."

He knelt before her. "I know it to be more than true that you are my One and Only. I hear the song in my heart when I see you. I feel the heat in my blood when I touch you." He brushed her cheek with the back of his hand. "I know well the ache of my flesh when you are pressed near. I am yours and you are mine." He stared at her for a moment longer. "Do you not feel these things as well?"

She could only shudder.

"I will see you when I return," he moaned as he pushed to his feet. "Be well and safe, Ellianna." He stalked from the room with long strides.

Ellianna returned to her chambers. She soaked in a long bath and dressed in a simple gown. Naught interested her this sun. Not food, comfortable chatter with Palma, nor weaving—not even her garden could draw her from the formidable thoughts weighing upon her soul. She dismissed most of the maids and sat on a chair in a bit of sunlight between the bright corner of the balcony and the cool seating room. A cup of mead sat untouched on the flower table beside her. The bright colors taunted her inner turmoil through the glass top.

"My lady, Eton has asked if you will come speak to him," Avery whispered.

Ellianna shot to her feet. "Where is he?"

"At his chamber, my lady."

Ellianna ran from the room banging doors as she passed.

Eton stood not quite straight near his doorframe staring at the tile floor. His right arm lay bent over his chest wrapped in a length of cloth tied around his neck. He tried to bow.

"No, Eton, do not. Please."

"Are ye well, m'queen?"

"Quite well."

He sighed, and the resulting relaxation of his tight muscles tipped him into the doorframe. He leaned there using its strength to hold him up. "Praise the Merciful. I could think of naught but ye, m'queen, as I suffered in the dark, damp, stinking hole."

Ellianna failed to stifle a gasp and he looked up at her with a smile.

One eye was swollen shut, and a bruise lay partially hidden under his growing beard. "Do ye know why King Kaldreck chose me for the honor of yer personal guard?"

She shook her head.

"I trained as a warrior for the Lord High King's army when I met Dove. She insisted we were destined for one another. I avoided her—which was very hard. She was a beautiful woman, though most told me later they did not behold her beauty as I did. She followed me to every city where I trained. She worked in the kitchens for the barracks, and she watched me train every sun."

His voice took on a husky deepness as he remembered. "I told her I was called to be a warrior and, as such, she could be left alone if I were killed. I didn't want her to suffer." He smiled, his open eye looking far off beyond the walls enclosing them. "She wouldn't relent. Ye think too much Eton, she'd say.

"Me skill brought me into Lord Kaldreck's notice as he trained to vie for the throne as one of royal blood. He requested I be part of his guard and with the new position, Dove told me to stop fightin' the Truth. We were united the next moon. I loved her with all my heart. She consumed me, and I her, until we were one soul. She beamed brighter than the heavens on the sun when she told me of the babe growin' within her. I thought I would burst from the sheer joy."

His voice faltered, and he cleared his throat twice before he could continue. "She never made it to the time of her laying-in before something with the babe went dreadful wrong. The healer couldn't help, and the Divine called them both." He cleared his throat of the threatening tears. "She took me heart with her and I didn't think I could go on. I withered away in a hut for moon after moon, until Kaldreck came. He encouraged me and said he had an assignment only I could complete."

His gaze shifted, his eye glistening with unshed tears, as he smiled at her. "Ye see, he wanted me to guard ye, because he understands I cannot be tempted to pull ye from his side, nor could I take yer heart or give ye mine. I had a One and Only and as the name implies, I can have no other. There have been women who wished to partner with me in friendship, if not love, so we might each endure our loneliness. But I could never feel about them the way I felt about me Dove. There is no substitution for perfection." His gaze held hers for a moment longer.

"Kaldreck knew he could trust me to be so close to ye. Now, if I may be so bold, might I be askin' why ye don't trust him?"

Ellianna startled. "Did he speak to you?"

"Only to see after me health, but I have eyes and a bit of discernment. 'Tis clear ye come as a duty and not in love. Has

Kaldreck done somethin'…?"

"No!" She took a breath and continued with more calm. "No, he has been naught but kind and considerate to me. He seems quite perfect."

"He's perfect for ye, m'queen. No other will satisfy him. I can assure ye."

"Eton, I am a plain and simple girl from a far-flung insignificant village. I have naught to offer the Lord High King. What happens when he realizes this truth? If I give him my heart, he will trod over it as a bit of dust in the road when his eyes are opened. I cannot bear to waste away in pain as I watched my mother do."

Eton nodded. "Might I offer ye a bit of advice Dove gave me when I filled her ears with similar pathetic excuses?"

She grimaced at his chastisement but agreed.

"The connection between calgents is a matter for the heart, and the head only muddies the waters of the soul on the matter. Yer head will concoct every conceivable objection to the surrender of your heart to another, but in the end the mind is not the thing that experiences the joy—the sheer, all-consumin' bliss—of union. Union, in fact, is not possible if the heart is not surrendered. It must be the heart's choice. M'queen, in the suns until your calgent returns shut up the mind in a dark place in yer soul and let yer heart run free. See what it wishes and what it desires."

"You have no regrets, Eton, in loving only to have her taken from you?"

"The only thin' I regret is listenin' to my mind and runnin' from union nearly a full turn wastin' time we could have spent together. I would not trade one sun I spent with me Dove. Not a single tick of a single degree."

She nodded.

"Do ye wish to go out?"

"No. You are to go and rest."

He frowned at her.

"I have much to dwell on, Eton. I have no wish to go anywhere or do anything."

He nodded with a slim smile. "I am here to serve ye, if ye wish."

She turned toward the doors of her chambers.

"I will pray the Truth reveals His will to ye, m'queen."

"As I pray to the Healer to restore you. Thank you, Eton. Rest well, and may the Compassion grant you comfort."

Ellianna spent several suns trying to do as Eton suggested, but her mind was a ruckus, unyielding beast. Ellianna sat late in the afternoon staring out her balcony at naught, thinking of the king's words. *I know you are my One and Only. I hear the song in my heart when I see you. I feel the heat in my blood when I touch you. I know well the ache of my flesh when you are pressed near. I am yours and you are mine.* How could she be as sure when her blood did not burn as his, nor her heart sing? She did feel a strong tug in her flesh and remembered well the tremors of her body at seeing him bare to the waist. Why did her blood not boil at his touch if he were her true One and Only?

This question consumed her for many suns. Then her heart cried out over the din of objections and she knew.

Later one sunsleep, dressed only in her night clothes and robe, she raced to Eton's chambers. "Eton, are you awake?"

"Aye, m'queen. What troubles ye?"

"Naught is wrong—in fact it is all quite right." Eton came into view from the shadows of his chambers. "I must beg you for a very important boon."

"Ye have but ask, m'queen."

"You must tell me the moment Lord Kaldreck returns." He nodded rubbing his eyes with his good hand. "No matter the degree of the sun—or moon. I must know as soon as he returns."

A large grin filled his face as he gazed upon her. "I'll alert ye at once, m'queen."

Chapter 30

Kaldreck sighed, rolled his shoulders, and tipped his head from side to side. A chorus of pops and cracks filled the air causing Malic, riding to his right, to laugh.

"You getting too old for a battle tent and bedroll, my lord?"

"I am only two score and five, Malic. Three turns younger than you as I recall. Are you not anxious for your own bed?"

"Oh aye, most anxious, but not as much for its soft comfort as for the one I share it with."

Kaldreck frowned.

"Is she still distant, my lord?"

"No, she was eager to see me and begged to remain in my chambers so I could tell her all I had seen and done in our time apart. Even after I exploded at her in a hot venting of my wrath, she wanted to spend time with me."

Malic snorted a laugh. "It is a blessing she did not meet you a few short turns ago."

Visions of his hands around Ellianna's throat still haunted him. He hated the rage that took hold of him—overwhelmed him. "I plead with our great Forgiver to cool my wrath every sun. Still, she wanted to stay with me. If she had known the desire in my heart at that moment…"

"The Protector watches over you both, my friend."

"He does. Thank the One. He does protect me—even from myself. Lady Ellianna is willing, but her experience with liars and the unscrupulous has jaded her view of my claims of calgent. She does not offer me her heart. I know not what she thinks I might gain by lying. She has no wealth for me to claim as Villiant did with her mother. She does not seek a more prestigious social standing by offering to bear me sons as with Lady Zorgot." Kaldreck groaned his frustration. "Malic do you know of Sole and his spouse?"

The large man raised a brow.

"He is a tanner in the city?"

Malic thought for a moment. "I believe he is the one near the outer gate, my lord. Why do you ask?"

"Ellianna intimated Sole did not treat his One and Only well."

Malic grunted. "I will investigate the matter, my lord. If for no other reason than to ease my queen's heart."

"She is a kind and tender-hearted woman."

"Which may be why she is reluctant to surrender such a fragile thing to one who could so thoroughly destroy it. Be patient, my lord. I trust the Truth will reveal all to her soon."

"If He does not act soon on my behalf I shall burn from within."

Malic's boisterous laugh filled the air. "Many a man have thought so—but the Sufficiency will sustain you—even when you do not think it possible."

"From your lips to the Merciful's ears."

Kaldreck trudged up the many stairs to the second-floor landing. There was not a part of his body that did not groan with weariness. Eton's door stood open. For a moment he thought to inquire after Ellianna, but as the time was well after sunsleep, he moved to press on to his own chamber.

"M'Lord High King, is that ye?"

"Eton? I feared you would still be in Balmson's healing rooms."

The man came to the doorway. "I couldn't bear to leave her without protection another moment."

Kaldreck smiled and placed a hand on the man's shoulder. "You are a blessing from the One, Eton. Thank you for your service to her and to me. I sleep better knowing you are here."

"Thank ye, m'king. 'Tis me pleasure to serve."

"Can I ask how she fairs?"

Eton smiled gently. "She is hale and well, m'king, though she hasn't ventured out of her chambers much since ye last left us. I fear she worries over my fitness and doesn't wish to over tax me."

Kaldreck hummed his approval. "She is naught, if not thoughtful."

"'Tis true. Our queen has a compassionate heart."

"I look forward to seeing her at first meal. Rest well, my friend."

Eton smirked, "And ye as well, m'king. I wish ye a blessed sunsleep."

Kaldreck considered him for a moment longer, but the man turned and moved back into the darkness of his chamber. Kaldreck reached the top of the last stair and pushed open his door. Gwidus greeted him with a cool cup of ale and a tray of thin sliced meats and cheeses. He sipped from the tankard and set it aside. Pulling his overtunic free and untying the sash around his waist, he tossed the sack at the older man. He completely shed his overtunic next, followed quickly by his undertunic.

Gwidus took his garments without a comment though he shot him an exasperated glare.

Kaldreck ignored him and dropped to the sofa. His head fell back, and his eyes closed. He one of his feet rose and the laces of his boot were worked free. If Gwidus did not hurry, Kaldreck would fall asleep here long before he made it to his much-anticipated bed.

The second boot dropped to the floor and Kaldreck reached lazily for the tankard.

The door banged open.

Kaldreck leapt to his feet. The tankard clanked to the floor, spilling its contents with a splash over his bare feet. He reached for his sword realizing too late he no longer wore it around his waist.

Ellianna stood in the open door. Her small frame convulsing as she gulped air. Barely covered in her shear nightrail, Kaldreck's own body reacted at the sight of her. *Divine be merciful. I do not have the strength to resist her again tonight.*

Gwidus collected the discarded cloths and slipped from the room.

Kaldreck stood alone with the object of his desire and forced himself not to look at her. He could not bear the pain.

She waited until the door latched. From across the room, he could hear her take a single deep long breath. Next the slap of her bare feet on the tiles echoed in the room before the carpet covering the center of the room muffed their falls.

He dared glance up at her as she drew near.

She never slowed as she released the hem of her garment and threw herself into his embrace. Her arms wrapped tight about his neck, and her feet dangled above the floor brushing the tops of his feet with a feather light touch. Only the barest of fabric separated their skin and Kaldreck fought not to collapse consumed by his pain and desire.

The whisper of her words brushed his ear. "I am yours, and you are mine."

Kaldreck's heart somersaulted several times. The breath she drove from his lungs would not return. He reached to his neck and pulled her free and she slid to the floor, brushing her body against his as she dropped.

Her eyes were not still and yet did not swirl. As she gazed up at him the smoke of her eyes had cleared revealing pale periwinkle irises shining with a light all their own.

"I have your heart?" he dared ask.

Her lips twisted in a chagrined smirk. "In truth—you have had it a long time. I was just too dull to recognize it."

Her hands rested on his bare chest burning deep holes through him. His entire body shuddered. "You feel the heat in your blood at my touch?"

She shook her head. Her hands slid up to his shoulders, around his neck, and into his hair. She pulled him down toward her bringing his lips within a breath of hers. "The heat is not in your touch." He could smell her sweetness and almost taste her. "The fire is in your kiss."

She pressed her lips to his, and he felt her shudder. She pulled him down into a deeper more passionate kiss, and her whole body trembled. Now Kaldreck understood her quivering was not from fear or reluctance but from the heat he stirred in her. A heat they shared.

She deepened the kiss. She tasted like buzzers necter and he could not drink in enough of her.

His heart sang with a melody he only heard when she was near. His blood raged. His flesh rejoiced. He pulled from her and stepped away. She searched his face as he caught his breath. He put out his hand in offer and led her to his bedchamber.

Kaldreck woke as Ellianna stirred beside him. Their union took them well into the predawn degrees. She squirmed next to him again, and he thought she whimpered. Kaldreck parted the curtains surrounding them and pulled the candle from the bedside table. He held it above Ellianna and saw her face distorted in pain.

He feared his need and eagerness had hurt her. Her head thrashed from side to side, and she cried out in pain.

"Ellianna?" he stroked her face.

She pulled from him, slipped out of his bed, and dropped to the floor on her knees.

"Ellianna?" He followed her pulling a blanket from the bed to cover her.

She pressed the heels of her hands to her temples. Her eyes remained clamped closed. She whimpered again and cried. "Too many. Too much." Tears managed to escape their tight confines and trailed down her cheeks.

Setting the lamp on a table, he knelt in front of her covering her hands with his own. "Ellianna," he called to her again, but it did not seem as though she could hear him in her pain.

"Too many. Too much."

He pressed his forehead against hers.

Kaldreck found himself standing in a black empty place beside Ellianna. The only light came from their white glowing garments. Ellianna's hand lay entwined with his as they stood in the void.

"Too many. Too much."

As the words again tumbled over her lips the ring of light encircling them grew, stretching out into the blackness. As Ellianna whimpered and tightened her grip on his hand, the vague glimmer of light brightened. As sunlight chasing the darkness at every sunwake brings clarity and vision to the world, so the light grew around them until faces materialized. Hundreds and thousand of faces encircled them. Row upon row of people. And as he looked, he recognized many. Gwidus, Eton, Halfort, Malic, and the rest of his guard were among those around them.

These were their people. All of them.

As the faces went from a shimmer to solid form, the din of their many voices grew until it assaulted his ears. He understood her pain and her cries of too much.

Kaldreck wanted to pull her close and shield her from the cacophony around them, but she raised her free hand and pointed. The sea of faces she indicated parted like a river before a plow ship. Wave after wave parted until a dark spot came into view far in the distance.

The form remained still until Ellianna shouted above the noise.

"Show yourself, coward!"

The spot turned and grew as it drew near them, revealing the full form of a man draped in a black cloak. The head rose until the hood-shadowed face pointed towards them. Ellianna flicked her wrist from where they stood, and the hood flew off the figure's head paces away.

Ellianna gasped and pulled from Kaldreck.

They sat on their knees in his bedchamber. She panted for breath and shuddered as her gaze searched his.

"Renwald…"

"…is a black sorcerer." He completed her statement.

She reached out a trembling hand toward him. "He wishes you great harm. He seeks your throne and your life, Kaldreck."

Smiling, he cradled her face in his hands. "But the Provider has blessed me with a seer—a true seer. The person who loves me most, will protect me and reveal his evil before it can do us any harm."

Ellianna frowned and pulled from his hold. She wrapped the blanket more tightly around her shoulders and turned to the door.

A heartbeat later Gwidus walked into the room. He stopped short when he spotted them.

Ellianna swayed and her panting breaths returned. She looked toward the old servant, but Kaldreck was sure she did not see him as she again whimpered, "Too many. Too much."

"Gwidus send for…" Kaldreck realized that he did not know who tended her now.

"Ellianna?"

She whimpered.

He turned her face to look at him again, talking to her with gentle prodding. "Ellianna, find my heart, listen to our song. I am here. You are with me and no other. Ellianna."

Her eyes locked on his. The dark centers diminished revealing the pale color through a thin layer of gently swirling smoke. She gasped for breath.

"Ellianna, who tends you now?"

"Avery."

He pulled her close and held her in a tight embrace. "Gwidus get word to Avery to bring a gown for our queen. Inform Eton to prepare for a journey."

"A journey, my lord?"

"We go to the Fathers."

"The Fathers?" Ellianna pulled from his grasp and looked at him, with eyes squinting in pain.

"They will know how to help you harness these powers the Giver has gifted to you."

"The light high on the hill?" she stammered.

He remembered the vision they shared and the dull light that emanated from high above them. He nodded and pulled her close once more.

Gwidus left, and Kaldreck reached for his leather breeches. It would not be appropriate for Ellianna's maid to find him undressed as she came to assist her mistress. As he stepped from her, Ellianna swayed, and she nearly crumpled to the floor cradling her head again. When Avery arrived with Gwidus, Kaldreck finished dressing in the outer chamber.

"Gwidus, clear the castle of all within and make sure no one crosses our path as we move toward the trail."

Gwidus bowed and hurried away as Avery led Ellianna staggering toward him. He wrapped a strong arm around her waist and took her other hand in his to steady her. "Listen to my heart, my love. Focus on me and push out all the others. Only you and I are here."

She steadied and relaxed into him, and they moved from his chamber and out of the palace.

Chapter 31

Several times, as they hiked the ridge above the far northern tower, Ellianna felt as though she would drown in the sea of voices clamoring in her head. A seer—her—of all unworthy people. The Divine made less since to her by the degree.

She stumbled again. Kaldreck's strong encircling arm remained the only thing between her and the jagged rocky trail beneath her feet. The pain in her head forced her eyes closed against it. But she was a seer, and her gift had been awakened by the love she shared with Kaldreck. The thought eased the pain and brought a smile to her lips.

They came to a gate at a tunnel and a guard draped in Kaldreck's colors. He bowed and unlocked the iron barrier. It creaked with a loud protest as he pulled it open. Kaldreck led them into the dark passageway as Calla, now much healed, held a torch for them. Eton entered the black path last as the gate clanged shut behind them and the key secured the bolt once again.

They walked for many echoing steps as drips filled the silence between their footfalls until a point of light came into view around a bend. Another gate stood before them. The guard posted here wore a yellow tunic of the Divine Guard.

"It is Kaldreck, the Lord High King, and his queen come on urgent business with the Fathers," Kaldreck announced.

The gate swung open with a faint whine. "Yes, my lord. You have been expected."

Ellianna squinted in the bright light of the full sunwake as they emerged from the darkness. The gate lock again clanked behind them, a calm presence of three strangers filled her before the men in long white robes physical forms materialized in her clearing vision. New voices assaulted her and she cringed into Kaldreck's embrace. His presence alone kept them from crushing her from within.

The man in the middle—shaved bald and the tallest—approached her. He cradled her face in his long-fingered hands and brushed each of her temples with a kiss.

Kaldreck growled his disapproval. Every muscle in his body went ridged against her. He started to pull from her and one arm raised to lash out.

Ellianna pulled back into his protective arms, and they took a step back together as she clung to him.

"I mean no offense, Kaldreck. I only wished to ease Ellianna's pain."

Kaldreck looked down at her and she nodded.

"The voices are quiet." She turned and looked at the man.

"I have wrapped you in a thin protection of my own thoughts. In the next moons here with us, we will teach you how to do the same. You will harness your extensive power and all will come to Crag Haven to learn of the wisdom the Wise shares with you."

Ellianna shook her head and clung to Kaldreck until he took

another step from the white-robed men.

"I will not remain here. I belong with my One and Only." Her voice was thin and weak.

The tall one frowned. "You have been given a gift, Ellianna. A most holy and powerful gift from the Giver. You cannot hide it under a bundle plant."

"This gift only came upon me because of the love I share with my calgent. It would not have been gifted me without him."

"It may be so," the one on the left sneered looking down his raptor beak of a nose at her. "But it has now been given and must be shared."

Ellianna tightened her grip on Kaldreck's arm. "The royal palace receives far more visitors than this holy mount—hidden up here in these imposing peaks. I could see, and share, with far more from my place at the Lord High King's side."

"There is but One we are to service with the whole of our being, Ellianna," the tall one snorted again. "You must be in the Divine's holy house to serve Him or He may well turn your gift into a curse."

Voices erupted in her mind once more with the force of an exploding fire mountain. She screamed and crumbled into Kaldreck's arms.

"Stop it!" Kaldreck's order rumbled over the cacophony in her head.

"We did stop it, but she does not wish our counsel. She wishes to turn her back on the leading of the One and handle the matter on her own." Raptor nose sneered.

Ellianna listened to the drum of Kaldreck's frantic heart under her ear, within it she found the song their hearts sang together since their union last night. A two-part harmony that soothed her and gave her strength. She pushed to stand on her own trembling legs, drawing from Kaldreck the strength she needed to force the voices away. "If I am to be locked away here, how is the Lord High King to have his heirs?"

Both men shrugged. The third—short and round, looked on her with pity. His sadness filled her and added to her own aching heart a pain so powerful it threatened to shatter her into a million shards.

Raptor nose tossed his head, his words were cold and chilled her insides. "Kaldreck, it would seem has served his purpose. The Divine may have no further use for him."

"A threat has come to our land!" Ellianna bellowed stepping from Kaldreck's hold, toward them. Without her beloved's touch the voices pounded down on her once more.

The tall one nodded. "And the Divine has sent you to teach us how we might be saved, or how to endure if He should want to see Windmere fall to ruin."

Nestled back into the anchor of her love's strength, Ellianna ground words between her teeth. "And what if the Divine says Lord High King Kaldreck is the one who will save us."

"Then he will yet have a purpose." Raptor nose spat and turned with the short Father, who never spoke. They climbed the stairs and disappeared into the structure carved from the mount itself.

"Choose this sun whom you will serve, Ellianna, the king or the Divine," the one remaining Father said.

Kaldreck stroked her hair, and she turned to look up into his gaze. Tears pooled in his eyes. "I cannot bear to see you in pain, my love. If the Fathers can help you…"

"I do not want to leave you." She glanced at the dark entrance leading into a structure devoid of windows or light. "I do not think I can bear to live in there." She turned back to him, filling her fist with the fabric of his tunic. "Please take me home. Take me to my garden and the waterfall." Her head lowered and she groaned the next words. "Take me back to your bed and let me give you sons, beloved."

His arms encircled her, pulling her tight to his chest. Her body ached for him as it never had before. "Ellianna, there is naught in all my life that I do not want more. But I cannot help you master this gift. What if returning with me leads to our deaths and the kingdom falls to Renwald? Could we ever be forgiven such a decision?

"May we have but one more sun together?" Ellianna moaned to the remaining Father.

He frowned but waved his hand toward a trail leading off to the north. "Follow this path to the second hut on the left. You may spend your time there." His eyes passed over those standing with the king. "The rest may go. They will not be needed."

Kaldreck's finger wagged at the man. "You get her only if she is attended by her maid and protected by her guard." The Father opened his mouth. "You say she has a gift of the Divine, and you say she must stay here to learn from you. This is the only way—by the Divine's most holy name—I will allow her to remain. She is my One and Only. I still have claim on her and how she is to be treated as Lord High King of his land—and your ruler. Defy me at your own peril."

The Father pursed his lips and narrowed his gaze, but he nodded. "But in all other ways she will be treated as any other acolyte." He too turned and disappeared into the dark gaping hole.

Eton, Calla, and the handful of guards remained near the statuary. Kaldreck led Ellianna to the hut.

Chapter 32

As sunsleep approached, Kaldreck led Ellianna back to the holy hermitage of the Fathers of the Divine. She trembled as she clung to his hand. "I do not wish to leave you."

He squeezed her hand a little tighter. "I am yours and you are mine—and ever will it be so. Stay with the Fathers for a little while. Learn from them." He brushed away a tear. "And if you ever have need of me, send word, and I will come for you."

She rose up on her toes and pressed her cheek to his. "I have need of you," she whispered.

He encircled her in a strong embrace and the inner assailing voices dimmed once more.

"I have given you the sun, it is passed time to come to your destiny, Ellianna. The evening missives to the Merciful are about to begin."

Ellianna drew from Kaldreck's arms her fingers trailing down his arm, over his straight elbow, across his strong wrist, and through his mighty fingers. She slipped away from him toward the tall impatient Father she met earlier.

He frowned at her as she glanced up at him through eyes squinted in pain. He huffed his disapproval of those who came with her but brushed her temples again with a brief kiss.

The voices clamoring in her head fell silent and she relaxed in the relief of again being alone with her thoughts.

He crinkled his nose, "Your frippery will not be allowed inside." He waved a hand to a young woman with a shaved head. She wore a rough plain yellow kirtle and carried another for Ellianna. "All acolytes shed their worldly belongings and all that makes them an individual."

"You will not lay a blade to her head or shears to her locks," Kaldreck growled.

"It is our tradition, Kal—"

"I care not. She will wear your clothes, but she will not have her head shorn. Have I made myself clear?"

"You may hold title outside these walls—"

Kaldreck stomped up the stairs and stood eye to eye with the man. He leaned in punching each word until the Father stepped away from him. "I am Lord High King of all Windmere. And this holy hermitage exists by my patronage alone. You Fathers neither concern yourself with the health of my lands, my soul, or my people. If not for my continued support, you would starve. I have consented to the training of my beloved in the use of her gift—in hopes you are at least capable of providing useful instruction. But know this, if any harm comes to her or she is denuded of her lovely locks or any changes should be forced upon her—I shall rid myself of the burden of this place. Are we at an understanding?"

"Aye," the Father gave a curt nod as he waved Ellianna inside.

Kaldreck took her hand once more and kissed the palm. "If you have need…"

She nodded and entered her new home.

Ellianna woke to the bells echoing through the chambers and passageways carved into the mountain. How long had she suffered here? One moon cycle? Two? More? She pushed herself up and swayed as she sat looking at Calla who poured water in a pitcher for her to clean. The effort it took her just to raise from her thin mat on the stone floor, sent her heart to pounding and her breaths to forced puffs.

Calla helped her stand on wobbling legs. "Come, my queen. The morning entreaty to the One will soon begin. Father Matthas will be more displeased with you, if you are late."

"I am glad he will no longer be instructing me. How many more suns must I sit and stare at candle flames, hum, and chant rote dead words with no result? I have not been gifted with seeing what is yet to come." Ellianna's ire stirred her strength and Calla pulled the nightrail over her head. Ellianna took a bit of cloth, dampened it and soothed it over her pale lifeless skin.

"But the voices still come, m'lady?"

An exasperated sigh raced through her and she threw the cloth in the basin, splashing water onto the floor. "The voices of those within these walls, and in the beginning those from the king's city below us. But I grow too weak to hear those so far away now." The shapeless yellow kirtle slipped over her head. "I hear your heart's voice Calla," she finally admitted.

"M'queen?" Calla gasped.

Ellianna stroked her maid's arm. "I did not mean to intrude on your private longing, but I know you miss your One and Only as much as I. Forgive me for insisting you accompany me to this awful, lonely pit."

Calla knelt before her. "I am honored to serve m'queen, m'lady. Please do not send me away."

Ellianna reached to pull her up and almost tumbled atop her in the effort.

Calla sprang to her feet and steadied her. Ellianna clung to her for a moment waiting for strength to fill her legs once more. "Even if I wished it, my friend, I could not rise in the morning without your help. And though Eton has vowed never to love another—I cannot think he would favor coming to dress me."

Calla stifled a chuckle. "Oh, you would send the poor man to an early eternal sleep, m'lady to even suggest such a thing."

They walked to the door and Ellianna's cheeks heated as she faced the object of their jest. He waited in his doorway across the hall. She looked at Calla and they both giggled, holding their heads close together. When she glanced back at Eton, his brows were drawn tight and his head cocked at them.

"Good sunwake, Eton."

"The Divine's blessings be upon ye, m'queen. Are ye well?"

She reached for his steading arm. "As well as one can be, locked in a hole for the dead."

They walked with care down the stairs to the large chambers three levels below. Calla and Eton helped her to her knees and they chanted with the others the same words they spoke every sunwake. Ellianna already tired of them—surly the Divine covered His holy ears not to bear their droning one more time.

When the entreaty concluded they stayed on their knees and partook of the first rations—a stale biscuit and half a cup of foul wine. Ellianna gagged on it as it went down—but it was the only nourishment she received until sunsleep.

As Calla and Eton pulled her to her feet and turned her toward the learning chamber, she moaned her displeasure again. "The Almighty Divine has created all manner of purple, blue, red and fuchsia fruit and eatable orange thing for us. He created it for us to enjoy—and we waste away in sun's old bad bread and the worst wine I have ever tasted. How is it the bread is always stale. Must it not at some point have been fresh?"

"We deny ourselves to draw closer to the One, child." Father Johafamus scowled down his raptor nose at her as Calla and Eton lowered her to her knees in the middle of the room. They left her there and went to the wall at the back of the room. "They must leave," he pointed a boney finger at Calla and Eton.

"Yet they will remain," she said with a calm as strong as Kaldreck's blade.

"You have failed in all your training. They and all the other indulgences you must have are a distraction."

"I fail because I am weak from lack of proper food—I ate more with Villiant," she muttered the last under her breath. "I once walked the fields the Divine created, ate from the provision of His hand and drank of the cool purple streams He uses to water His people and His land." Again her anger fueled her— added to her strength and allowed her to sit straight, unbending as a jahala trunk. "And I learn naught, because I am not the type of seer you wish me to be. I do not see visions. The One does not reveal His will to me. I say it yet again: I see into men's souls."

He waved a flippant hand at her and took to pacing back and

forth in the front of the chamber. On his second circuit, he clasped his hands behind his back and glared at her. His hatred and loathing shot at her like a flyer's arrows. He came to a stop and stared down his nose at her where she knelt below him. "I have heard such things reported to me about your sight, but no one has ever—in all the recorded history of Windmere—ever possessed such a sight. Seers are given the sight of what is to come—that is the way of things. So you are not doing as you are being instructed. Matthas could not get through your obstinate spirit— you will not find me as kind hearted an instructor."

Ellianna snorted and muttered again, "Kind hearted? A hamsouls stench is more kind."

A hand flew, colliding with her cheek sending shock waves through her entire body. Moonstar blooms danced in her vision as she swayed from the force.

"Ellianna!" Calla screamed "Oh, m'queen," she stammered kneeling next to her.

"There are no queens in the Divines house!" Johafamus roared.

Ellianna blinked as Eton took up position between her and the Father. His legs blurred in her dazed vision. "I may not have me sword, sir. But ye lay another hand on yer queen and I'll wrap it around yer neck till it breaks and ye're strangled with it."

"She must learn to be obedient. I call the starry host and terra firma to record this sun against you. The Divine has set before you life and death, blessing and cursing: therefore choose life, that you may live. By loving the Divine, by obeying His voice, and by cleaving unto Him: for He is thy life, and the length of thy life."

"I cannot conjure visions I have not been given. The Divine showed me the man who is a threat to King Kaldreck, to Windmere—and even to you Father. But the One does not speak to me as you wish Him to."

"You are unbending of neck and will, Ellianna of Illgrove." He whirled wagging his finger at her. "And the Divine chose poorly in selecting you. It is my contention that your disobedient heart has caused the One to remove His hand from you. This is why the visions do not come. This is the reason you waste away when you are given the sustenance you need to survive." His arms flew out at his side and his voice rose, bouncing off the carved walls of the small chamber, and thundering into her head. "These…these uncalled, who accompany you, do not suffer the weakness from which the Divine has cursed you. They are faithful to Him and you are not."

Father Johafamus whirled on his heel, sending his white robe spinning with the force, and stomped out the door at the front of the chamber. It banged closed rattling Ellianna's already frail nerves.

She crumpled into Calla's arms, tears flowing without care. "Oh please, Holy Divine, do not curse me. Show me what I must do?" She held her aching head.

"Should I send for the king, m'queen?"

She reached her hand out to lie on Eton's strong arm. "If there are to be no interminable lessons this sun, may we go outside?"

Eton's arm was around her back before she finished her words. His strength brought her to her feet. She clung to his neck as he held her tight and led her from the mountain stronghold. Calla followed down the narrow hallways and twisting stairs, through the meandering chambers until they stepped out into the glaring sun at its zenith.

Ellianna raised her hand to shield her eyes but sighed at its glorious warmth.

Calla came to her other side and held her up as Eton led her feet to the tiny patch of young orange grass at the bottom of the four stone steps. She wiggled her toes in the thin blades and a smile pulled at her lips.

With her eyes closed, she threw back her head, and her voice sang out in praise. "Oh Holy Divine, Merciful and Mighty. You are the One. You are all. The Creator of all good things, the feathered beasts and the furry, the two legged and the multi-legged. The Provider of every sweet and nourishing food. You have given me all things. My heart sings praises to Your name and none other. I will seek Your face." Tears choked her next words. "I will follow You Divine. I will do as You wish." She crumpled to her knees and raised her quaking arms toward the purple sky. The green slivers of the two moons low on the horizon still visible under the full light of the blue sun. "Please Holy One, show me what I must do to please You."

Her hands dropped to her lap and her shoulders slumped forward. Calla sat beside her and drew her near so she did not fall. A gentle mountain breeze caressed her face as Calla rocked her and sleep pulled her into a blanket of peace.

Chapter 33

Ellianna rose stronger the next sunwake for her time out in the glory of her Maker's creation. She walked under her own strength to the entreaty and ate without comment of the biscuit washing it down with the wine. She entered the learning chamber before the Father and sat in the middle—not on her knees, but on her rump with her legs crossed comfortably before her.

After half a degree, Father Johafamus entered. He sneered at her, but she sat with her back straight and peace flooding her heart. "Are you ready to receive instruction this sun?"

Ellianna nodded and repeated the mindless script. While her mouth spoke the words, she found no meaning in, her mind worked on a structure within her as real as any surrounding her. Finding herself in the empty other-place where she had stood with Kaldreck when her sight first awoke, she set about building a wall around her spirit. Rocks of every hue and shade appeared in a heap between her and the faces that jabbered at her unconscious. One-by-one she chose a rock and set atop another. They fit together as if chiseled from one source.

Sun after sun as she sat before Johafamus and babbled, the wall grew. The only stonewall she ever favored. And no matter the height, she could still reach to lay the next stone. She fashioned a door and hung it in the wall, which now encircled her. When she laid the last stone, it closed a dome over her head. She stood within the tower surrounding her and marveled at the peace and the quiet. No voices filtered through. Here she was alone—but a light filled the space. A light that spoke of love and a Presence Who cared for her more than even Kaldreck.

She found solace and respite in her inner tower within her mind, and real sleep came to her—restoring her and soothing her temperament so she no longer looked for fault in all those who chose to live in the hermitage.

Strengthened and more herself than since she entered, Johafamus believed he was successful where Matthas had failed. "You are most dutiful in your lessons, child." Though his words were kind, his tone remained dismissive and belittling. "Your willingness may yet move the One to bless you with a true vision."

Her answer slid calm and unbothered across her lips. "I will never see what you wish of me, Father. The sight of the-yet-to-come is not my gift."

Johafamus' fists clenched and his arms went straight at his side. "You horrid little pretender. I cannot bare the sight of you anymore this sun." He stormed from the room.

When Ellianna took her place in the learning room the next sunwake, Johafamus burst in dragging a young man. He tossed the lad to his knees a half a pace in front of her. Johafamus' finger wagged at her nose. "You say you have the sight of seeing a man's soul. Tell me of this boy. Make me believe you see inside his heart."

Ellianna's gaze shifted to the young man. His shoulders were slumped, but he looked at her. He could not have been more than two turns younger than her. Ellianna looked back to the Father and shook her head.

"As I thought. You are a liar. The Divine has not gifted you."

The young man swept long strands of brown hair from his eyes. "Please, my queen. Do what he asks. Show him your gift," he said with a pleading that pulled at her heart.

"Are you sure, my friend?"

Joy parted his lips. "Oh yes. Prove him wrong, my queen," his grin turned into a roguish smirk.

Ellianna rested her hands on her knees as she stared at the youth's eyes and opened the door of the inner tower around her spirit. She saw only his spirit and not his physical face. Images floated around her, swirling in disjointed happenings until she looked on one and forced it to be still. She looked through the lad's eyes at a much younger Johafamus, who stood, arms crossed, tapping his foot, next to a woman crying in a chair.

"Please, stay with us," she begged.

"I will not waste another moment with you, Ferma. You have served your purpose. I have the prestige of your family and a son for an heir—such as he may be. Boinn will come with me to Crag Haven, and he will learn to be a man—not a simpering fool," Johafamus snarled.

Ellianna spoke to the Father though she did not see the man he was now. "This youth is Boinn, your true son, Johafamus. You claimed his mother, Ferma, as calgent though in truth her title is what you lusted after. You desired, naught her love but, only to grow your power. You stole the boy from her—caring naught for the emptiness you inflicted. You left her to die of loneliness. Though he is your son, you care naught for him either—his needs and desires are of no consequence. All that matters is how he reflects on you."

The vision shifted from the distraught mother, and she focused on another time in Boinn's miserable life. "You make a point of berating him before all the other acolytes. Never will you discipline him in private. In fact, if you are not yelling at Boinn and speaking hate and venom over him, you have naught at all to say to him. Ugly words spew from your lips that ought not ever be given breath and life— 'worthless, a waste of a life, good-for-naught, laze-about, fool, my biggest mistake'.

"He is a man of intelligence, and you resent how easy he learns, Johafamus. He is kind—though he has never received kindness from any here. His heart is yet tender, and while he should hate you, yet the Merciful has shown him how to forgive."

"M'queen."

"Boinn does everything you ask—though you offer no gratitude, not a single word of praise. He is far better a man than you—and you loathe him for it."

"Ellianna!"

The images swirled and danced. Her head spun and her breaths came in shallow puffs.

"Queen Ellianna! Stop, m'lady!"

She felt the weight of hands gripping her. Some shook her. Others patted her face. The images of Boinn's past darkened and faded. Calla and Eton materialized above her. She lay on her back gasping for breath as their worried faces stared at her.

"M'queen, are ye hale?" Eton groaned.

She managed a nod as her heart slowed, and her breaths came with more ease. She reached out to him to help her sit. He pulled her up and supported her with a firm hand on her back. The warmth of his touch thawed her chilled body.

Her gaze found Johafamus first. He sat on the instructor's stool, eyes wide and mouth agape. She looked to Boinn next. Tears streamed down his face.

She gasped trying to reach him. "Oh Boinn, did I hurt you?"

He shook his head refusing her hand as the quiet cries turned to deep sobs. "You saw true, my sweet queen. You spoke of the injustice to my mother—giving voice to her pain for the first time. You saw my pain deeper than I would ever allow myself to admit. But wherever you saw the pain, your spirit gave comfort. Like a healing balm for a wound, you ministered to my tormented soul, and it is healed. Thank you…I know not what more to say. Thank you, my queen."

Johafamus sprang to his feet, causing the stool to clatter to the stones. "Foul creature," he screamed at Ellianna, his finger pointed unmoving like a flier's bolt. "Never has such been done. 'Tis evil. This is not a gift from the Divine but from the dark one. You have ruined my son. My precious boy must be cast far from here—if he is even to live."

Ellianna's spirit flew at him. She held him by the throat in an unyielding grasp penning him to a wall. He writhed in her grasp, choking for air.

"M'queen."

She snarled. "You are the foul intruder in the Divine's holy house. Your greed for power has turned your soul far from Him." She glanced up seeing a spiral shelf that encircled the entire room that had never been there before. Upon it lay scrolls beyond counting. She could read the bold labels of those nearest her: Love, Respect, Service, Believing, Truth, Wisdom, Sacrifice… They went on until she could no longer see them.

"M'lady, please."

"You study all these things," she waved her hands at the scroll, "not for the purpose of becoming a better man, but only to keep others under your disapproving thumb. They are of no value to you and therefore wasted." Her hand flew out again, and the scrolls were swept from the shelf to the ground where they turned to dust.

"Queen Ellianna you must stop!"

The vision left her. She fought for breath as her entire body trembled. Her heart beat so hard it shook the solid ground beneath her. Calla and Eton hovered above her. She raised her head to glimpse Johafamus. He lay far from her, crumpled on the ground, coughing and sputtering, as his hands gripped at his throat.

Her gaze returned to Eton's, as she fought to keep her eyes open. "I am so very tired, Eton."

"Let us return to yer chambers at once, m'lady."

"I have not the strength," her head lulled onto his shoulder.

Eton paused only a moment before he slipped his arms under her and cradled her. He carried her to her mat.

She roused for only a moment as he lay her down. She took hold of his sleeve with a weak grasp. "Eton, see to it King

Kaldreck has that awful man removed and banished from the Divine's house."

"Aye, m'queen."

Consciousness invaded her oblivion each time Calla forced broth or wine into her. But it never lasted long. She lost count of the intrusions until something caught her attention when the cup of broth was drained.

Calla laid her back, and as she welcomed the nothingness, she heard it. A few notes of a song. A familiar and cherished melody. The music grew, and her heart joined with it creating the beautiful harmony of their love song. Kaldreck drew near.

She set her spirit free, soared along the hallways and through doors. She burst outside and to the tunnel, passed the Divine guard who did not see her—and the song grew. Passed the king's guard and down the winding path. She saw him and the harmony thundered in her heart.

The corner of his mouth turned in a smile. He heard it too.

I am here, beloved.

His smile grew.

Can you hear me, Kaldreck? I am with you.

His lips parted. "Oh aye, I can hear you, my love."

Darkness engulfed her. The melodies fell to discord. Chill filled her bones. *Danger! Kaldreck there is danger.* She could no longer see him as her spirit was yanked from the in-between back to her body. *Protect yourself, beloved!*

Chapter 34

Ellianna sat upright screaming Kaldreck's name.

A thud pounded on the door. "M'queen?"

"Do not enter, Eton," Calla ordered.

Ellianna yanked the nightrail from her quaking body. The kirtle barely lay over her hips before she flung the door open and pushed past Eton. "Kaldreck comes and evil follows," she called over her shoulder as she ran down the stairs. Now in her solid form with her spirit firmly locked inside her body, others blocked her path and doors slowed her progress.

"Make way!" Eton yelled racing on her heels. "Get out of the way of yer queen!"

Her heart pounded faster than her feet: she could not capture enough air in her lungs. Then, delayed at a door and hemmed in by two children, it came. The melody returned—strong, sure, close. She burst through the exit, sailed down the last few interior stairs, and out into the early sunwake glow. Two final steps and she flung herself into his arms.

Kaldreck engulfed her in his arms and spun her around clutching her to his heart.

She clung to his neck, pressing her cheek against his rough

stubbled jaw. She couldn't speak.

His fingers laced into her hair, pulling more of it loose from the braid. He drew back and his lips pressed to hers. Fire filled her. His lips pressed harder, as his kiss grew in passion and hunger.

"What is the meaning of this disruption?" Matthas grumbled.

Kaldreck pulled from her lips and rested his forehead against hers.

"You are hale, beloved?" she gasped looking at the blood on his doublet and hands, which now stained her kirtle.

His eyes closed. "I am whole of body, my love, but… Oh, Ellianna, I am to blame."

Her hand stroked his cheek.

He took it and kissed her palm pulling from her a little.

"I demand to know…" Ellianna heard no more of the Father's rant as she lowered the inner wall protecting her spirit and drew Kaldreck in with her love. She cradled his spirit within her and he gulped at her intimate touch.

His eyes looked on her with such love as he kissed her hand again. "It was Brayden."

"Brayden?"

"Aye," he choked on his pain. "I knew in my head, he was not the one who handed you a sword and inflicted injures upon you. 'Twas Renwald who stole his image. But the very sight of Brayden stirred anger in me—blinding me to the man I knew and trusted." Kaldreck's head shook back and forth, and Ellianna shared more of her love for him. He squeezed her hand at her touch to his spirit. "Brayden came at me on the trail shouting his hate. He said he had now become the man I silently accused him of being. In the end, he welcomed evil into his heart, Ellianna."

She touched his face again. "It was his choice to make, beloved."

He held her hand to his skin, and the flame her touch stirred in him mingled where their spirits lingered entwined.

"…back in this house now, child!"

Matthas' words filtered back to her. She sighed and turned. Kaldreck still held her about the waist and she leaned into his embrace. She wound her fingers in his, as she looked at the Father standing with his fists on his hips.

"No, Matthas."

He grumbled at her use of his name, and not his title.

"I am done cowering to your useless lessons another sun. I have learned, on my own, how to shield myself. And, I again feel the strength that had failed me. It fills me now as I stand with my calgent. The Lord High King is the other half of my soul. I cannot exist apart from him. My gift is strongest and most controlled when he is near. I belong to Kaldreck and must be with him."

She took a steady breath and looked up at the man perched on the top step. "You have lost the Way, Matthas. The Divine wants a heart after Him not mindless words and struggles for power. Clean His house of all that is not of Him—or He will destroy it, and you with it."

Matthas pointed his finger at her. "How dare you speak to me thus. You ungrateful, child. The Giver of all Justice, deal with you." He stomped into the dark confines of the holy house.

She pulled from Kaldreck, turned, slid her arm around his waist, and rested her head on his shoulder. "Take me home, my love."

He pulled her nearer yet and they turned on the path.

Boinn dropped to his knee before them. "Please my king, I beg you, allow me to come and see to my queen's care in any way you deem me worthy. She has ministered to my soul and I love her."

Kaldreck's eyes moved from Boinn to Ellianna. Before she could speak, Eton stepped beside the kneeling lad.

"Queen Ellianna was challenged to prove she had the sight of seeing a man's soul. Boinn was brought forth for her. Our queen—to her own determent—looked into his heart. She learned he was the son of one of the Fathers. She saw the evil this Father inflected on the one he claimed calgent and on the boy. Our queen's kindness to the lad and testament to the strength of his character has endeared Boinn to her."

Kaldreck looked to her again.

She nodded her head. "'Tis true, but Boinn, I cannot ask you to give up your life for me."

"You did not ask, my queen. I come to you of my own desire."

"But what of Niaria?"

Boinn's head shot up and he stared at her. A smile parted his lips. "Johafamus forbade us union, for she did not have the family name he desired. But now Johafamus controls my destiny no longer. Niaria agreed to go wherever I go, to love whomever I love, and serve whom I serve. We were united a few suns after Johafamus left the mountain."

"My Lord King," Eton spoke again, "as there is much danger surrounding you both, and I am a man of some turns, it would be prudent to bring another into the guard of our queen. I believe

Boinn would be a good replacement for me when it comes my time to step aside. And I would welcome his aid now."

Kaldreck reached out his hand, grasped the lad's forearm, and pulled him to his feet. "You swear to protect your Lady High Queen—"

"With my life—to my very last breath and the final beat of my heart. I will see no harm comes to her. This I swear to be true before the Truth, and all here. May death be my punishment if I should ever fail my queen."

"Then collect your things and bring your One and Only. We leave for home, Boinn."

The boy bowed and a grin split is face as he dashed down the path in the direction of the honel hut Ellianna had shared with Kaldreck.

Kaldreck glanced down at her. "It is long past time we return home."

Calla appeared in their path next. She bowed. "Forgive me, my king, but Queen Ellianna cannot return to the castle—"

"By the Holy's Name, why not?" Kaldreck yelled.

"Until she changes her gown." Calla finished with a bowed head.

Kaldreck pulled from Ellianna and they both glanced down at her blood spattered, shapeless kirtle. "Of course, this would not be fitting. But were not all her gowns returned to the palace?"

Calla reached into a bag slung at her shoulder and unrolled one of her simpler gowns.

Ellianna followed Calla back into the holy house to the first chamber they found with a door. Eton stood outside while

Ellianna changed quickly, and Calla worked the knots from her hair. When it lay unbound in gentle waves she moved toward the door. "Kaldreck prefers it down," she grinned

Calla nodded dropping the brush back into her bag as they stepped from the structure once more.

Kaldreck smiled, inclining his head toward her, and offered his arm. She did not take it, slipping instead under his arm to nestle back against him—her arm around his waist.

"I am ready to return home, my love," she whispered.

Boinn and a girl with a pretty oval face appeared over the rise moving toward them with haste.

"Alcoff, Nafwin, lead us home. It is time our queen resumes her proper place."

Ellianna snuggled in closer to him, her feet skimming around the jagged rocks in her growing joy.

Emerging from the tunnel out into the warm glow of the blue sun now risen high above the mountain peaks, Ellianna savored the strength and love she shared with Kaldreck. Truly, she was never stronger than when she was with him.

They wound down the path only a short distance before they came to Kaldreck's cloak covering a body. Only the toes of the fallen man's boots could be seen. Kaldreck's hold tightened around her as his muscles drew taunt and eyes squeezed shut.

"Please bring him home," he told the guards. "I failed him in life, but I will see he receives a decent burial. I owe him at least as much."

A trumpet called in the distance. Then another and another. The jubilant blasts continued until Ellianna and Kaldreck stood on

the battlements above the city.

Kaldreck pushed her forward a step and shouted to the throngs of people calling and waving to her. "My people, your queen has returned!"

"Long may Queen Ellianna live. Long may she rule beside King Kaldreck. Long may the Divine bless her with wisdom, kindness, and sons," the people chanted.

Their love flooded her spirit even through the inner wall. The combined power of it overwhelmed her and pushed grateful tears to her eyes. The weight of it too much to comprehend.

Kaldreck's strong arm encircled her once more. "Will you walk the wall once more with me and allow your people to see you and welcome you home?"

As deep as the longing to be alone with him pricked her, she nodded and slipped her arm around his. Standing on the inner side of the walkway atop the battlements, she waved to those gathered. Their cheers increased as they took steps forward.

Kaldreck spoke over his shoulder to those who followed. "See all is in preparation for our queen's return. Alcoff, once Brayden's body is delivered for burial, please seek Halfort and have him find accommodations for Boinn and Niaria."

The guards nodded and all but Eton and Calla turned to descend the tower.

Ellianna pulled Calla close and whispered in her ear. "I will not have need of you this evening, my friend. Go to Oswin."

Calla shook her head in protest.

"Please, I know well the longing of both the heart and the flesh for one's other heart. Go to him. I insist."

Calla bowed her head with a muttered, "Thank ye, m'queen." Then she too followed the men down the tower.

Ellianna and Kaldreck circled the city high above waving at all who lived within their walls. Her heart danced at the windows lined with flowers and the pots full of a variety of plants everywhere in the city. She smiled and, again, laid her head on Kaldreck's shoulder as they came toward her own garden.

"Your need for nature has almost strangled the city," Kaldreck chuckled.

She raised her head to look at him. A quizzical flutter pulled her from her thoughts.

"They so want to please you and emulate you, near every path has some pot in it—if not several. Carts can no longer go down some lanes." He smiled as they walked down the stairs of the tower nearest her garden. "I will admit I favor the change. I never saw the need until you revealed it to me." He pulled her close and kissed her soundly. The roar of her waterfall competed against the pounding in her ears with the blood he stirred.

"Should we go inside?" His breath lay husky and dripping with need as it brushed her cheek.

"Please," she begged.

Their steps hastened as they struggled to make their way past well-wishers. As Kaldreck turned her from the hall and toward the stairs, she pulled to a stop. Her eyes scanned those gathered inside and her spirit trembled.

"My love?" Kaldreck drew her toward him.

She took one step. Opening the protection around her inner sight—she looked again.

"Are you hungry?"

Her eyes went to his and she brushed her hand across his face. "Desperately," she groaned. "But evil sits in your hall, beloved. At least one inside does not give their oath to you."

Kaldreck's eyes flew over those gathered within the great hall as they stepped to the doorway. "What do you advise?"

"I cannot locate him with so many." She moved forward through the crowd, climbed to the dais, and took her place at his table. "Let us eat, and I will see what might be learned."

Chapter 35

As they ate, Ellianna focused on one group of people at a time. Kaldreck held her hand acting as her anchor in the sea of voices and emotions. The one she sought did not dine among the wealthy merchants from the city; nor did he reside with those who served and worked within their home.

She tightened her fingers on his. "Beloved, the one who has surrendered to evil is to be found among your men-at-arms."

Kaldreck nodded. He waited until the meal concluded and some stood to return to the sun's activities. "Fighting men of Windmere, come, present yourself to your queen and speak again the oath of loyalty to her now that she has returned to us."

The men glanced at one another. Some muttered. Others shrugged. But they came forward forming a line. Each bowed, spoke their oath, and exited the hall.

Ellianna smiled and inclined her head, as man after man she saw their good and true heart.

Her senses buzzed and her heart fluttered. A chill rose freezing-bumps on her flesh. Darkness assailed her spirit. The evil one came near. As Nafwin took a knee speaking his fidelity, the one behind him came into view. "You!" Ellianna stammered.

His gaze narrowed and he flinched.

Kaldreck twisted throwing his upper body across her. Becoming a shield between her and the threat, his left arm grabbed her right shoulder and pulled her tight to himself.

A small dagger flew through the air at them. It sunk deep into Kaldreck's left shoulder as he covered her.

Boinn burst from the line, leapt on a bench, and came down on the attacker. They tumbled to the ground in a heap as others piled on the man. Daggers rose in the air, plummeting to the fray below, and came up bloody.

Ellianna could no longer sense the evil as the man's life fled.

Kaldreck groaned.

Someone shouted for Balmson but the healer was already on his way to the dais.

Kaldreck straightened with a wince his eyes searching her face. "Are you injured?"

"No." She stared at the hilt of the weapon protruding from high on his shoulder as Balmson examined him. "Thank you, Kaldreck."

His hand closed tighter about hers. "'Twas my duty and my honor to protect you."

She inclined her head and turned back to the blood splattered men before her. They grumbled at the man who sparked the melee and scanned one another for injuries. The dead man—whose name Ellianna did not know—was carried from the room. Free of the darkness she had sensed, she allowed the others to filter out without their oaths. There was one she called back.

"Goffray, stay. I would speak with you."

"Not him. Please tell me he does not—"

Ellianna patted Kaldreck's hand with one hand as he still clung to her other. The pain of Balmson tending to his wound pulled a groan from deep within him. Ellianna was sure the ache was in her own flesh. "Peace, my heart. Your armor bearer, Goffray, possesses a good and true heart, but it is broken by his duty."

Goffray dropped to one knee. "'Tis not true, my queen. I hold it as an honor to serve my king. I would never do anything to bring shame to him or my own name."

Ellianna stifled a sigh. "Peace to you as well, Goffray. I make no recriminations of you. You are ever faithful and true. But your heart longs to serve your king in another manner. You are not the warrior everyone wishes you to be. Goffray, your father was the king's friend from his youth—a strong sword at his side always. When he died King Kaldreck took you into his home to honor your father—"

"I raised you among the warriors. But I am not your father, lad. I did not think to ask what you wanted for your own life."

Goffray remained on his knee, only the top of his head showing. It shook back and forth. "I count it an honor to serve— first as your page and later your armor bearer, my Lord High King. There is no greater call for me."

Ellianna stroked Kaldreck's hand her eyes fixed on his. "He tells the truth, my king. He is ever grateful, but his heart cries for more."

"Speak of your wish, Goffray. You have found favor here."

His head continued to shake as it bowed ever lower.

"Music," Ellianna whispered.

The young squire's back went rigid.

"Music?" Kaldreck played with the word on his tongue and glanced between Ellianna and Goffray.

"Aye, music, my love. There are great compositions in his heart, my king. Oh, that you could hear them. They are a wonder."

The lad's head rose and his gaze held her with awe.

Kaldreck tried to shrug and air whistled through his tight jaw. He swallowed hard and took a slow breath. "If music stirs the longings of your heart, my boy, I can see no reason to bind you to a service you feel not called to. The Creator did not make all to be warriors. Some he gave the gift of building, some in tending the flocks, some in crafting of fine metals, some in hides." His gaze shifted to Ellianna, "To some, the love of all growing things."

She smiled at him.

"And to others the talent for music. Are we not told to make joyful noise unto the One? Goffray, you have my leave to go and follow your heart. I make no claims on the man the Divine calls you to be."

The lad rose on trembling legs and bowed deep. His tears choked his words. "Oh, my Lord High King, you are ever kind and generous to me. I could not have been treated better by even my own father. I thank you for your lasting favor." He paused and sniffled. "If I might be granted one final boon."

"Ask, Goffray."

"Might I be allowed to remain in your service until such a time as you have selected the one who will now serve you? I will train him in all he is required to do so my king will never lack in his care."

A smiled tugged at Ellianna's lips and joy flooded her heart.

"It will be done to you as you have requested, my friend."

"Thank you, my lord." Goffray spun on his heal and bounded from the room.

"Well, sire, if this mundane business is concluded, might we retire to my chambers to see to your treatment," Balmson huffed.

Kaldreck rose to his feet pulling Ellianna up as well. Servants milled about clearing the trestles and removing the blood-soaked reeds. His uninjured arm encircled her waist as he led them down the steps from the dais. "You may tend to me in my own chambers, healer. Bring whatever you need."

Ellianna sat atop of the quilted cover of Kaldreck's bed, her legs stretched out in front of her. Kaldreck lay face down, bare to the waist. His arm on his injured side hung over the far side of the bed, while the other lay heavy across her lap.

Balmson finished the last stitch, stood, and rolled his shoulders and neck as he straightened. "'Tis finished," he whispered. "Our king should sleep yet a little longer from the tea." He placed a jar on the bedside table. "This is to cover the wound three times each sun as the soiled cloth is removed and a clean one is added." A small leather pouch, bound with a thong, plopped next to the jar. "And this is the tea for the pain."

Ellianna nodded her understanding as the man collected his supplies.

Gwidus—who had stood guard at the foot of the king's bed through the entire procedure—came forward. He collected the soiled rags and Kaldreck's tunic before the two men left the inner private chamber.

Ellianna rested her head back against the carved board at the head of Kaldreck's bed. Her eyelids slid closed as the song of their hearts lulled her to sleep, as a babe in her mother's arms. Her muscles relaxed and her fingers slid through his silken locks. They danced and frolicked in the golden waves atop his head as her soul sang praise to the Restorer for bringing her back home.

Kaldreck's arm seized her around her waist and before her eyes had time to open, she lay on her back beside him. She stared up into hungry eyes.

She blinked, trying to find the air that had leapt from her lungs by his sudden action.

His head moved with the slow stalk of a hunter after alert prey. His lips brushed hers. The heat made her quiver. "I thought the man would never be done."

Chapter 36

Ellianna straightened her skirt and pushed her hair back over her shoulder. She turned to leave Kaldreck's chambers the morning following her return, but he caught her hand. "Not that way, beloved." He pulled her toward the wall opposite his bed.

They stood before a huge tapestry depicting a hunt in a dark forest. He smiled at her confusion before he pulled the heavy cloth aside to reveal a door in the stonewall behind it. He pushed it open and lit the torch that rested in an iron holder a step inside the opening. The flickering light uncovered steps curving downward into the darkness.

Ellianna looked at him.

He kissed her temple. "I love your willingness to come to me, beloved."

"I have displeased you, though."

"Displeased is too harsh. I have been…concerned."

She tilted her head searching for understanding.

"You traverse the halls scantily dressed, my love. It has not yet come to anyone's notice, as we have not entertained any of the noble families who would also stay on the second floor. I first thought to move you into my chambers so we might live like so many of our subjects, but I was advised of a queen's need for maids and attendants. The only other possible solution was a direct path between our chambers."

He took her hand and led her down the narrow stairs as they made one complete turn. "I had men carve out this route so you may come to me anytime you desire, beloved." They stopped at another door. Kaldreck pulled her close kissing her. "I will always welcome you."

Ellianna cradled his face in her hands for a moment before she turned and pushed open the door. Brushing aside another tapestry, she found herself at the of the hallway directly across from her private chambers. She smiled back at Kaldreck as he closed the door leaving her alone.

In the near cycle of the larger moon since Ellianna returned home she was rarely far away from Kaldreck's. But during that same time his war host had begun to arrive filling the city wall and in the fields around it. Kaldreck trained often with his men as more arrived every sun. At those times, Ellianna sought out her garden. It lay ablaze with every color under the heavens, and the waterfall bubbled in contented merriment. Yet Ellianna found no solace—even with her One and Only.

Ellianna looked out over her balcony railing. The sun kissed the waking sky with shades of deep purples and hues of blue. The growing season brought few winds with the warm sun, but now one stirred her hair. The few maids she still retained scurried about her chambers, making her bed, drawing a bath, and preparing her clothes for the day. She watched them for a moment as she hugged her heavy robe about her. It was not as though anything disappointed her but… something was missing.

A longing had grown in her heart since the day she left the Crag Haven. How was it she missed the times set aside in prayer to the One? The need was not in the mindless droning of words but for a true connection between her and her Maker.

Ellianna tossed her head at her own foolishness. Why would the All-Powerful and Holy want to commune with the lowly of His creation? Yet the need remained.

After first meal, Ellianna wandered her garden. The benches did not draw her, nor the waterfall, nor the lovely blooms.

"Eton?"

"Aye, m'queen?"

"When I traveled with the Lord High King, we passed a Sanctorum. Are there any near the city?"

"I am unsure, m'queen. I can seek someone who might know."

"Please, Eton. If there is any within half a sun's ride I wish to visit it."

He bowed, "When would you like to travel?"

"Now."

Eton straightened and stared at her for a moment. "Aye, m'queen." Boinn took his place as Eton left to see to her request.

Within two degrees of the sun, Ellianna sat atop her mount surrounded by a small contingent of Kaldreck's men and all of her personal guard. They headed south on the main road past the walled city she now called home. A league beyond the wall, they turned west again onto a smaller lane and stopped not long after.

Eton helped her from her saddle, and Ellianna walked toward the dull brick building covered in bright splashes of moss and lichen. The roof was caved in on the front corner and only one of the two wooden doors remained—though it hung from only one hinge.

"M'queen, why have we come?" Eton asked walking beside her as the rest of their contingent took positions of a protective perimeter.

"I wish to go inside."

Eton stood in her path. "I can nay allow it. 'Tis likely danger inside."

She smiled at him. "'Tis naught but an old forlorn building, Eton. Not a battlefield. No one waits inside to do me harm. No one has been inside for over a generation, I fear."

He eyed the building over his shoulder. "The danger is in the building itself, m'queen. 'Tis unsound. What if the roof were to fall while ye were within?"

Boinn stepped beside them. "I will go inside and see to the dangers of anything falling. If it does collapse at my entry, our queen will not be in danger. If the structure doesn't fall, it will be safe for her to enter."

Ellianna and Eton both agreed. Boinn disappeared within, and she turned to look at the creation surrounding the quiet place.

A prick of cold brushed her arm. Renwald. She closed her eyes and searched for him. The taint of his evil now growing familiar. But he was not near—and he remained beyond her grasp. His spirit had only come close enough to make her aware of his presence.

"The building is safe for you to enter, my queen."

She turned and inclined her head to Boinn. Both men followed a step behind her on either side. She stopped at the door. "I wish to be alone for a moment."

"But m'queen," Eton started to protest.

"Boinn assured its safety. I will only be a few steps away. Please?"

Eton nodded.

Blue sunlight trickled between the tree branches above and washed through the hole in the ceiling. It bathed the room in a murky light. Boinn's footsteps marred the floorboards creaking beneath her. Dust he had awakened swirled in the air.

Long wooden benches lay in heaps with leaves and other clutter on either side of the room. Ellianna looked down the center aisle toward the high table at the front. The dust moved, as though blown on a wind. Ellianna followed.

Climbing the three small steps of the dais, she looked down on the table. A thick blanket of time covered it. She reached out her hand needing to brush it away—free it. A swipe revealed a carving etched deep into the wood. Her heart leapt into her throat, as lightening flashed in her skull. Two more passes of her hand and the image of two beams crossed over one another with a crown looped over the top of the upright one could be clearly seen. An image used to represent the Holy Lamb who was to have died in sacrifice, yet Who was not dead.

Using her clean hand, she reached out to lay her trembling fingers in the deep grooves. With her hand pressed into the carving and her eyes closed—she waited. She knew not what for, but she waited.

One single full breath filled her. Warmth caressed her skin.

Peace more overpowering than an ocean wave flooded her soul.

And there, in the quiet of her spirit, she heard it. *My beloved child, when you seek Me, you will find Me.*

Ellianna dropped to her knees in worship.

Chapter 37

The darkness grew. A cold froze her blood. Her head ached. Her heart struggled to beat.

"You think you are capable of fighting me, little girl?"

Yanked from her protective inner wall, her spirit floundered in the grasp of evil. Sinister malevolence swirled about her loosed soul and pulled her consciousness far from her physical form. Darkness, stronger than a mighty storm, crushed her from every side.

"You are a weak child, no match for one as skilled as I in the ways of the spirit."

With no feeling of a body to quake, Ellianna fought the pull of Renwald and his evil.

"Struggle as you might, infant, you will never escape."

Strength fled from her as rodents from a fire. If he continued to pull her asunder, she would die.

Renwald's pull on her broke. Like a run-away carriage hitting a fallen log, she stopped in the void between them. Her thoughts lurched. Her heartbeat continued resilient. Music, strong and clear, overwhelmed her. Her love song. Kaldreck held her fast. The malicious grip on her evaporated, and she followed her melody back until she opened her eyes and stared up at her love.

His brows were knit together forming huge furrows in his forehead. His bright eyes were shadowed as they bore into her. "Ellianna, are you hale?"

She blinked. Her strength returned. Her heart and breathing slowed. She nestled into his arms as she lay across his lap—his warmth driving out the last of the chill.

"Ellianna?"

"Kaldreck," she managed despite her parched lips clinging to her teeth and her tongue sticking to the roof of her mouth.

"Are you hale?" he asked again nearly shaking her.

Her vision cleared more, and she beheld what lay behind him. "Kaldreck? You are in the women's chambers." She could not contain a smile from dancing about her lips.

A scowl marred his features. "As your maids came to me frantic that my love collapsed in her sitting room, and would not respond, I could not tarry for the time it would have required to bring you to me. Now, tell me true—are you hale?"

A shudder skittered over her flesh remembering Renwald's hold on her. She pulled from his arms and sat beside him taking the drink her maid offered. "As you have prepared, gathering the full fighting force of Windmere, I have sought to learn Renwald's plan. I wished to know where he hid that we may vanquish him and route this evil from our home."

"Ellianna, 'tis too dangerous! You will stop at once!" Kaldreck ordered.

She offered him a slim sideways nod. "'Tis true I grew proud of my skill and over confident of my gift from the Giver. After besting the Fathers with such ease, I believed I was ready for whatever Renwald could offer me. For suns I have felt him on the edge of my awareness lurking in the shadows beyond where I could see. I exposed more of my spirit to clear the vision."

"You will never do that again!" Kaldreck's volume grew with each word.

As Ellianna drifted, the chill from her memory raised the hairs on her neck once more.

He took her hand and brushed her cheek with his other hand bringing her back from the memory consuming her. "Tell me what he did to you."

Her gaze shifted back to him and she focused on the present —once more grounded in the moment. "He pulled my spirit away —taunting my inexperience. I would have been lost, save your strong presence bringing me back to myself."

Kaldreck rose to his feet, straightened his doublet, and looked about the room with fleeting glances. His eyes found nowhere to land and they returned to her face. "You will stop seeking out our enemy, Ellianna. My army will put an end to him." He turned to leave and nearly stumbled over a chair. Righting himself, he straightened his garments again and cleared his throat. With a small toss of his head, he squared his shoulders and headed again for the door.

"When do you plan to leave?"

"We depart at first light two sunwakes from now."

Ellianna pushed to her feet. "I will join you."

Kaldreck whirled, stomped back, and towered over her.

Maids, who had tried to draw near to attend her, scurried away.

"You will not! If you are in danger within our walls—" His hand went to the back of his neck and his eyes squeezed close. When next his spoke, his words were grave and heavy. "I would never—could never—so endanger your life and gentle spirit as to take you to a battlefield and expose you to the horrors of war."

She laid a hand on his arm.

His eyes opened, but his scowl remained.

"I know I gave my oath to hold my tongue until my council you sought, but would you walk with me and hear my thoughts?"

Kaldreck started to pull from her.

Her head lowered. "I have truth you must hear, my king."

A huff of air leapt from his lips. One foot tapped for a moment. He extended his arm and led her to the battlements.

"The Queen is to join us on the battlefield?" Malic stumbled as the words exploded from his lips. He stood stalk still for a moment before taking great strides to catch up and keep pace with Kaldreck.

"Aye, 'tis as I said. Took her near four degrees of the sun to convince me, but I see the merit in her arguments."

"Might you be of a mind to share them with me, my Lord High King, for truly I understand not the benefits of having a woman in battle—no matter her skill with a sword."

"Renwald seeks to keep us apart. Do you not recall his pleas to keep us from Illgrove? He sensed her there and knew the power within her. He foresaw what would awaken when we came together. Even the attacks on our journey home—which occurred when we were not yet together—were contrived to keep us from ever enjoying union. If he had succeeded in killing Ellianna before such a time, he would have already won this battle. She is the key to defeating him—though I know not how. And I must be at her side, for even this very sun, Renwald took her spirit from her body while she remained within her chambers." Kaldreck again rubbed at the knot at the base of his aching skull. "She spoke of feeling his presence for suns, but he waited until she was in a place he believed I would never venture."

Kaldreck stopped outside the armory to address Malic face-to-face. "The bond the Divine has knit between Ellianna and I is… profound. I hear her thoughts in my own head. I feel her heart beat as my own. She has said my touch anchors her spirit within the confines of her body. If I leave her here, Renwald will pull her apart. She must be where I am. For her sake and mine. She is a powerful seer and, while she cannot see what is yet to come, she sees what is now. We will have need of such on the battlefield."

Malic nodded. "We will need additional guards, for her and those who attend her."

Kaldreck smiled. "She brings only Niaria. As Boinn's calgent she insists the young woman come since Boinn will join Eton as her guard." Kaldreck's arms crossed. "She may have been long in coming to believe the truth of calgent love bonds, but now she defends them with the same strength we saw her battle the monsuit. As such, Calla is no longer allowed to serve her at sunsleep. She only permits the unbound women to attend her at all degrees." Kaldreck chuckled.

"Concerning the matter of our queen's feeling of the bonds between mates, I have spoken to Sole on her behalf. The woman with him at the tannery is not his calgent, but his sister. Seems as no other is eager to be tied to the disagreeable man. He is now most aware of the queen's thoughts on his treatment of Cami. I deem he will endeavor to avoid our queen and behave better."

"Good, I will inform Ellianna. The news should ease her concerns." Kaldreck turned and entered the armory. Beads of sweat formed almost instantly and soon dripped down his skin. He noted the stacks of blades, mountains of shields, and piles of armor.

"Good sunsleep to you, my Lord High King." Forger bowed with a red-hot blade in one hand and his hammer in the other.

"The Divine bless you."

"How might I be of service, my lord?"

"The queen needs armor. She will ride with the army into the coming battle."

The hammer dropped to the ground and the sword almost followed. The slender smith blinked at him a couple of times, snapped his slacking jaw shut, and nodded. "Aye, armor for our fair lady." The words did an odd jig on the man's lips as though he ate something sticky.

"As we leave in two sunwakes and this one is nearly asleep, will there be time for a breast piece to be fashioned, or would a shirt of mail serve her better?"

The blade cooling in his hand drew his attention, but he turned back toward the king and then looked at the stacks of armor. His mouth opened, then closed, as his gaze bounced from one thing to the other.

Kaldreck held up his hand to stay the man the next time his eyes lighted on him. "Hold Forger. I wish not to perplex you.

Think on the matter, and I will come to you on the morrow. You can inform me of how best to proceed to assure the queen's safety."

"Leave her in the castle," the man muttered as Kaldreck stepped from the armory. Had the breeze not kissed his sweltering face bathing him in its cool refreshing breath, he may have taken the man to task. Naught could be gained in the exchange though. To those who did not understand Ellianna's gift, and the threat against her, their present course would forever be unwise.

Malic's hand landed hard on his wounded shoulder. Though the skin was nearly knit together in the moon's passing since the injury, the muscle beneath still protested.

Kaldreck winced and shot his friend a disapproving look.

"One more task complete in your preparations, my king." Malic's gaze moved to the rising smaller moon, its green pallor lighting the southern sky. "Shall we enjoy a good meal in your hall while we yet may?"

Kaldreck nodded, and they walked together in silence. The weight of the trials to come strangled any words between them.

Chapter 38

On her mount near the camp, Ellianna sat high above the battle for another sun with Eton on her right and Boinn on her left. Niaria was on her own mount behind her. Renwald lurked at the edges of her consciousness menacing her waking and sleeping thoughts. She again pushed him aside and focused on Kaldreck. He battled his own people—given over to evil—and an equal number of foreign warriors.

She would alert him to danger and inform him which way the enemy planned to move. With her aid for the good and Renwald's assistance on the other side, the armies fought every sun—turning the orange vegetation beneath their feet crimson red—stalemated. They collected their wounded and dead in equal numbers to their opponents, slept, and arose at sunwake to do it all over again.

The weariness ate away at every soul—including her own. Renwald afforded her little sleep as he fought against her internal protections. She jerked her head up and opened her eyes. Now is not the time to sleep.

Boinn considered her.

She tossed her head and fought for alertness. Kaldreck and their people needed her. She could sleep when the battle was won.

Again, she shook off the drowsiness threatening to overcome her and righted herself in the saddle. Her only saving grace lay in the stiff and stifling armor covering her and preventing her from crumpling from the saddle.

So, you still fight me, little girl, Renwald crawled into her thoughts. *You are a stubborn thing.*

She tossed off his voice and turned back to the battle.

'Tis been a fortnight and still you resist, little one.

She closed her eyes and tossed her head, hoping to rid herself of his foreboding presence. She focused on the melody she shared with Kaldreck to bolster her strength.

Renwald stood before her. Black hair, long and greasy, clung to his head. His smile revealed pointed teeth and sent a shudder through her. "Get out of my mind, Renwald!" she screamed.

His menacing laugh made her blood chill. He distracted her— but for what purpose. *You will never defeat me.*

"I need not defeat you. Kaldreck and our good people fight. He will win the victory." She tried again to push him from her mind.

He will only defeat them if I am defeated, for my magic keeps them alive —feeds them—sustains them—makes them powerful—and is set by my will.

She fought for breath as he grappled with her within her own mind. She summoned her strength from her bond with Kaldreck.

He can't help you, child.

"You know naught of what we can do together." She listened for their song. The one their hearts sang. She felt his heart pound as though it resided in her own chest. Ellianna harnessed his warrior's heart and turned it on Renwald.

Like vapor he vanished before her.

She went sprawling across the landscape of her mind, kicked from behind. Falling to her back she looked up and twisted away from a boot ten times too large. She sprang to her feet lunging at him. Again, vapor hovered where he stood. Staggering forward, her head swiveled in both directions trying to find him again.

She focused on her feelings of Renwald and went to the in-between to engage him and to steady herself she listened to their song. Whirling with the heel of her hand up, she caught him in the nose. They may only be fighting within their minds—with mere thoughts—but they still could injure one another.

Renwald bellowed, charging her.

She spun from him and kicked at his backside as he passed. Pity she did not have a sword in this internal world. The hilt of a blade filled her hand. She stared at it as Renwald laughed.

"You are so young—thinking the weapons of the real world can help you here in the Land In-Between. What I could have taught you." His image shimmered, dissolved, and reformed into a great winged serpent with black scales. It belched fire and melted her blade.

She dropped the useless hilt that remained. The next blast of fire hit a wall of ice as thick as the battlements around her home. As he spewed flames, she allowed the ice to concave, then flung it out sending shards hurtling into his scaly flesh.

Renwald stood as a man and brushed the ice crystals from his clothes. "You learn quickly, child. But not quick enough." He materialized behind her. His hand clamped down on her throat, and he wrapped his other arm around her waist strangling the life from her.

Her mind filled with thoughts of heat.

Then she heard it.

Another heartbeat—small and quick.

Kaldreck felt Ellianna's scream tear apart his mind in the middle of the battle. The pain nearly tore the blade from his hand. He bellowed her name, slashing out at the next three enemies he encountered rending them asunder. He turned his mount and charged up the hill—away from the battle—away from his men.

He leapt from his charger before it fully stopped and dropped to his knees beside her prone body. Her skin was pale. Though she breathed, he could not hear her—their song had fallen silent.

He looked to Eton. "What happened?"

"I know not, m'king."

"She has not slept well, sire," Niaria said. "I thought when her head drooped she slept while still in the saddle."

"I watched her closely. She tossed her head often as if trying to ward off an irritating pest," Boinn added. "Then she remained still for some time."

Eton cleared his throat. "Without warning, m'king, though no one injured her, an unholy scream was rent from her, and she collapsed in a fit of shaking. Boinn caught her before she could fall. We laid her here, and thus she has remained until ye arrived, m'lord."

Kaldreck touched her face. She felt cold.

"My king, mayhaps the Fathers…" Boinn offered, but shrank from his glare.

The sun travelled two degrees with no change in his beloved.

No song, no heat, no life—other than weak shallow breaths. Kaldreck rose to his feet—the sounds of the battle below returning to his ears. "Take her to Crag Haven. See if the Father can at last be of some aid."

"Aye, m'lord," the three said as one.

The following sunsleep, as Kaldreck returned to camp, Boinn charged out of the growing darkness. Both he and his mount were coated in sweat.

Boinn dropped to the ground and stumbled toward him. "My king, I bring word," he panted and dropped to his knee.

"Bring water! See to the destrier." Kaldreck stepped down from his own mount and lifted the cup to Boinn's lips. When he had his fill and again breathed with some steadiness, Kaldreck raised the man to his feet, and led him into his tent, leaned back against the table with the war charts, and asked. "Is she?"

Boinn shook his head. "Nay, my Lord High King, your queen yet draws breath."

"Is there any hope?"

Boinn's head rose slowly and at some length their gaze met. "My Lord High King, Queen Ellianna's life lies in her own hands. Father Gramphill says the energy of a lifetime was stole from our Queen."

Kaldreck stared at him, understanding would not come.

"She is not dead now, for she carries another life within her, my king."

"A babe?" Kaldreck said the words in awe.

Boinn nodded and his head drooped once more. "Aye, my king. But there is only enough life within her to allow one of them to survive." A deep sigh fled from him nearly collapsing him from the stool where he sat. "It may be some time before we know what she decides."

"Thank you, Boinn. You may eat and rest. When you feel strong enough, return to our queen. I do not wish her to be without those who love her in the end."

Boinn rose to his feet, brows drawn together pinching his face.

"I know my beloved, Boinn. Though I may wish for her to spare herself, knowing we could have more children, she would never sacrifice that child for herself—or me."

When Boinn left, Kaldreck moved around the table, dropped in a chair, and buried his face in his hands. *Merciful, please.*

Chapter 39

Ellianna lay on her side, her babe nestled in the crook of her arm. Beyond her elbow a face came into view from the darkness. The round-faced Father she saw when she first came moon cycles ago looked at her. His eyes were hooded by heavy lids and glistened with unshed tears.

"Hello," she greeted him. It seemed he was the first person she had seen for many sunwakes. "Have you come to see Kaldreck's son?"

"I have come to see ye, child."

"Me. Why ever for?" She shifted a little so he could look on the infant's tiny face. "Is he not as handsome as his father? Will not Kaldreck be proud?"

"Where is Kaldreck? Should he not be here with ye, child?"

The peace fluttered from her for a moment. "He is near, I am sure he will be along shortly." She released a slow breath. "Yes, Kaldreck is on his way. I am sure of it."

"Where are ye, child?"

"I lay in my room in the palace." Her smile grew. "That is why Kaldreck is not here. I lie in the women's chambers." She tried to raise her arms with the infant but all strength fled from her. "Will you take him to Kaldreck? Let the Lord High King meet his son."

The old man shook his head. "Who am I, child."

"You are one of the Fathers who lives in Crag Haven. When I first arrived, you greeted me standing with Fathers Matthas and Johafamus."

"And why would I be in yer chambers?"

Peace fled, and panic stirred her heart to a frantic beat.

"Again, child, I ask ye, where are ye?"

"I… I do not…" She gasped for breath as she looked around. She saw naught but black. "Father, where am I?"

He patted her hand, "Hush, child. Ye are safe in the holy mountain."

"I do not understand. Why am I here and not with Kaldreck? He must know of his son."

He continued to pat her though his words became quiet and kissed by sorrow. "Child, what is the last thing ye remember? Why were ye brought to us?"

She shook her head.

"Why has the wee babe never woken, never suckled?"

"He is alive. I feel his heartbeat. See… he draws breath." She struggled to quiet the heart that thundered in her head to the point it nearly drowned out his words. Wisps of thoughts danced on the edge of her awareness, but naught could be caught. "Father, please tell me. What is happening?"

"Renwald…"

Images assailed her like a gale-force wind on the seas. They stole her uneven breaths. She felt as though she would drown under the waves.

The Father's hand caressed her face. She found air. Calm settled on her. "There now." He brushed his hand over her forehead and a gentle smile crinkled his face. "Ye remember now."

"Renwald attacked me while I tried to help Kaldreck in the battle. He invaded my mind. Then we grappled in the in-between, where he choked the life from me. We heard it. Both of us, at the same moment, heard the babe's first heartbeats." She ran her finger down the side of her son's face. "I fought for us, but…" Her gaze shifted back to the elderly man. "What has happened to us, Father?"

"Renwald succeeded in stealing a life."

"I do not understand. Whose life? The babe and I yet draw breath so—No! Father tell me it is not Kaldreck. Please—"

He threw up his hand and shook his head. "Nay, child. The Lord High King is quite well."

"Then who?"

Tears again filled his eyes, "Only one of ye will survive, child. Either the babe will die or ye."

She looked down at the wee life in her arms. "Him. I choose him to live."

"Kaldreck thought ye would choose the babe."

Her heart tore within her. "Will he be all right?"

"Nay, Ellianna. Even now his heart is so broken he loses hope. The war can nay be won without him, and he cannot find victory without ye."

"How can I…?" Sobs wracked her body as she gazed at the babe. "He is an innocent."

"Peace daughter. Peace. The Divine has given me a chance to

redeem myself."

"I do not understand, Father."

"I know child. I have failed ye in so many ways." A tear slid from the corner of his eye. "Truth, daughter. It is time for the truth. I am your two father."

"Two father? … Boppa?"

"Aye, daughter, I was yer mother's sire. I could never call myself her father." He shook his head. "I joined with yer two mother and, I tell ye true, I loved her with all my heart. But the sight of things to come awakened in me when our love joined. I came to the Crag Haven—as ye did—to control this power. And like with ye, they required I stay and learn and share my gift with all here. They insisted I leave all behind. I believed it to be the will of the Divine that I remained here apart from my One and Only, but my heart ached for her.

"When I learned she carried my child, I wanted to go to her, but the Fathers forbade it. I did not have yer strength, daughter. I allowed them to convince me of things my heart said were untrue. I hid here and felt the loss of everything. With my gift, I could not see anything of value—only the hurt happening to my own family. I watched from this prison as my love slowly wasted away and died. I saw the evil showered upon both my precious girl and ye by that wretched man Villiant. How I hate him. Yet I cowered here, too afraid of loosing my gift to come to either of yer aids. In the end, what was once a gift turned into a curse for me."

When next she looked at the Father he lay on his side next to her. She laid her hand over his and shared a calming thought with him.

"No, don't ye go using yer gift on me, daughter. Ye have not the strength to be giving it, and I have not the worth to be receiving it." He stared at her for a long time.

"Ye are so much stronger than I, daughter. I am so very proud of ye. When forces tried to separate ye from yer love ye fought them. Ye showed them the power with Kaldreck far exceeded what ye could do on yer own. Oh Ellianna, my dear child. Ye have brought life and hope back to an old dried up shadow of a man."

He pulled from her touch and laid his hand on the side of her face. "I have loved ye from the moment I first saw ye, daughter. I have followed ye through the fields and hills of yer home. I have watched ye grow and cherished yer strength and the beauty of yer soul. There is much left for ye to do, my child." His voice grew faint. "I give back to ye that which was taken. Restore what was stolen. Rebuild what was torn down. Take my love, save yer babe, and give hope back to our king. Use the Holy Script to free the land."

His words faded away and his hand slid from her face.

"Boppa? Boppa?"

Chapter 40

"Ellianna? Oh, the Merciful be praised. My Queen, are you yet with us?"

Ellianna opened her eyes to stare up at Nairia. The woman snatched up a cup, helped Ellianna raise her head, and pressed it to her lips. "All glory to the Great Healer. He has restored you to us."

Ellianna drank and turned her head to see the old man lying lifeless beside her—eyes open yet staring at naught.

"He has come ever sun to inquire after you. This sun I was drawn away, but both Eton and Boinn were to stay. Yet they too were directed elsewhere, each believed the other, remained. When I returned, I found him lying with his hand on your face. A holy glow filled him, my queen. I do not know what happened, but the glow faded and you called out. The first words in near three moon crossings."

The babe stirred within her. She rested her hand on the bump at her middle.

"Is the child…?"

"Peace, Niaria, we are both quite well." She pushed herself up to sit and looked back at the old man. "He was my Boppa, my mother's father, and he gave his life to restore us. Greater love than this hath no man, when any man bestoweth his life for his friends." The words tumbled off her lips with ease, but they sent a thrill through her that caused the babe within to leap. Where had those words come from? Why did they make her entire spirit sing?

Niaria stared at her wide-eyed. "Are you well, my queen? Mayhaps you should lie down and rest."

"I must work the works of Him that sent me, while it is sunwake; sunsleep cometh when no man can work." Again the words, came from somewhere deep within and filled her with such excitement she rose to her feet. "There is something which must be done. And it must be done quickly. Help me dress."

"My queen—"

"I feel the Divine stirring in me, Niaria. Help me dress so we can be about it."

The woman hesitated.

Ellianna took her hands. "My strength and life have been restored to me in full. I am well and in my right mind, but now my soul is filled with wonders I cannot describe. Let us go, discover them, and share them with our people."

Niaria nodded slowly, took up the simple gown from the peg on the wall, and helped her pull it over the chemise she wore. It lay overly tight at her middle but naught could be done about it just now. Niaria ran a brush quickly through her hair and lashed it with a thong.

Ellianna made the few steps across the room to the door and flung it open. Both Eton and Boinn leapt so abruptly seeing her they nearly collided. "My queen," they stammered as one and bowed—again almost knocking heads.

"Sirs, we have a mission. One of greatest importance and secrecy. Come with me."

Eton put his hand out. "My queen, ye have just now risen from the sleep of death. How have you come by this important mission as no one has spoken to ye in over two moons?"

She smiled laying both hands on the sides of his face. "The Divine has spoken to me through my two father." She released him to start down the stairs.

"Two father?" Boinn asked racing to keep up.

"Aye, Father Gramphill," Niaria called as she fell into line on the narrow stairs.

Eton squeezed past her and pulled Ellianna to a stop at the next landing. "Gramphill? Yer two father? When did ye learn this?"

"He met me in the land-between where my spirit communes with the souls of others. Boppa told me of his life here, his gift as a seer, and he gave his life to restore ours." She slid her hand over her middle. "With his last breath he said, 'Use the Holy Script to free the land.'"

"The Holy Script?"

"Yes, Eton."

"What is it?"

"I know not, but he left a vision in my mind the path to follow to find it."

"M'queen—"

"Eton, I know how I must sound, but I feel it inside me like a glorious sunwake. Will you trust me and see that we are safe as we go and seek it?"

He did not hesitate, "Aye, m'queen. But I'll leadin' the way. Tell me the path to follow."

She told him where to turn, directing the little group from one corridor to the next. She opened her mind and listened for the nearness of others living in the holy mount. They slipped into shadows to avoid meeting anyone or being stopped.

They came to a narrow, low-ceiling passageway with what appeared to be only one route ahead. Eton moved toward it.

"Nay," Ellianna whispered. She closed her eyes and walked the path again Boppa left in her mind. Opening her eyes, she turned to the right.

"There is no opening there, m'queen."

She stared at it a moment longer and moved all the way to the left. There, in the narrow corner between the two rock faces, a slender opening could be seen. "'Tis here." She put her arm in the opening to prove it.

Eton shifted around her to peer into the narrow passage himself and turned back, his gaze dropping to her middle.

"Gramphill was wider than I and he came this way." She protested in a huffed whisper.

He nodded and moved into the hidden corridor.

Ellianna squeezed in behind him and stooped under the low ceiling. Niaria and Boinn followed.

Down more stairs and two more hidden passages, they came to a dark tunnel. Ellianna pulled Eton to a stop. "A guard waits for us around the next bend. He guards a wooden door. We must subdue him but not harm him. He believes he works for the Divine and does not know he actually works against the Holy One's will. He cannot be allowed to raise the alarm, but we need his key to open the door."

Eton nodded and glanced back to Boinn. The younger man shimmied past the two women with apologies and came to Eton. They talked in hushed tones for some moments before Eton raised his hand, "Wait here, m'queen. We will see what can be done."

"The Way go before you and make your path straight. Thou hast enlarged my steps under me, and mine heels have not slid." Every time the strange words came to her lips she could not stop them. Though she had never studied them, they were familiar. Though she had no recall of reading them, they danced before her memory from an old, aged parchment.

Voices drifted back to her. First Eton's. "Truly, your father allowed you to come here?"

"He was a braggart. He thought to impress me by showing me how he traversed the secret passages regularly. Truth was, I had found them on my—" Boinn's answered as though he talked with Eton while they explored.

"Hold! Who goes there?" This voice was deep, commanding, and unknown—though somehow familiar. Kel. His name was Kel, but how did she know?

"This is Boinn and I am Eton. The queen's private guard."

"What are you doing here? Is not the queen lying on the brink of death in her chamber?"

"I was showing my mentor the secret passages."

"I know you… you're Johafumus's boy. You don't belong here. No one is allowed here but the most senior Fathers."

"And when was the last time they came, Kel?" Ellianna stepped from the shadows.

"Ellianna, my queen—majesty," Kel stumbled over his words and started to bow, then straightened.

"Only Father Gramphill came regularly, but Father Matthas forbade anyone enter many cycles ago. I cannot remember the last time someone entered this door."

All four of them moved closer to the guard.

Kel backed away and reached for his horn.

Boinn jumped toward him securing his arms behind his back. Eton covered the guard's mouth with his hand.

As Eton slipped his arm around the man's neck and began to cut off his air, Ellianna reached in the guard's pocket for the key. "The Divine has said it is time to read the Words once more."

The man dropped unconscious to the floor, and she handed the key to Boinn. The lock gave with a whine and a clack that reverberated off the walls. The hinges cried in protest, but the door opened, and they looked into the pitch-black opening. Eton pulled a torch from the wall and stepped inside. He held the light up, and Ellianna looked down a twisting narrow staircase hugging the wall of a round shaft leading deep into the earth.

She nodded and followed as he led the way slowly to the bottom.

Chapter 41

The stairs wound around endlessly. Ellianna placed her hand on Eton's shoulder as dizziness danced. Her legs bellowed their discomfort by the time they reached the bottom and another wood door. There was no lock, and Eton pulled it open slowly and led the way inside. Eton and Boinn circled the odd shaped room at the bottom of the shaft and lit the many torches standing idle in rings hammered into the rock.

The light flooded the space revealing a single, long table atop a narrow rug twice Ellianna's height. On the table stood a single object covered in cloth. A heavy grime shrouded everything so thick it obscured the color of the cloth and rug, and even the type wood from which the table was hewn.

She moved with a reverent awe to the table and pulled off the covering. Dust filled the air, and they all erupted into fits of coughing, which lasted several ticks of the sun.

Beneath the cloth lay a scroll rolled from both ends to the center. The two sides were the same size as her upper arm. Ellianna removed the scroll from the stand and laid the heavy rolled parchment on the table opening it. She read out loud the words. "That the Divine, the Father of glory, might give unto you the Spirit of wisdom, and revelation through the acknowledging of Him, that the eyes of your understanding may be lightened, that ye may know what the hope is of His calling, and what the riches of His glorious inheritance is in the Saints, and what is the exceeding greatness of His power toward us, which believe, according to the working of His mighty power."

Ellianna dropped to her knees.

The men both took a knee beside her.

Niaria knelt as well, her face nearly touching the dusty earth. "These are holy words," she whispered. "We should not be here."

Ellianna rose to sit tall on her knees and moved the scroll to another passage. "Yea, I have loved thee with an everlasting love, therefore with mercy I have drawn thee. Again I will build thee, and thou shalt be built, thou shalt still be adorned with thy timbrels, and shalt go forth in the dance of them that be joyful." Ellianna drew in deep breath. "Nay Niaria, the Divine called us here so that all may know His words."

Again, she rolled to another place in the scroll and read the words that leapt to her eyes from the dry skin—bringing life to her soul. "And thou shalt love the One thy Divine with all thy heart, and with all thy soul, and with all thy might. And these words which I command thee this sun, shall be in thine heart. And thou shalt rehearse them continually unto thy children, and shalt talk of them when thou tarriest in thine house, and as thou walkest by the way, and when thou liest down, and when thou risest up; And thou shalt bind them for a sign upon thy hand, and they shall be as frontlets between thine eyes. Also thou shalt write them upon the posts of thy house, and upon thy gates."

Ellianna stood. "Yes, I will obey," she sang out. Rolling the scroll closed, she cradled it in her arms and prepared to climb the stairs.

"What are you doing in here?" A door, on the other side of the table they had not noticed, flew open and Father Matthas stormed in. "This is a most sacred place. The likes of you are not allowed in here."

"I am taking the Holy Words, given to us by the very hand of the Author, and sharing it with all people."

He blocked her path. "I forbid it!"

Eton and Boinn moved across the room and took their places between the Father and Ellianna.

"Yet the Divine has ordained it."

"Those who wish to study the Words can come here to hear of them."

"'Ye are the light of the world. A city that is set on a hill, cannot be hid. Neither do men light a candle, and put it under a bushel, but on a candlestick, and it giveth light unto all that are in the house. Let your light so shine before men, that they may see your good works, and glorify your Father which is in heaven." The words etched into her soul came from Boppa. He'd studied here. He knew of the Divine's Truth hidden away. Now they spilled from her lips.

"Matthas, I was here for moons, listening to the dead words that droned on without life. These Words," she held up the scroll with both hands, "were never spoken. And our people do not live here. The One said to talk about His laws while we are at home, or on the roads: when we rise and when we lie down. We are to have them on our hand and engraved on our gates. They must not remain here hidden and ignored."

"If you take them from this place, the mountain will crumble."

"So be it." Ellianna moved forward, and her guards pushed the Father out of her path allowing her to proceed. Carried on eager feet she moved toward the outdoors. Excitement and joy welled up in her until she thought she would burst from it. At the same moment she saw the light from the sun, the cavern rumbled. Eton grabbed her hand and steadied her.

She proceeded with more care, but the closer she came to removing the scroll from the mountain the more the stone house shook. Small rocks fell from the ceiling. Acolytes screamed in fear.

"I told you, the scroll may not be removed." Father Matthas came up behind them and reached for the scroll.

Ellianna pulled it away from him. "It must be removed and shared. It *will* be removed." Turning to her guards and maid. "Go through the entire mountain. Send up the alarm. This house has served its purpose and is no longer needed by decree of the Most Holy One. They must leave now or forfeit their lives."

"M'Queen—"

"I will be safe here, and I will not move until you have returned. Please—go and warn the innocent."

They raced off leaving Ellianna standing before Matthas. Again, words she had never read leapt to her lips. "For a Shepherd is come to seek, and to save that which was lost," she told him.

Father Matthas did not move. He stared at her. "You are ruining everything."

"I am bringing into the light that which has been hidden far too long. 'All power is given unto Me, in heaven, and the land below. Go therefore, and teach all realms, baptizing them in the Name of the Father, and the Son, and the Spirit. Teaching them to observe all things, whatsoever I have commanded you; and lo, I am with you always, until the end of the world, Amen.'"

The mountain groaned and creaked. Dust rained down on them. Terrified people fled past.

As the last of her detail to arrive, Eton reported, "That should be everyone, m'queen,"

"Then let us return home and to the work needing doing." She moved to leave. Niaria stepped out first followed by Boinn. She turned back to Matthas who remained rooted where he was. "Come Father. Teach the Word with us, everywhere in the land."

"No, I belong here in this mountain."

Eton turned to collect him, but Matthas raced out of sight.

"Leave him, my friend. He has chosen his path. It is not with the light."

They stepped from the opening and hastened down the stairs The mountain groaned. The house shuttered and shook. Rocks cascaded down. All of it collapsed in on itself. A plume of dust settled over everyone huddled outside.

When the air cleared, Ellianna turned to the path. Walking, she called out. "I go to spread the Good News, all who wish to serve their Maker, and their king, are welcome."

Chapter 42

Ellianna descended the stairs from the battlements and swept through the inner ward.

"It's the queen."

"Queen Ellianna has returned."

"The Restorer has returned our queen."

People called out all around her, but she paid them no heed for the moment.

"Boinn?" she called without slowing.

"Aye, my queen."

"Go to the armory and have the smithy adjust the shape of my breast piece." She ran her hand over her belly.

"Aye, my queen."

"Niaria?"

"Yes, majesty."

"Take some of my simpler gown to the needle woman and have her do the same."

"Yes, my lady."

She headed up the stairs toward the hall as the din of well-wishers grew. "Eton, tell the guards to prepare for us to join the battle within four sunwakes."

"Aye, m'queen." He remained near but waved over a guard and passed the instructions along before they entered the great hall.

"Halfort?" she called as she stepped inside. "Halfort, where are you? I have need of your assistance."

"Aye, aye I am here, what—" he broke off as he came around the corner and saw who called him. His mouth gaped open, and the man stared at her unmoving as though turned to stone.

"Halfort, I have instructions I require you to attend to immediately."

"Majesty, you are home."

"Yes, sir, now to the tasks at hand."

"But the Fathers said…Oh my queen—the babe."

Eton patted the man on the shoulder to pull him from his deep perplexed babble.

"My old friend, the Merciful has been most gracious and kind to us. He has restored both our queen and the heir she yet carries."

Halfort's gaze shifted from one to the other. "The Healer be praised," he stammered.

"Indeed. We praise His most holy name. Now to the needs of your queen. Will you assist her?"

He nodded vigorously. "Aye, aye, of course. What do you require, my queen?"

"I need every scribe of skill to come to the palace immediately. Tell every tanner within the kingdom to prepare parchment of the finest quality in great quantities and send it to the castle. Along with them, we need bindings and covers prepared. We will require an endless supply of quills and ink as well."

"It will be done, my lady."

"Also send word throughout the town and the surrounding villages; all who can be spared should come to the great hall and hear the reading of the Words left to us by the Author."

The steward gasped. "From the Divine, my lady?"

"Yes, my friend." She patted the scroll cradled in her arm. "It has been hidden away in the Crag Haven for generations. Now it will be read aloud for all the people to hear and copies made to distribute to every village in the kingdom."

"The Mighty One be praised. What an extravagant gift He has given us."

"It is a gift, Halfort. And unlike the Fathers of old, it will not be locked away but shared with all."

"Aye, my queen."

"I require all who can read to make their way to the hall. We will begin reading at evening meal this very sun."

Halfort glanced out a window. "In two degrees, my lady, all will be prepared to begin the reading."

He hastened away to see to her many requests as Eton stepped forward. "Ye should rest, m'queen."

She shook her head. "I could not if I tried. The Almighty has stirred such an excitement in me… I feel I shall burst should I be still."

Eton smiled. "Then might I encourage you to eat something while we wait for the reading to begin?"

At the mere suggestion of food her stomach rumbled. "Yes, I would welcome some cheeses and meats." She moved to the front of the hall as Eton informed the kitchen of her request.

"Men and women of Windmere, I welcome you to the Lord

High King's hall. For as many suns as are required, the Word of the Divine will be read from sunwake until sunsleep for all to hear. I know there are many tasks and responsibilities to attend to in your sun, but I cannot urge you enough to be present at the reading of this holy missive, which for too long has been lost to us. The Provider has now restored it. These are the Words of the Lover of your soul, written for you that you may know Him. And in knowing Him, serve and honor Him all the more." Ellianna had rolled the scroll to the very beginning and laid it on a low table. Now she knelt and began to read.

"In the beginning the Divine created the heaven above and the land below. And the world was without form and void, and darkness was upon the deep, and the Spirit of the Divine moved upon the waters. Then the Divine said, 'Let there be light; And there was light…'"

Everyone dropped to their knees and listened in rapt attention as Ellianna read for the next two degrees of the sun. When her voice grew hoarse, Halfort stepped forward, knelt in her place, and continued the reading.

Ellianna moved off the dais to the floor below and knelt with all the other worshippers.

For two full suns, from wake to sleep, the eager came and listened to all the Words of the Divine. And for the two additional suns to follow they came to hear again the Truth. Each sun more came to hear. The business of the city ground to a halt as everyone hungered for the truth from their Holy One.

On the fifth sun after her return, Halfort greeted her. "All is in preparation, my lady. The scribes and the first of the vast supplies are here. What are your instructions?"

"Bring everything and everyone into the hall."

"Aye, my queen."

As he left, she turned to Eton. "Tell all who go with us to the battlefield to prepare. We leave within the degree."

"Aye, m'lady."

When the scribes sat around the outside edge of the room, three to a table, Ellianna stood before them. She turned first to Halfort. "How many scribes are there?"

"Sixty-six, my queen."

She smiled, "And how many villages of ample size are there in Windmere?"

"About one hundred, my lady."

She nodded and turned to the men gathered before her. "Noble scribes of Windmere, you are called here on the most sacred of duties. One that will require your utmost skill at all times. No errors can be allowed as you are to copy the Divine's Holy Words."

A murmur fluttered around the room in a mixture of excitement and trepidation.

"There is no higher calling than this." She paused to look on each one in turn.

Each agreed with a single nod.

"As there are sixty-six divisions to the Holy Text and the Provider has seen fit to have a like number of you, each will be responsible for making one hundred copies of one division. This is your task: copy a single page, have five others verify it for accuracy—not a hash or marklet is to be out of place. If any error be found, the page is to be burned. There is to be no exception."

"Aye, majesty," they intoned as one.

"For those who have smaller divisions, when all your section is copied one hundred times, see to the verification of the others' pages as they complete their assignments and to the binding when a full copy is complete."

She turned toward the steward again, "Halfort, I to return to the king. I pray with the Divine's aid, Lord High King Kaldreck can now make a quick end to the evil in our land. I leave you in charge of this most holy work and the hands that labor at it. As each copy is complete, see to it they are distributed to all the towns in our land. Later we will see to the grand task of making a copy for every household."

"Aye, my queen. May our Protector go before you and grant you and our king the victory, through His mighty hand."

She strolled from the hall. Boinn assisted her into her armor, and they mounted to return to the battlefield.

Chapter 43

Kaldreck fought waking—but it came nonetheless. He pushed himself up and sat on the edge of his cot. His hand rubbed over his beard. He kept it trimmed but had not shaved since Ellianna was attacked. Three moons had past since he sensed her loss. Every sun he expected word of her final death, and every night he found her in his dreams. Oh, to live in his dreams and never wake. Why could this not be so?

He feared when the news did come, he would not be able to continue. It took a monumental act of will to keep him fighting each sun—while not allowing the enemy to run him through. How did Eton manage? Would he be able to live on without his love? If the babe survived, will he love him or her or only see in them the loss they caused?

As it so often did, when he thought on Ellianna, the melody of their heart-song struck a few chords within him. He doubled in agony. He pushed it aside, rising to his feet. He reached for his gambeson. The heavy padding warmed his skin though not his aching heart. Prepared as much as he could without the aid of his armor bearer, Kaldreck summoned the strength to call the youth.

The chords struck again but louder this time. He staggered

from his tent noting where the black sky had now turned violet. The sun would soon be up—and the battle begin again.

Kaldreck took a faltering step. "Tyne, my arm—" The blast of horns cut him off.

Someone approached.

Two of the palace guards came into view over the rise behind them. *This sun is the one then. Ellianna is*—

Next over the rise appeared Eton, Boinn, and between them—

It cannot be. Kaldreck dropped to one knee as Malic came to stand beside him. "Malic, do you see her? It is not a trick of my mind, is it?"

Malic pulled him to his feet and pounded him on the back almost driving him back to his knees. "It is she."

Crying out for all to hear, Malic bellowed. "Hail, Queen Ellianna. She is returned to us."

A shout that shook the mountain erupted from the men of Windmere.

Eton helped her down, and she floated to him as though from his dreams. A heavy wool cloak covered her. She came, but he did not reach for her fearing she would vanish like the vapor of a vision.

"Hello, beloved."

Her voice was sweet to his ears. The warriors mingling about drifted away, joyfully patting one another on the back. Hope returned to the camp. But Kaldreck could not breathe. "I too mourn for the babe, my love. But the Creator will bless us again."

She parted the cloak revealing the bulge created in her armor to accommodate the child still growing within her. "The Merciful has already blessed us."

"I do not understand. How can it be both of you still draw breath? The Fathers said—"

"The Fathers and Crag Haven are no more."

"What has happened to them? Were they attacked? How could a mountain be no more? How is it you are here?"

Ellianna stepped close and seized the front of his gambeson. She pulled him down until his lips hovered over hers. "Do you intend to interrogate me all sun, my love, or will you welcome me with a kiss?"

He pressed his lips to hers and the fire he believed dead, burst to life once more. The song he had tried to stifle blared in his heart with a new chord added to the melody.

"You have a beautiful son, Kaldreck. I have seen him. I have held him in the secret place between. At the reading of the Divine's Words, he has stirred in me. He will lead our people like none before him."

He rested his forehead against hers, felt her in his arms, gazed into her eyes. "Have you now the gift of seeing what is to come?"

"Nay," she giggled. "Father Gramphill was in fact, my two father. Boppa had the gift of the seers of old. As he gave his life for ours, he left me with images of what he had seen."

The horns rang out again for the calling of formations.

"Your majesty." Tyne stood holding his armor.

"No time to rejoice when the enemy will not relent," Kaldreck grumbled. "Mayhaps with our queen's return, victory can yet be won."

"Might I be allowed a moment to speak to our men,

Kaldreck?" she whispered.

His brow rose, but he nodded.

With all the men in formation before him, Ellianna rode to take her place along side alongside Kaldreck. She reached for his hand and closed her eyes. Like a whisper on the breeze her words floated from her mind to each heart.

With a strength not her own, words sang from her lips—loud and clear reaching every ear on the mountainside. "Brave men of valor—hear my heart. The Words of the Divine have been found hidden in the holy mountain. They were read aloud in the great hall for four suns and now, even as you prepare for another day of battle, copies are being made for every village. The Divine loves His children, and He will fight for us.

"For thou hast girded me with strength to battle: them, that rose against me, Thou hast subdued under me.'"

The men pounded their swords against their shields.

"Our Protector, the Mighty One, has prepared you. Now He, and He alone, puts your enemy under your feet. Fear you not, neither be afraid for this great multitude: for the battle is not yours, but the Holy One of the Angel Army. Surrender your hearts to Him, and He will fight for you."

The cheers rose.

Swords were hefted into the air.

"For the One, King Kaldreck, and Queen Ellianna. Forever may they reign in glory."

The battle cry rang out, and through Ellianna's connection, even Kaldreck felt Renwald tremble.

Chapter 44

The men prepared to charge.

The enemy stood ready to defend.

In the void of the in-between, Ellianna met Renwald.

"So, the whelp returns." Renwald loomed twice his natural size.

Ellianna did not quake. She spoke the words hidden in her heart and trusted in the Faithful One. "It is not I who fight, but the Mighty One of the Angel Armies fights for me."

"You think the Holy Words frighten me. Do you not remember what I can do to you?"

"The Protector is with me: therefore, I will not fear what man can do unto me." She stepped toward him. "For I am persuaded that neither death, nor life, nor angels, nor principalities, nor powers, nor things present, nor things to come, nor height, nor depth, nor any other creature, shall be able to separate us from Love, which is in the Sent One our Savior."

Renwald gave her ground and his size diminished. "I could give you the world."

She pressed her advance, her words growing in strength. "Avoid the evil one. For it is written, thou shalt worship the Holy thy Savior, and Him only shalt thou serve."

"I control this world! I am master here." He continued to shrink.

She stepped nose to nose with him and with an intensity not her own, Ellianna said, "You have no power over me."

Renwald stumbled away and a deep red, wet stain darkened his black tunic. He looked down at it, and back to her, and down at it again. He staggered back another step.

"It would appear, while you pitted yourself against me here in the in-between, an arrow has found its mark. Victory be praised."

He fell back and his image shimmered. "I cannot be bested by a mere arrow," he protested as his image became fainter.

"If it flew at the Divine of the Angel Army's bidding, you most certainly could."

He was gone before she finished speaking. She opened her eyes to see the enemy being routed before Kaldreck and his men. Though they scattered and tried to go to ground, they were pursued and dispatched with great prejudice.

Kaldreck returned to the camp. Niaria and Boinn sat near a fire preparing a small meal. "Where is the queen?"

"She rests in your tent, my lord high king." Boinn said as he stood and bowed.

"We prepare her meal," Niaria tried said as he raced passed. Eton stood outside his tent.

"Is she well?" Kaldreck's heart would not be calm as sweat pooled in his hands and ran down his neck. He feared his legs would not carry him.

"Aye, m'lord." Eton smiled. "She is great with child and merely weary. She asked to rest until you returned. I will wake—"

Kaldreck put his hand on Eton's shoulder. "Nay, my friend. Help me off with this armor and I will join her."

Eton nodded and assisted to free him of the cumbersome metal. Once in his tent, he further rid himself of the gambeson and slipped in to lay behind her. His hand slid over her wide belly causing her to stir.

"Shhh, my love. Rest. I did not mean to wake you."

She put her hand over his and laced their fingers together. She moved it down and back a little and he felt the life within her kick at his hand. She sighed and pushed against him until her entire back rested against him. "I have missed you desperately, Kaldreck."

He kissed her neck. "No more than I you, Ellianna."

He lay with her in his arms for some time unable to sleep for the joy overwhelming him. The scent of her hair was like the colorful blossoms of the waking season: the smoothness of her skin like the fine marble in their home. The warmth of her body comforted him, soothing frayed nerves and mending broken places within. Her even, rhythmic breathing like the gentle breeze. The life within her, the hope of a long future by her side—everything about her brought him joy.

The tent flap parted. "Forgive me, my lord," Malic whispered.

Kaldreck rose and met him outside.

Malic spoke in hushed tones. "The men have cleared the field and are returning to camp."

"Tell them, we return home at first light."

Malic's shoulders relaxed. "Glad I am to hear it, my lord."

"You shall see your One and Only within two suns."

"Possibly three," Ellianna said as she joined them blushing.

"Why is it a woman with child spends so much time in the privy?" She moved away from the tent with Niaria, while Eton and Boinn trailed behind—ever her faithful guards.

"She is well?"

"Aye, my friend." Kaldreck put his hand on Malic's shoulder. "The Gracious One has been so very kind. I cannot put to words my gratitude. I thought I could not know more joy than when I saw her, but to know my son yet lives too… it is beyond joy."

"A son?"

Kaldreck chuckled, "Aye, she says she has seen him."

"I praise the Faithful One with you." Malic turned and meandered off to deliver his news.

Kaldreck turned to his men as they prepared to head out. "Mighty men of Windmere, I give my thanks for your faithful service and praise the Provider for bringing you to fight at my side. I welcome you to come and celebrate at Hearthrop. But I also know the call of the heart when it misses its calgent. I give you leave to return to your homes. It matters not the destination— stories of your prowess, your faithful service, and the victory you achieved with the Mighty's aid, will be sung until the time of our children's, children's, children."

"Long live Lord High King Kaldreck. May he rule a thousand years in the service of the One, and for the love of his people!" the men called back.

Afterword

In due time, Ellianna bore Kaldreck the first of three sons, Chanan. She also blessed him with two daughters. Chanan was so named for 'The Divine was gracious' to them in sparing both his life and Ellianna's. Chanan grew in the ways of the Divine and led his people—though not as Lord High King, but as the first High Priest Windmere had seen in twenty generations. The sanctorums were reopened, and more built, as Chanan brought the hearts of all the people back to the Lover of their souls and taught them true and proper worship.

Glossary for Seer of Windmere

*__Bot__ – animals the size of ponies who are good for meat and wool

__Braies__ – medieval underwear: Varying in length from upper-thigh to below the knee, closed with a drawstring at the waist

*__Bristlemit__ - butterfly

*__Calgent__ – the lifetime spouse of a person, their One and Only

*__Centerworm__ – caterpillar

__Dalmatic__ - a wide-sleeved overtunic-like vestment open at the sides,

__Destrier__ – large war horse

__Gambeson__ – is a padded defensive jacket, worn as armour separately, or combined with mail or plate armor.

*__Hamsoul__ – pig-like animals

*__Honel__ – a mud wall hut with thatch roof. Can have one room for the poor and many rooms for the wealthy.

*__Jahala__ – sweet, juicy fruit

__Kirtle__ – a woman's loose gown, worn in the Middle Ages.

*__Koi__ – a purple mash made of blood, animal inners, and inferior grain

***Manga Foot** – a foul but edible root

***Minsome** – herb

***Monsuit** – large six-legged bear type creatures with green fur

Needlewoman – seamstress

Pace – five-feet

Rod – measurement of land, 16 1/2 feet

Sadesmen – old English for messenger

***Saltars** – money of the realm

***Sanctorum** – a house for worship

Stays – corset

Surcot – an expansive, unfitted ladies gown with flowing sleeves.

***Volif** – wolf like creatures

***Yorn** – tree

* words of my own creation

About the Author

Michelle Janene (Murray) is a church secretary by day and writes Christian fantasy and historical fiction in all her free time. She lives in Northern California with two crazy dogs and the characters of her imagination.

If you enjoyed *Seer of Windmere* please review it on your favorite site.

You can connect with Michelle on:
Facebook: MichelleJaneneAuthor
Instagram: MichelleJanene_Author
Twitter: @MichelleJaneneM
Pinterest: www.pinterest.com/michellejanene
Goodreads: Michelle Janene
StrongTowerPress.com

Other Books

Check out these books also by Michelle

Mission: Mistaken Identity

The Changed Heart Series:
God's Rebel
Rebel's Son
Hidden Rebel

Barbarian Hero

Guardians of Truth

Culling a Miracle

Lost Stones

The Last Good King

The King's Vengeance

Thice a Bride

Dragon Fire